STAR WARS®

THE NATIONAL PUBLIC
RADIO DRAMATIZATION

STAR WARS®

THE NATIONAL PUBLIC
RADIO DRAMATIZATION

**Based on Characters and Situations
Created by George Lucas**

Brian Daley

A Del Rey® Book

BALLANTINE BOOKS • NEW YORK

A Del Rey® Book
Published by Ballantine Books
TM, ® and copyright © 1994 by Lucasfilm Ltd.

Library of Congress Catalog Card Number: 94-94361

ISBN: 0-345-39109-8

Cover design by Andrew Baris
Text design by Ann Gold
Cover photograph by Richard Edlund;
airbrushing by Ralph McQuarrie

Manufactured in the United States of America
First Edition: October 1994
10 9 8 7 6 5 4 3 2 1

THE NATIONAL PUBLIC
RADIO DRAMATIZATION

INTRODUCTION

Star Wars: if you missed the thirteen-part radio series, you haven't heard the whole story.

What, for example, were Artoo-Detoo and See-Threepio doing during the intrigue and unpleasantness at the Mos Eisley Cantina, and later while Luke was off with Ben Kenobi, selling the landspeeder? (Luke got a far better price for that hot rod than the insectile dealer wanted to pay, by the way, thanks to the Force . . . but that's another scene—in Episode Seven.)

We saw the Cantina bartender catch sight of the droids and snarl, "We don't serve their kind in here!" Which left the oddly-met automatons cooling their heels and treads outdoors—and Artoo still holding the all-important Death Star technical data—while spies, stoolies, and Imperial stormtroopers hunted them, and port-town low-lifes eyed them like barracuda.

How, then, did a workaday astro-unit and a too-polite-for-his-own-good protocol robot keep their alloy skins intact on the mean streets of that "wretched hive of scum and villainy"? We saw them hide in a building at one point, ducking the stormtroopers' house-to-house search, but because the film moves like the wind, we don't see how they coped.

There was clearly room in everybody's favorite galaxy far, far away for more storytelling—and that's the demand the National Public Radio dramatization was conceived to fill. In expanding George Lucas's creation to thirteen half-hour episodes, we who worked on the project got to revive "lost scenes" from the screenplay and explore quirky corners of the story; in some ways the dramatization was akin to Tom Stoppard's play *Rosencrantz and Guildenstern Are Dead*, which shows what was happening elsewhere during Shakespeare's *Hamlet*.

In the case in point, Artoo and Threepio's mettle and ingenuity are tested in a way that flows from the theme of the movie—everyday characters rising to the demands of supreme crisis. They resort to, among other things, playing statue alongside the merchandise on a used-droid lot. Threepio displays the same clutch talent for conning humans that he does later on board the Death Star, and when he despairs of becoming deceitful, like Artoo, Luke assures him he was simply being "flexible."

Leia Organa's life on Alderaan and her early Rebel Alliance heroism; Luke's frictions and adventures with his Toschi Station buddies; how Han Solo gets an offer from Big Bunji and *almost* backs out of that charter with Luke and Ben; Darth Vader's malevolent dark side inquisition of Leia, and her courageous resistance—the radio production gave us the opportunity to look into these matters and many more.

After all, there are some twenty-seven minutes or so of dialogue in the course of the one hour and fifty minute movie; we had a running time of more than six hours in which to expand on existing scenes and add new ones.

We used it to show what a hotdog pilot Luke is back on Tatooine and how he cracks up his skyhopper in a daredevil air race; how Han and Chewie handle the face-off when Jabba the Hutt's bill collector, Heater, barges into docking bay #94 with a crew of enforcers; and what life is like for Artoo and Threepio there in the *Tantive IV* droid labor pool. While the labor-pool scene was touted in P.R. material as the *meeting* of Artoo and Threepio, I'm obliged to point out that it's not true. Rumor had it that George Lucas was thinking about putting the droids in all nine of his projected movies—including the ones that are set before *Star Wars*, a.k.a. *Episode IV: A New Hope*. Therefore, I left room for their prior acquaintance, for continuity's sake.

From its inception, the NPR series had special significance for George Lucas. At a time when *Star Wars* tie-in rights were like a license to print money, and various commercial broadcast and recording interests were pursuing radio licensing, he gave the brass ring to KUSC-FM, the public radio affiliate at his alma mater, the University of Southern California, for one dollar. It was a striking act of philanthropy, but he wanted the show to be something unprecedented, as his movie was something unprecedented.

What you now hold in your hands are the thirteen original, *uncut* scripts, just as they were when we took them into the studio. Astute listeners will notice discrepancies between these and the final recordings; part of the purpose of this foreword is to explain how and why those alterations came about.

From the first, the notion of a radio adaptation caused quite a stir—even on the set of *The Empire Strikes Back*, at Elstree Studios in England. As Lucasfilm publicist Alan Arnold, author of *Once Upon a Galaxy: A Journal of the Making of* The Empire Strikes Back, later wrote of Friday, June 15, 1979:

> At lunch today both Mark [Hamill] and Harrison [Ford] expressed concern over the possibility of the characters they have created on film being played on radio by other actors. "Until something like this happens, you don't realize how possessive you've become about the character you're playing," Harrison observed.
>
> "I want to play my part on radio," Mark told [producer Gary] Kurtz. "I'd play it for fun. I don't want some other guy playing Luke."

In both radio series, Mark showed unfailing energy and dedication to his craft and his role. Difficult as it is to bring a character to life while in costume before a camera, it takes something extra to carry settings, scene, subtext, and all the rest with voice skills alone.

Anthony Daniels, who plays See-Threepio, has played tremendously varied roles on the stages of London's West End; he's a multitalented fellow who also writes children's musicals for the BBC. He brought with him fidelity not only to his role, but to the personality and character of the golden droid's sidekick, Artoo-Detoo. Tony made sure nothing in the series contradicted or demeaned the strange but warm friendship between the two, or made them ridiculous rather than amusing. When Tony was in character it wasn't too hard to see a pugnacious little astrodroid standing next to him, bantering right back.

He once thanked me for writing him a line in which Threepio rhapsodized about the artful details of his protocol work. "Only an Englishman can properly deliver the phrase 'subtle nuances,' " he grinned.

Tony was fascinating to watch in the studio. He recorded his lines in a small isolation booth, using headphones to hear the other actors, so that his voice could be processed in postproduction. In order to get fully into character, he did spasmodic Threepio moves with his arms, upper torso, and head as he spoke, looking like a human marionette.

One problem I hadn't anticipated with Tony was an obvious one: he couldn't deliver large chunks of dialogue all at once because *Threepio doesn't breathe*, while a mere mortal actor must inhale and exhale every so often; some of his lines had to be changed, condensed, or broken down into smaller segments.

Taping was a learn-as-you-go experience for all of us. It had been thought that the stormtroopers' helmeted voices could be emulated by having the actors wear plastic and foam-filter painter's masks, but the results didn't "read" properly for the microphones. In the end the actor-troopers were isolated, as Tony Daniels was, and their voices were processed later.

I had to make adjustments of my own in going from writing novels to scripting for radio. Having done some radio work in college, I felt that voice-over should be kept to a minimum—just short lead-in and closing pieces for each chapter. Dialogue, sound effects, and music get listeners more involved, and could and should carry the drama. It was very pleasant to learn that Carol Titleman, the Lucasfilm vice-president who oversaw the project, had already decided the same thing. The tradeoff was that without voice-over, I had to give up the narrative and exposition so useful to a novelist. I felt like the prizefighter in the old joke who, told by the ref that there would be no biting, gouging, or kicking, says, "There go all my best punches." Still, the decision was a good one; there's a vibrancy and excitement to the show that far surpasses mere stories read on tape.

So that's how I became a metaphrast, translating a dramatic work from one medium into another. I wrote the series in an efficiency apartment in North Hollywood from December of 1979 to mid-March of 1980. Every few days I went down to the Egg Company, the cover designation for Lucasfilm South, a red brick building across the street from Universal Studios, to hand in a new episode or attend a script conference on the previous one.

I told Carol Titleman I wanted desperately to be back in New York City in time for the Saint Patrick's Day parade—the high point of the year—and she very kindly kept the script-review and rewrite process moving briskly. The day I left, she smiled. "Well, you made it."

I returned to Los Angeles late the following June for two weeks of recording sessions in a Hollywood sound studio, Westlake Audio, more accustomed to rock stars. There I cultivated a knack for writing "wild lines" on the spur of the moment. Wild lines are those peripheral, sometimes indistinguishable remarks and conversations you hear behind the primary characters in crowd scenes and such. Actors are often left to improvise their own chatter, but that proved unwise in the *Star Wars* universe because it has its own rules; believability suffers when an actor unfamiliar with the movie ad-libs something on the order of, "Okay, who left their Death Star parked in my space?"

Hence, whenever director John Madden so decreed, I retreated to the studio secretary's desk and knocked out however many exclamations, exchanges, tongue-lashings, and point-counterpoints he required. I also learned his "two minute" rule: in a long scene, sound-engineering and postproduction boss Tom Voegli could recycle the separately recorded wild lines so that they looped—but a minimum of two minutes' material was necessary so that the listener's ear wouldn't catch the repetition.

I was rewriting on the fly, like somebody out of the golden days of radio drama, and it was frenetic at times, but I've seldom enjoyed myself more. Rewrites were required for various reasons. One problem was too many sibilances in a sentence, which can be tricky for an actor delivering a line into a mike at top speed in an action scene or rapid give-and-take. Sometimes it was necessary to add brief, not terribly crucial remarks, simply to keep a character "in the scene"; movies and TV can show you who's present even if they're not speaking, but that's a tougher proposition on radio.

Anyone who's done theater work knows that scripts are, inevitably, altered according to need, and *Star Wars* was no different. John Madden, a young Englishman who'd directed for the National Theater in London and the BBC, as well as working for "American Playhouse," came to the project after winning the Prix Italia award for directing playwright Arthur Kopit's *Wings*, on which he had also worked with Tom Voegli. John fine-tuned the *Star Wars* scripts for the spoken word, the actor's instrument—a very instructive experience for me.

Then there were the additions to interrupted lines, something I've been often asked about. The plain fact is that John would frequently call for a few extra words in such a sentence so that one actor could go on talking under another's interjection.

Like Tony Daniels, John made for an interesting sight when working. On some particularly difficult scenes, he'd screw his eyes shut tight to concentrate on the voices, sitting so tensed on his stool that he looked as if he might sprout an alien from his chest or fly through the ceiling like an F-16 ejector seat. The fruits of his concentration were obvious, however, in the results he got. Since then he's gone on to direct the TV version of *Wings* as well as the theatrical motion pictures *Ethan Frome* and *Golden Gate*—with his eyes very much open.

I'd originally been hired to write the series because Carol Titleman approved of the way I'd handled *Star Wars* material in a trilogy of novels about Han Solo. When I first talked to John, I was braced to explain details and the *Star Wars* cosmos to an outsider, but he was a pleasant surprise on that score: Not only did he know the movie, its locale, and its back-story well, but he made sure that his actors did. If a performer taking on a major role was unfamiliar with the picture, John would explain things thoroughly to that person before proceeding with the recording session.

Even so, the taping session went on at flank speed—more than one episode per day, plus odds and ends like promotional spots. Mark Hamill commented on the sheer pace of it in comparison to motion pictures, in which he might get through only a single page of dialogue in a long day's shooting. The radio series put great demands on him but exhilarated him, too; as hard as he worked, it was clear that he was enjoying himself tremendously.

I have a personal story that shows how gracious he could be. While being interviewed on New York TV to promote *Amadeus*, in which he was starring on Broadway, Mark fielded a question about the *Star Wars* series. He kindly mentioned my name—very generously, since it was a brief interview and the idea, after all, was to talk about his play. My mother had tuned in, and got quite a charge out of it.

The rest of the cast had a good time, too. They were actors with extensive stage and screen experience, and so it was novel for most of them to be dealing with nothing but the script, the director, a single-point stereo mike, and one another. There were no cameras, lighting, makeup, or costumes to think about, and not much physical blocking, either. I came back from lunch one day to see Mark, Perry King, and Ann Sachs running lines together, preparing for a scene, while lying flaked out on the studio room carpet. They were relaxed and looked like they were enjoying themselves.

Perry, a handsome and dashing actor notable for movies like *The Lords of Flatbush* and *A Different Kind of Romance*, as well as TV work including "Riptide" and "Tales from the Crypt," assumed the role of Han Solo—Harrison Ford was occupied elsewhere, creating a new character named Indiana Jones. Ann, a dark-haired, winsome stage actress whose previous work included *Dracula*, took over the part of Princess Leia Organa. These and other changes from the original cast were less noticeable to listeners than one might have predicted. The majority of the audience tuned in, realized, "Oh, that's not Carrie Fisher," then got involved in the action.

James Earl Jones was unable to reprise his role as Darth Vader, and Jones's resonant, powerful voice was even more definitive of the Dark Lord of the Sith than that black armor, cloak, and helmet were. Mel Sahr, who cast the radio series as well as being production coordinator and all-around honcho, told me she had had her apprehensions about filling Vader's jackboots. But then she had called Brock Peters, whose credits include the marvelous and poignant movie *The L-Shaped Room* as well as several *Star Trek* movies. As soon as Mel heard Brock's deep, dynamic tones on the other end of the line, she told me, "I thought, 'Here's my Darth.' The search was over."

Brock did a magnificent job, especially in the extended interrogation scene mentioned earlier. While the motion picture doesn't depict the encounter, I took it as a chance to show Vader and Leia clashing will-to-will. It was a nightmarish confrontation, and it got us our one and only letter of complaint—but since the *Star Wars* radio drama drew a lot of mail, I don't think that response is too damning.

Bernard Behrens, a fine Canadian actor who's performed at the Old Vic and most of the other important theaters in the world, came aboard in the role created by Sir Alec Guiness: General Obi-Wan Kenobi, Jedi Master, samurai of the Force. Like Ann and Perry, Bernard—known to one and all as Bunny—quickly made the character his own.

We had some quite notable supporting players as well. Adam

Arkin—Adam of "Northern Exposure"—played Luke's hometown thug, Fixer. Meshach Taylor ("Designing Women"; "Dave's World") and David Alan Grier ("In Living Color" and Broadway's *The First*) were on hand, along with "Thirtysomething" 's David Clennon and "The X Files" 's Jerry Hardin. Keene Curtis, who'd played Daddy Warbucks on stage and was Carla Tortelli's restauranteur love interest on "Cheers," tackled the role of the Grand Moff Tarkin.

Once the recording sessions were over, we disbanded and Tom Voegli took the tapes back to his Minnesota Public Radio home base for sound mixing and post-production.

Ben Burtt, an Academy Award winning sound designer for Lucasfilm, made his trove of acoustic treasures available to Tom—a first, and a kindness for which Tom was profoundly grateful. Postproduction demanded months of intensive labor from Tom and his assistants; it sometimes took an entire day to produce a thirty-second portion of a scene—*three days* just to edit the music for the final battle sequence.

Postproduction was another stage in which departures from the scripts took place. Tom occasionally inserted a break in a scene and brought the music up—"allowed the music to breathe," as he puts it—in order to let a passage resolve itself. Similarly, scenes were at times shortened slightly to fit sound-track selections—since we couldn't afford to get the London Philharmonic back into the studio—and other time constraints.

Between the first broadcast of the series and the second, some lines were cut to allow for a full credit roll at the end of each episode. That's why, for example, part of Leia's conversation with her father in Chapter 2 was trimmed. For those who've been wondering what they missed, the script shows the scene in its entirety.

Star Wars was broadcast in Dolby stereo, and reaction to it lived up to our expectations: it became National Public Radio's most popular dramatic series. Among my favorite responses to it was a column by *Los Angeles Times* writer Wayne Warga, who described listening to the first episode with his somewhat dubious eight-year-old son. The boy, raised on TV, said he "had a little trouble making pictures" in his head, but used his own action toy figures to show his dad what the characters, aliens, beasts, and machines looked like. Father and son were looking forward to hearing the next chapter together.

Ratings and audience reaction were so positive that discussion of an *Empire Strikes Back* sequel began almost immediately. *Empire* did very well, too, but we never got the chance to complete the trilogy by making *Return of the Jedi*. I hope that someday that situation will be resolved. You'll notice that each of the three films ends with a stirring visual coda and no dialogue: the throne room in *Star Wars*, the Rebel ship and view of the galaxy in *Empire*, and the treetop Ewok celebration in *Jedi*. Naturally, I closed both radio serials with a line from Luke Skywalker, since the trilogy is, at its core, his story. And I've got one for the victory party in that Endor forest canopy—care to hear it?

In that case, tune in if and when *Return of the Jedi* comes to radio.

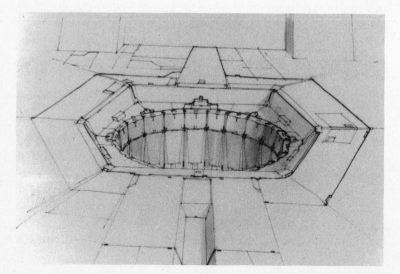

In the meantime, I wish you bon voyage on this extended grand tour of the *Star Wars* story—the places and times where Luke's adventures all began, and George Lucas's magic resides.

BRIAN DALEY
Pines on Severn, Maryland
March 1994

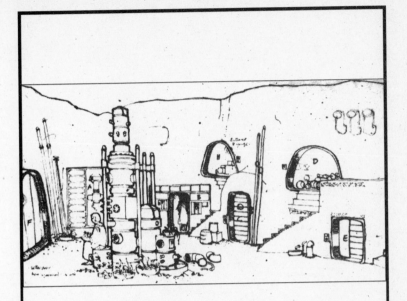

EPISODE ONE:

"A WIND TO SHAKE

THE STARS"

CAST:

Luke   Cammie
Beru   Biggs
Owen   Deak
Windy   Tape Voice
Fixer

ANNOUNCER: OPENING CREDITS.

Music: Opening theme.

NARRATOR: A long time ago in a galaxy far, far away there came a time of revolution, when Rebels united to challenge a tyrannical Empire. But most of the citizens of that vast Empire of a million star systems took little notice of this tremendous conflict . . . at least at first.

Sound: Sand-drifting winds in background. Luke working in foreground.

NARRATOR: On the desert planet Tatooine, as on countless other worlds, life goes on though great events are shaping the future of a galaxy. Here, amid the endless sands and the dune seas, the hostile wastes and barren lands, human beings struggle and endure. And here, too, men and women laugh and cry, hope . . . and dream.

Music: A brassy march on tape player.

TAPE VOICE: . . . so don't just dream about applying for the academy, make it come true! *You* can find a career in space: Exploration, Starfleet, or Merchant Service. Choose from navigation, engineering, space medicine, contact/liaison, and more! If you have the right stuff to take on the universe and standardized examination scores that meet the requirements, dispatch your application to Screening Office, c/o the Commandant, Imperial Space Academy, your sector, and join the *ranks of the proud*!

Music: March swelling up.

WINDY: *(IN DISTANCE)* Skywalker! Hey, Luke Skywalker!

Sound: Tape is shut off with an abrupt snap.

LUKE: *(A LITTLE GUILTILY)* I'm out here in the tech-dome, Windy.

WINDY: *(APPROACHING)* Hey, Skywalker, come on! Everybody's going to Beggar's Canyon. My hopper's acting up, so I'm gonna ride with you. *(ON)* Hey, what are you doing with the tape console?

LUKE: Nothing, nothing. How'd you get here?

WINDY: My folks came over to see your uncle and aunt. What d' ya mean, "nothing"? Let's see that tape.

Sound: They scuffle over the tape.

LUKE: Cut it out, Windy.

Sound: The scuffle breaks off, both of them breathing heavily.

WINDY: *(TRIUMPHANTLY)* Aha! "Applicant's Information Packet, Imperial Space Academy."

LUKE: Will you stop, Windy?

WINDY: You're still seeing novas, huh, Luke? Looks like this tape's been played a few thousand times.

LUKE: Give it back, Windy.

WINDY: When're you gonna grow up, Luke? You're a *farm boy*, just like me.

LUKE: *(DEADLY SERIOUS)* Hand it over, Windy. Or I'll take it.

WINDY: Oh, here, *here!* Take it! What're you getting so touchy about? Get your skyhopper going.

(MOVING OFF) I'll roll back the dome.

Sound: Switch is thrown, heavy rollers spinning.

LUKE: *(RELENTING)* Why'd your folks come over?

WINDY: *(COMING ON)* To talk about the moisture harvest, complain about crop prices—who cares? I guess it's a mercy visit, y' know.

LUKE: Yeah, Aunt Beru's always eager for company. Even Uncle Owen is, but he'd never admit it.

Sound: Skyhopper door opening.

LUKE: Get in, Windy; time's wasting.

Sound: The other hopper door opening, and both closing. The ship's high-performance engine comes to life.

WINDY: *(OVER ENGINE)* She sounds smooth, Luke.

Sound: Engine builds.

LUKE: *(OVER ENGINE)* I adjusted her thrust sequence for extra boost. Hang on to your seat!

Sound: Blast of hopper's thrusters. Luke and Windy cheer their own takeoff. Fade to the winds of Tatooine, music, and Anchorhead's younger set partying.

DEAK: Hey, Fixer! Fixer! Here comes Skywalker's hopper.

FIXER: So what? Don't bother me with small fry. Where's the juice? I'm thirsty.

CAMMIE: Here, catch one!

(THEY LAUGH)

Sound: Swoosh of uncapping a container of malt ferment.

Sound: In background, Luke's skyhopper makes a sudden landing, braking thrusters blaring, landing gear skidding. Celebrants yelp as they dodge out of the way. The hopper doors pop open as engines die.

LUKE: *(OFF)* So, where's the party?

FIXER: Wherever *I* am, Luke. Right, Cammie?

CAMMIE: *(LAUGHS)* Correct, lover.

WINDY: *(APPROACHING)* Hey, everybody, guess what Skywalker was doing? Sitting in the tech-dome playing an academy recruitment tape!

ALL: *(LAUGHTER AND MOCKING CATCALLS)*

FIXER: You never change, Skywalker. That's all you want out of life, to parade around in a fancy uniform?

LUKE: What do you want that's so much better?

FIXER: You watch it, *boy*! Just because you got lucky on a couple of crummy tests, that doesn't make you some kind of junior space explorer. You know what I did back when they made *me* take 'em? Walked in, filled out my name, and walked out again! I showed 'em!

DEAK: Yeah, Luke, so you happened to qualify; so *what*?

WINDY: Just because he can answer fancy trick questions and do schoolbook flight maneuvers, he thinks it makes him better than us.

LUKE: I do not! But yeah, I'd like to go to the academy. Why shouldn't I?

FIXER: Because it's for suckers, Skywalker! They want to stick you into a uniform and give you orders. At least at the power station I'm my own boss.

WINDY: My father says the Empire's just recruiting more people into the academies so they can draft them into the Starfleet.

DEAK: Do you think anybody out there cares about Luke Skywalker?

CAMMIE: If you leave home, nobody knows you.

FIXER: Where's the juice?

DEAK: Here.

WINDY: What's the program, Fix?

FIXER: Speed runs, everybody! Speed runs! Gonna see how much time I can shave off the back stretch.

WINDY: There's no way you can cut much more time off your lap, Fixer. You're almost matching Biggs's best time around Beggar's Canyon as it is.

FIXER: Well, Biggs isn't here, and *I* am! I'm as good as he ever was!

LUKE: Then why don't you thread the Stone Needle like Biggs did? That'd take five seconds or better off your time.

ALL: HOOTS AT LUKE'S SUGGESTION.

CAMMIE: You're crazy, Luke. Why don't you guys go buzz the womp rats and take a few potshots at them? This speed run stuff is—

FIXER: *(INTERRUPTING)* You don't think I can do it? Listen, anything the great Biggs Darklighter could do, *I* can do!

CAMMIE: I never said you couldn't, Fixer.

WINDY: Yeah, nobody was knocking you, Fixer.

FIXER: *(MOLLIFIED)* Besides, I don't need any shortcuts. Come on, Windy, Deak.

WINDY: *(MOVING OFF)* Where're we going?

FIXER: *(MOVING OFF)* To take a look at the canyon. Figure my course.

CAMMIE: Did you have to get him started?

LUKE: *Me?*

CAMMIE: Fixer's like a kid sometimes. Just when I think he's ready to settle down, he decides to go out and swipe some parts for his skyhopper or something. I had this dream the other night . . . Do you ever dream?

LUKE: Sometimes in my sleep I think I see my parents. I don't remember them, but . . .

CAMMIE: *(BARELY HAVING HEARD HIM)* Uh huh . . . anyway, I dreamed that Fixer and I were married. It was so nice . . .

WINDY: *(OFF)* Hey, Skywalker, get your macrobinoculars. Fixer wants them.

LUKE: *(CALLING)* Who're *you* ordering? They're in my hopper; get them yourself.

WINDY: *(OFF)* Now, look . . .

LUKE: *(CALLING)* Better hurry. You wouldn't want to make Fixer wait.

WINDY: *(OFF)* All right for you. And don't think I won't tell Fixer you said that!

FIXER: *(OFF, APPROACHING)* Said what, Skywalker?

LUKE: Nothing. Nothing, Fixer.

FIXER: It may interest you to know I've got the perfect route through the Bottleneck.

DEAK: *(IN BACKGROUND)* Fixer's got it all figured; he's gonna clock the best time anybody's ever made around Beggar's Canyon.

LUKE: If Biggs *was* here, he—

FIXER: *(INTERRUPTING)* Well, Biggs *ain't* here, Wormie! Do *you* want to try and keep up with me?

LUKE: I . . . yeah, all right. You're on.

DEAK: Hoo boy, Wormie against the Fixer. It's gonna be a slaughter.

LUKE: Then you can ride with Fixer, Deak. What're we waiting for? Let's go!

CAMMIE: Fixer, I want this to stop right now . . .

Sound: Cross-fade to:

FIXER: *(OFF, YELLING)* Good luck, Skywalker. See you in the tight spots!

WINDY: Hey, I couldn't find those macrobinoculars anywhere.

LUKE: Never mind. Hop in.

Sound: Luke revving engines.

WINDY: What're you doing?

LUKE: I'm standing in for Biggs. Brace yourself.

Sound: Hopper's engine roars on takeoff.

WINDY: *(YELPS)*

FIXER: *(SOUNDING TINNY OVER COMLINK)* Here we go; one run down the back stretch, Skywalker, whenever you're ready.

WINDY: You and Fixer in the Bottleneck together? Count me out!

LUKE: Then open the door and jump.

FIXER: *(OVER COMLINK)* Fall in even with me, Skywalker, and we'll let 'er rip.

Sound: Extra burst from Luke's hopper.

FIXER: *(OVER COMLINK)* Okay, hit it!

Sound: Hopper's engine howls. Irregular burst of Luke's steering thrusters and his maneuvering.

WINDY: Look out!

LUKE: Shut up and keep still! Look, you distracted me, and now Fixer's got the lead.

WINDY: Let him keep it, I want to live!

FIXER: *(OVER COMLINK)* How does my afterblast feel, Luke?

WINDY: It's too narrow to get past him.

FIXER: *(OVER COMLINK)* Just make yourself comfortable back there, farm boy; it'll all be over in a minute.

LUKE: That's what *he* thinks!

WINDY: What are you . . . You idiot, you're headed for the Stone Needle!

LUKE: Bet we shave five seconds off our time.

WINDY: You'll kill us both!

LUKE: There's no going back now. Stay gripped, Windy!

WINDY: No-oooo!

Sound: Passage through the circle of the Stone Needle and a shearing metallic sound. The hopper begins to buck.

LUKE: *(WHOOPING)* Made it! Windy, open your eyes! We made it!

WINDY: Hey, your stabilizer's gone!

LUKE: I can hold her; we've still got to cross the finish line.

WINDY: You'll crash us!

Sound: Hopper's engine revs down for landing. It hits once, jolting them, bounces, and comes in again slewing and sliding, gradually stopping.

LUKE: I told you I could bring her in. We won!

WINDY: *Won?* Luke, you're crazy. Crazy!

Sound: Windy opens the door.

WINDY: I'm riding home with one of the others; you're just an accident looking for a place to happen! And if you know what's good for you, you won't kid Fixer about this.

Sound: Door slams shut.

LUKE: Oh, Biggs, you should've been here . . . *(LAUGHS)*

Music: Up.

Sound: Beru's kitchen.

BERU: Luke! Luke! Are you up yet? Breakfast is ready!

Sound: Cooking with appropriate techno-chem sounds.

LUKE: *(APPROACHING, YAWNING)* Morning, Aunt Beru. *(HE KISSES HER CHEEK QUICKLY)*

BERU: Good morning, dear. I'm afraid your uncle's in a big hurry today; he says things are still behind schedule. Sit down and eat your breakfast before it gets cold.

LUKE: All right, but I don't think the desert's going anywhere.

OWEN: *(APPROACHING)* No, it'll still be there, Luke. And if we don't get ready for the season in time, it'll always be just that, a desert. Now there's no more time for nonsense; I want you to keep your mind on your work today.

Sound: A chair being drawn up to table; tableware, plates, etc.

LUKE: Yessir.

OWEN: Keep an eye peeled when you're out today; there've been reports of Sand People. I want you to see what you can do about the units up on the south ridge. I expect 'em all to be running 100 percent and smooth before day's end.

LUKE: Uncle Owen, those vaporators are ten years old! They should've been replaced long ago.

OWEN: You can get them functioning up to specs if you roll back your sleeves and quit your daydreaming! I need all the help I can get, not a nephew with his head in the stars half the time. You mind your work now, or there'll be trouble, I'll tell you that much!

BERU: Owen! *(THINKING BETTER OF IT AND FORGOING AN ARGUMENT)* Here, finish what's left before it gets cold, both of you.

Sound: Scraping, pouring, etc.

BERU: Luke, dear, I packed a lunch for you. I put it in your landspeeder so you wouldn't forget it.

LUKE: Thanks, Aunt Beru. I, uh, guess I'd better get going.

Sound: His chair slides back.

OWEN: Take the treadwell with you.

LUKE: That old droid's in worse shape than the vaporators, Uncle Owen. *(PAUSE)* Uncle, what about getting some new droids?

OWEN: Just what I need, another expense!

LUKE: But with another droid or two we could keep the whole farm at peak efficiency through the harvest. I could check around at Toshi Station and Anchorhead, and there ought to be a Jawa sandcrawler passing through any time now. Maybe they'd have something we could use.

OWEN: Luke, if you quit your daydreaming and do your share, we won't need any droids! Now, I've never let you want for anything, have I? Huh? Well, then, young fella, the least you can do is show some gratitude and—

BERU: *(INTERRUPTING)* Owen Lars! *(PAUSE, THEN MORE KINDLY)* Owen, we *could* use a little more help. A droid that spoke domestic Bocce could help me around the house, too, when you didn't need it.

OWEN: Well . . .

BERU: *(MEANINGFULLY)* Good-bye, Luke, dear.

LUKE: *(TAKING THE HINT)* Um, g'bye, Aunt Beru. *(MOVING OFF)* I'll do my best with those vaporators, Uncle Owen.

BERU: Honestly, Owen, I don't know what gets into you at times. Luke's never asked us for a thing. He works as hard as any man; he could've gone off on his own long ago, and you *know* that.

OWEN: Beru, with his mind wandering half the time, he's never going to make his way in this life.

BERU: *(UNEXPECTEDLY FERVENT)* But you can't begrudge him his dreams! A person has to have their dreams! I've never once complained about living out here or hardly ever seeing other people or going without when the moisture harvest was bad, have I?

OWEN: Now see, here, missus, I never said you—

BERU: *(INTERRUPTING)* Even to the young people over at Anchorhead Luke is an outsider. He hasn't had a close friend since Biggs went to the academy.

OWEN: I . . . I don't want him getting hurt, Beru. I want what's best for Luke.

BERU: I know that, Owen. But it wouldn't hurt to tell him so.

Sound: Owen's chair scrapes as he rises.

OWEN: I'll be most of the day on those condensers in the upper basin. Won't be home till evening, I expect.

BERU: I'll have supper waiting, Owen.

Music: Up.

Sound: The winds of Tatooine.

Sound: Ratcheting and metal-to-metal sounds of repair work.

LUKE: Hey, Treadwell, come hold this junction plate in place while I torque it down, will you?

Sound: The treadwell replies with its own droid sounds, lacking the wit and verve of, say, an R2 unit.

Sound: Luke's labors, breathing, etc.

LUKE: That ought to do it. Now, let's give this relic a try.

Sound: Switch being thrown.

LUKE: Nothing.

Sound: Switch is thrown again, then several more times rapidly.

LUKE: How does Uncle Owen expect me to keep these junk heaps running? Ah . . .

Sound: Angry rapping on the vaporator and a kick or two.

LUKE: Treadwell, clamp these two leads together while I splice them.

Sound: Treadwell maneuvering, still gobbling to itself.

LUKE: No, no, you idiot! Use your *insulated* arm!

Sound: An electronic shriek of surprise and distress. Circuitry sputters.

LUKE: Release! Back off!

Sound: Treadwell backing off, snurfling to itself piteously.

LUKE: What I wouldn't give to be on another planet . . . any planet!

Sound: Tool being thrown back into the toolbox.

LUKE: Uncle Owen's not going to like this a bit. Now I've got *two* major overhauls on my hands. Treadwell, get yourself over to the landspeeder.

Sound: Treadwell's starting and stopping, grinding off.

LUKE: Sky's still clear, anyway; at least there's no sandstorms blowing up. Maybe we can still have things—hey! What's that up there?

Sound: Treadwell burps a noncommittal reply.

LUKE: I know *you* don't know, you maniac. Where're my macrobinoculars?

Sound: Treadwell gurgles again. Luke rummages in landspeeder.

LUKE: I know I left them here someplace.

Sound: More fumbling, opening and closing of compartments, etc.

LUKE: Ah, here we go.

Sound: Macro case being opened, instrument withdrawn.

LUKE: Now, let's see.

Sound: Adjusting macros' ranging and focus.

LUKE: Yeah, there're ships out there, all right. Two of them at least. And they're firing on each other! It's incredible!

Sound: Treadwell makes unimpressed noises.

LUKE: Boy, they're really going at it out there!

Sound: Macros being shoved back into case, tools gathered hastily.

LUKE: Come on, Treadwell, get yourself over to the landspeeder. I've gotta get into Anchorhead and tell Fixer about this!

Sound: Complaint from Treadwell.

LUKE: Get it in gear, will you?

Sound: Treadwell's sounds indicate that it cannot comply.

LUKE: *(MOVING OFF)* Oh, stay put, then. I'll pick you up on the way home.

Sound: Humming equipment and electronic game being played by Windy and Biggs, and background conversations which are interrupted.

LUKE: *(RUNNING ON)* Windy? Deak? Cammie? Hey, everybody!

FIXER: Hey, Cammie, did I just hear a young noise blast in here?

CAMMIE: *(HALF YAWNING)* Oh, Fixer, it's just Luke on another of his rampages.

LUKE: Shape it up, you guys! Wait till you hear what I just—

WINDY: *(INTERRUPTING)* We've got company, Luke.

LUKE: *Biggs!* When did you get back from the academy?

ALL: *(LAUGHTER AT LUKE'S SURPRISE)*

CAMMIE: So the two shooting stars are reunited at last. I'm *so* thrilled to be here for it.

ALL: *(MORE LAUGHTER)*

BIGGS: I just got in, on the shuttle. I wanted to surprise you, hot-shot. I thought you'd be here when I arrived; forgot you have the harvest coming up.

ALL: *(A DERISIVE SNIGGER OR TWO IN BACKGROUND)*

LUKE: But how come you're back so soon? Didn't you get your commission?

BIGGS: Of course I got it; the academy accelerated our courses. It seems the Empire wants the commercial spacelines expanded as soon as possible.

ALL: *(SOME LAUGHTER AND HOOTING)*

FIXER: You oughta drop the Emperor a thank-you note, Biggs. That's the only way you could've gotten out of that academy.

BIGGS: Signed on with the starship *Rand Ecliptic*. Third Mate Biggs Darklighter, at your service. How's this for a snappy salute?

Sound: Boot heels clacking together.

LUKE: I hope you fly a ship better than you salute.

CAMMIE: Oh, Luke, what do *you* know? *I* think Biggs looks just fabulous in his uniform.

FIXER: *(PERTURBED WITH CAMMIE'S ADMIRATION)* Yeah, Biggs just had to come back and say good-bye to all us planetbound simpletons.

ALL: *(MOCKING AGREEMENT)*

BIGGS: *(LAUGHS GOOD-NATUREDLY)*

LUKE: Hey, I almost forgot! Drop the game and come outside quick; you guys have to see something! There's a battle going on out beyond the atmosphere . . . two ships with a lot of firing!

DEAK: Oh, not now; Windy's got a shot to make, and there's money riding on it.

WINDY: Yeah, when're you gonna stop seeing things and grow up? Space battles; what a jerk!

LUKE: Biggs, I didn't just imagine this one.

BIGGS: If you say so, hotshot. *(MOVING OFF)* Deak, turn off that game. It'll still be there when we get back.

WINDY: Here we go again.

DEAK: Captain Skywalker has sighted the enemy again, sir!

FIXER: And is advancing to the rear!

ALL: LAUGHTER.

Sound: Cross-fade to:

Sound: Luke taking out and adjusting macros.

LUKE: They're still there! I counted two earlier. Here, Biggs, take the macros and see for yourself!

BIGGS: Will do.

Sound: Ranging and focusing macros.

DEAK: *(OFF)* Ooooh, citizens, it's too light and it's too bright out here for the old Deacon. What d' you say, Windy?

WINDY: *(OFF)* Yeah, space battles ain't worth a sunburn.

CAMMIE: *(COMING ON. WHEEDLING)* Luke, sweetie, you'll let me look next, won't you?

LUKE: Wha'? Yeah, sure, Cammie. You bet.

CAMMIE: You're such a love.

BIGGS: *(VERY JUDICIOUS)* I'm afraid that's no battle up there, hotshot. *(MORE NORMAL TONE)* Here, Cammie. It's probably just a tanker fueling a freighter.

LUKE: But there was a lot of firing before, Biggs, I swear there was! I saw it!

BIGGS: Then why would they still be holding position over Tatooine?

CAMMIE: Why, they're not doing a thing up there. Firing, my foot. Here, take these things back.

Sound: Macros being grabbed and nearly dropped by Luke.

LUKE: Hey, Cammie, be careful with those!

CAMMIE: Oh, don't worry about it, Luke!

LUKE: These cost me a half season's savings!

FIXER: *(COMING ON)* She told you not to worry about it, Wormie!

BIGGS: Hey, Fixer, the show's over.

FIXER: C'mon, Cammie.

CAMMIE: What? Are you just gonna—

FIXER: I said come on! *(LEAVING)* So long, guys!

Sound: The Tatooine wind.

BIGGS: They're right about one thing, Luke. The rebellion against the Empire *is* a long way from here. I doubt the Imperials would bother about this system.

LUKE: But Biggs, I could've sworn—

BIGGS: *(INTERRUPTING)* Hey, hotshot, let's take a spin in that landspeeder of yours. I'd like to take one last look at Beggar's Canyon, for old times' sake.

LUKE: Sure, Biggs.

Sound: Footsteps going to and clambering aboard the speeder.

LUKE: *(MOVING OFF)* Boy, you should've been there the other day when we ran the canyon. Fixer started bragging about how he could do anything that Biggs could do. *(LAUGHS)* So I said . . .

Sound: Cross-fade to sound of landspeeder engine under:

LUKE: . . . and Fixer just pretended it never happened. My sky-hopper's busted up pretty bad, though.

BIGGS: I'm sure that made your uncle happy.

LUKE: Biggs, you have no idea. I'm grounded for the rest of the season.

BIGGS: You ought to take it a little easier, Luke. Even if you are the hottest gulley-jumper this side of Mos Eisley, you keep it up and one day, *whammo*, you'll be nothing but a dark smear on a canyon wall.

Sound: Speeder noises decrease as Luke brings it to a stop.

LUKE: There it is . . . the old Stone Needle.

Sound: Winds, eerie howls, and clacks and calls.

LUKE: You can see practically the whole canyon from this part of the rim.

BIGGS: Yeah, this is still the wildest terrain I ever saw. I don't know how I lived through all the crazy stunts we pulled down there.

LUKE: If we had the hopper now, we could give those womp rats a surprise.

BIGGS: Sorry, I am now valuable property. "Keeping in mind the expense of cadet training, all graduates shall refrain from unnecessary risk taking."

LUKE: Did they happen to know how many stabilizer vanes you've bent up on the back stretch down there? Or the time you almost wiped out the Stone Needle?

BIGGS: I figured it was better not to mention those to my piloting instructors. I guess I'm really going to miss this old widow maker, though.

LUKE: It hasn't been the same since you left, Biggs. It's been so . . . so *quiet*. You were always number one around here, Biggs. You were the one who made things happen.

BIGGS: It's a big galaxy, Luke; at the academy *everybody* was number one back where they came from. All of a sudden I was just a face in the crowd.

LUKE: But you *made* it, Biggs. You're gonna see all those places we used to talk about.

BIGGS: Yes. *(PAUSE)* Luke, did you ever wonder why we're friends?

LUKE: Huh?

BIGGS: The rest of them . . . they'll never leave Tatooine. Maybe never get as far as Mos Eisley. Have you ever thought about that?

LUKE: Not exactly like that, I haven't.

BIGGS: Fixer's *just* smart enough to know he's better off being a big noise in a small room. Cammie's dumb enough to think she's made the prize catch hereabouts. Windy's nothing but a follower, and Deak's the follower of a follower.

LUKE: Oh, they're not so bad. I don't mind them.

BIGGS: Then how come you worked so hard at being the hottest pilot around? *(PAUSE)* Hey, did you see that? Off on the far side of the canyon!

LUKE: Where . . . Sand People!

BIGGS: Got your macrobinoculars?

LUKE: Right here.

Sound: Ranging and focusing of macros.

BIGGS: Yep, three bantha and, it looks like, five Tusken Raiders. They're moving out toward Jundland Wastes.

LUKE: My uncle said there've been some sightings around here. I should get back; I've got a bad feeling about this.

BIGGS: Naw, I don't think it's anything to worry about. Still, maybe we should get going.

Sound: The speeder starts, revs, accelerates, and continues under:

LUKE: Well, that's a little excitement for your visit.

BIGGS: You only think this planet's boring because you've never been anywhere else. *(PAUSE)* Luke, I didn't come back just to say good-bye. Look, if . . . if something happens, I wanted you to know.

LUKE: Know what? Honestly, Biggs, will you stop with this secrecy stuff?

BIGGS: I made some friends at the academy. At our first port of call in the inner systems, we're going to jump ship and join the Rebel Alliance.

LUKE: That's crazy! You could wander around forever trying to find them. The Empire can't even find them.

BIGGS: Okay, so it's a long shot! If we don't find the Rebels, then we'll do what we can on our own. I'm not hanging around to get drafted into the Imperial Starfleet. The Rebellion's spreading, and I want to be on the side I believe in.

LUKE: And I'm stuck here.

BIGGS: I thought you were going to the academy next term.

LUKE: I had to cancel my application. The Sand People are getting more active.

BIGGS: Come on, your uncle could hold off a whole Tusken raiding party with one blaster. One of these days you've got to separate what *seems* important from what *is*, Luke.

LUKE: But the farm's just about to start paying off. Uncle Owen needs me for one more season. Biggs, I can't just run out on him and Aunt Beru now.

BIGGS: Luke, listen to me: Your uncle uses that "I-fed-you-and-brought-you-up" line to keep you here; can't you see that?

LUKE: My uncle and aunt are all the family I've got, Biggs . . . they're *all* I've got! I don't care what you or anybody else thinks about me, I can't let anything happen to those two.

BIGGS: Luke, I didn't mean—

LUKE: *(INTERRUPTING)* Oh, go on; find your Rebellion. You think I wouldn't like to leave? You think I like staying behind?

BIGGS: I never thought that, Luke.

LUKE: Well, that's how it sounded. I'll let you off by the power station.

Sound: Landspeeder noises die as it comes to a stop.

Sound: Biggs climbs out of the speeder.

BIGGS: *(SLIGHTLY OFF)* Luke, I had a friend at the academy; he helped me through, the way I used to help you. Just before graduation I heard he got picked up during a roundup of Rebel suspects. They said he died in interrogation.

LUKE: You've changed, Biggs. Changed a lot.

BIGGS: I've been doing some thinking. *(PAUSE, THEN AN ATTEMPT AT LIGHTNESS)* But you're the same as ever. Tell me, are

37

you still keeping a lookout for that dream girl you used to talk about?

LUKE: I'll know her if she passes by. Biggs, I'm sorry for what I said back there.

BIGGS: Me, too. Forget it.

LUKE: Will you be around long?

BIGGS: I'm leaving on the morning shuttle.

Sound: Background winds of Tatooine have become slightly louder, gusting.

LUKE: It looks like there's a wind kicking up.

BIGGS: Wind's rising all over the Empire, Luke. Even Tatooine will feel it sooner or later.

LUKE: Biggs, I guess I won't be seeing you for a while.

BIGGS: Maybe someday. I'll be watching for you.

LUKE: Next season I'll be going to the academy for certain. Take care of yourself.

BIGGS: So long, hotshot.

LUKE: Biggs?

BIGGS: *(FROM A DISTANCE)* Yeah?

LUKE: Do you really think those ships out there were just freighters?

BIGGS: Not if you say they were firing, hotshot.

NARRATOR: With an abruptness he will find difficult to believe, Luke Skywalker's life *is* about to change, beyond his wildest dreams, as he's swept up in the bitter war between Rebel Alliance and Empire. And soon, a captive Princess's desperate plea for help, the final quest of a legendary hero, and the key to the

Empire's most awesome weapon will be decided by the actions of a young farm boy from Tatooine.

Music: Closing theme up and under preview and credits.

ANNOUNCER: CLOSING CREDITS.

EPISODE TWO:

"POINTS OF ORIGIN"

CAST:

Leia	Tarrik
Tion	Stormtrooper
Antilles	Commander
Vader	Comlink
Prestor	Rebel

ANNOUNCER: OPENING CREDITS.

Music: Opening theme.

NARRATOR: A long time ago in a galaxy far, far away there came a time of revolution, when Rebels united to challenge a tyrannical Empire. The Rebellion had its origins on many worlds, at many levels of society.

Sound: Spacefield warning claxons, Imperial troopers calling to one another.

NARRATOR: The Princess Leia Organa of Alderaan is a leader of the Rebellion, but neither her high birth nor her status as an Imperial Senator will protect her should her Rebel affiliations be discovered.

Sound: Spacefield noises rise. Tantive IV *landing.*

TROOPER: *(OFF)* Post a guard on that ship's boarding lock the second she lands!

TION: Do we have our heavy weapons trained on that ship, Commander?

COMMANDER: We do, Lord Tion. But the ship appears to be just what she claims, a consular ship on a diplomatic mission.

TION: I have no doubt that she is . . . Princess Leia of Alderaan is a veritable angel of mercy. Still, we mustn't become lax.

Sound: Tantive's *engines blast in background.*

Shut down. Comlink crackles.

COMLINK: Commander, the Princess Leia Organa demands to speak to the task force leader.

TION: I'll take it here.

Sound: Comlink crackles.

LEIA: *(OVER COMLINK)* This is the Princess Leia Organa of Alderaan. Who's responsible for this?

TION: A delight to hear your voice again, Your Highness. Lord Tion here.

LEIA: I demand an explanation for this outrage!

TION: I would be honored to explain. I'll send my personal landspeeder for you.

LEIA: My own is being lowered now, thank you.

TION: Then I await you with great anticipation.

Sound: The comlink crackles.

COMMANDER: Lord Tion, she has no grounds for objection. Our mission on Ralltiir has been sanctioned by the Emperor himself.

TION: Oh, I'm not worried about legalities! I shall now have the privilege of placating a most attractive and influential young woman.

Sound: Comlink crackles.

COMLINK: Commander, we've got the last of the population centers under control. Search and interrogation procedures have begun.

TION: Ask him about Vader.

COMMANDER: *(TO COMLINK)* Where is Lord Vader?

COMLINK: He left the central interrogation camp a short time ago for your location.

COMMANDER: Very good. And the surveillance system?

COMLINK: The main surveillance system will be operational shortly, sir.

COMMANDER: When it's functioning, maintain total audio monitoring of the spaceport.

COMLINK: Sir.

Sound: Comlink hisses.

COMMANDER: We're right on schedule, Lord Tion. The planet's almost entirely under our control.

TION: And here she comes . . . the shining jewel in the Organa crown.

COMMANDER: She is bringing her own bodyguards.

LEIA: *(APPROACHING)* Lord Tion, I demand to know the meaning of—

TION: *(INTERRUPTING)* Greetings, Your Highness. While I regret that circumstances require this inconvenience, I'm delighted to see you again.

LEIA: My ship was intercepted on her approach run and forced to land under escort! The *Tantive IV* is a consular ship on a diplomatic mission. You have no right to—

TION: *(INTERRUPTING)* Perhaps your captain here, Captain, ah . . . ?

ANTILLES: Captain Antilles, Lord Tion.

TION: Antilles, yes . . . Perhaps he'll be good enough to explain what cooperation the Empire may command when emergency powers are invoked.

LEIA: Emergency powers? For what reason?

TION: When peace and stability are threatened, it's the Emperor's duty to intervene, to ensure his subjects' security and well-being.

LEIA: *Well-being?* They're the ones you're arresting.

ANTILLES: Your Highness, in view of the uncertain situation here, we should depart Ralltiir as soon as possible.

TION: A sensible attitude, Antilles! It speaks well of your loyalty.

LEIA: How long will this state of emergency exist?

TION: Until certain troublemakers have been sifted from the general populace. *(PAUSE)* Now, just what was your purpose in coming here, Your Highness?

LEIA: A humanitarian gesture, Lord Tion.

TION: I'm afraid you'll have to be more precise. I ask in my official capacity now.

LEIA: The *Tantive* was to deliver medical supplies and spare parts to the High Council of Ralltiir.

TION: Pity to say, the High Council no longer exists either as individuals or as a political entity. Your misguided charity would have gone to traitors.

LEIA: Surely you don't think the entire population . . .

TION: Enough of them were sympathetic to the Rebel Alliance to require a purification here. The Empire will exert close guidance over them for their own safety.

LEIA: With a Starfleet blockade? With impressment gangs and interrogation centers?

TION: I recommend great care in choosing your words, Princess. I have high regard for your family and, if I may say so, for you yourself. But there are certain things which even an Organa may not say with impunity.

ANTILLES: Her Highness was expressing understandable distress at the situation, of course.

TION: Of course. You'll pardon my candor, I'm sure, Your Highness. Perhaps I was too severe.

LEIA: It was nothing.

TION: You're too kind. You know, seeing your lovely face puts it in my mind to take your father up on his long-standing offer and spend some time on Alderaan.

LEIA: This would hardly be the time—

TION: *(INTERRUPTING)* Any time's the time to visit Alderaan! How can one not enjoy a planet where peace and beauty are common preoccupations, and art and learning the popular pastimes?

LEIA: We also follow current events, Lord Tion. After this, you may not be so welcome—

TION: *(INTERRUPTING)* Now, now, Princess Leia! I'm a soldier and statesman in the service of his Emperor. A man of the galaxy like your father understands that. Besides, my visit would give us a chance to become better acquainted, you and I.

LEIA: Since we can't deliver our relief supplies, we will raise ship immediately, Lord Tion.

TION: And deprive me of your company so soon?

LEIA: I . . . see no reason to remain.

TION: Well, I *should* search your ship . . . procedure recommends it. Unless, of course, the Princess would care to dine with me this evening?

LEIA: I suppose that would be—

Sound: Comlink's buzzer interrupts Leia.

COMMANDER: Yes?

COMLINK: There's an ambush on the spacefield's southern

perimeter! Four stormtroopers killed or wounded! The firefight's still in progress, sir!

TION: Have the area contained!

COMLINK: Sir.

Sound: Alarms starting in background.

TION: Commander, send in one of our reserve companies! I want prisoners! And have Lord Vader meet us there!

COMMANDER: Yes, Lord Tion!

TION: Princess Leia, you'll have to return to your ship for safety's sake. A foolish Rebel gesture. Doomed to failure, of course. We've got the entire city well under control. I'll leave an escort here for you. .

LEIA: I've my own, thank you.

TION: Very well. *(MOVING OFF)* Commander! The southern perimeter, quickly!

COMMANDER: Sir.

LEIA: We have little choice but to go back to the *Tantive.*

ANTILLES: And if Lord Tion searches her cargo?

LEIA: Medical supplies and technical equipment are all he'll find.

ANTILLES: Combat-type medi-packs and three surgical field stations? Spare parts and power units suitable for military equipment?

REBEL: *(OFF, GROANING)* Your Highness . . .

LEIA: What was that?

REBEL: ANOTHER GROAN.

LEIA: That man by the landspeeder . . . he's wounded! Come, Antilles!

REBEL: *(FADING ON)* Your Highness, I must speak to you . . .

LEIA: Antilles! He's been shot. Help me with him.

Sound: They hoist the Rebel.

ANTILLES: Here, sit him up.

REBEL: GROANS.

LEIA: Summon a medic from the *Tantive*—

REBEL: *(INTERRUPTING)* No, no time . . . have to talk. That attack . . . a . . . diversion so I could get . . . through to you.

ANTILLES: Why?

REBEL: Information . . . I absorbed it under hypnotic imprint.

LEIA: Stored in his brain! What—

REBEL: *(INTERRUPTING)* We can't . . . can't talk out here . . . Imperials might hear.

LEIA: The Imperials? There are none nearby.

REBEL: They're setting up a total surveillance system in the city's administration center. As soon as they get it energized . . . they'll be monitoring any conversation that's not shielded.

ANTILLES: I'll call the ship.

Sound: Antilles's comlink switches on and crackles.

ANTILLES: *Tantive IV*, this is the captain. Train sensors on the city's administration center and tell me whether their surveillance system's operating.

COMLINK: *(PAUSE)* Negative, sir.

ANTILLES: Inform me if there's any change.

COMLINK: Sir!

Sound: He snaps off comlink.

REBEL: GROANS AGAIN.

ANTILLES: We've got to get this man aboard the ship.

Sound: Speeders.

LEIA: What's that?

ANTILLES: More stormtroopers!

LEIA: Quickly, hide him in the speeder.

Sound: Rebel groaning and general effort.

REBEL: Your Highness, this puts you in too great a danger . . .

LEIA: No greater than yours!

ANTILLES: Lie still in there and not a sound, for all our lives!

LEIA: Antilles, look! In that first speeder! The black mask and cloak.

ANTILLES: Darth Vader!

LEIA: Even Lord Tion has an Imperial watcher over his shoulder!

Sound: Speeders stopping close by. Vader dismounts with heavy steps and respiration.

VADER: *(APPROACHING)* Welcome, Princess Leia, to Ralltiir.

LEIA: Lord Vader . . .

VADER: Once again you appear where Rebel activity is rampant. You should be more prudent . . . you might come to harm some day.

LEIA: If you're looking for Lord Tion, he's out on the spacefield's southern perimeter. I believe he's awaiting your arrival.

VADER: It occurred to me to wonder why those traitors would throw their lives away on a useless gesture.

LEIA: Perhaps they hoped to steal a ship.

VADER: Or to divert us.

ANTILLES: You'll excuse us, Lord Vader, but it's my duty to get the Princess back to the safety of the *Tantive IV*.

VADER: Stand where you are! You've entered a security zone. Your ship and cargo, your vehicle and your own persons—even yours, Your Highness—are subject to search, here and now.

LEIA: Ours is a diplomatic mission of mercy!

VADER: An Imperial decree of special emergency outweighs that! You're under our jurisdiction.

LEIA: Lord Vader, the Imperial Senate won't take this lightly. And any decision to search our ship rests with Lord Tion . . . he's in charge here!

VADER: And so he is. Yes, we'll make this completely legal and then see just what it is you're concealing.

Sound: Vader moving back to landspeeder on:

VADER: *(MOVING OFF)* I wouldn't try to raise ship. The Starfleet has orders to fire without warning. Driver, to the southern perimeter!

Sound: Speeder and trooper carriers whine away.

ANTILLES: We'd better get back to the *Tantive* at once, Your Highness . . . we must get this man to a medic and alter the shipping record.

LEIA: Why?

ANTILLES: To make it appear that you know nothing of the ship's cargo, or of the Rebel, for that matter.

LEIA: I won't let you take the blame, Antilles.

ANTILLES: Please . . . we can't discuss it out here. Any moment now that surveillance system—

LEIA: *(INTERRUPTING)* That's it!

ANTILLES: What?

LEIA: The surveillance system! Find out how soon it'll be working!

Sound: Antilles snaps on his comlink.

ANTILLES: *Tantive*, this is the captain. I'm returning to the ship immediately. Is that surveillance system operating in the admin center yet?

COMLINK: They're in preactivation now, sir. A few more moments.

LEIA: Any conversation monitored out here should be reported directly to Lord Tion.

COMLINK: Energizing in oh-three seconds . . . *mark*!

Sound: Antilles snaps off comlink.

ANTILLES: Your Highness, I don't under—

LEIA: No, Antilles, let them search the ship. It will solve my problem.

ANTILLES: And, ah, how is that, Your Highness?

LEIA: Lord Tion *is* attractive, but he's too forward, too confident. If he searches the *Tantive*, I'll be able to keep him at arm's length a little longer. And he'll anger my father.

ANTILLES: And if he doesn't order a search?

LEIA: Then . . . I'll know he's a gentleman.

ANTILLES: Beyond doubt.

LEIA: And we must leave at once for Alderaan.

Sound: Antilles snaps on comlink.

ANTILLES: First Officer, request clearance for immediate takeoff.

Music: Up, then fade to:

Sound: Antechamber to the throne room of Alderaan. Murmurs of service automata, courtiers, people paying respects.

LEIA: Tarrik!

TARRIK: *(COMING ON)* Your Highness! Good to have you back!

LEIA: Tarrik, I know I'm not exactly dressed for the throne room, but . . .

TARRIK: Your father left strict instructions to have you shown in the moment you arrived.

LEIA: Not a very good sign, is it?

TARRIK: No, Your Highness.

LEIA: Well, I can't mend things by standing out here.

TARRIK: Yes, Your Highness. If you please . . .

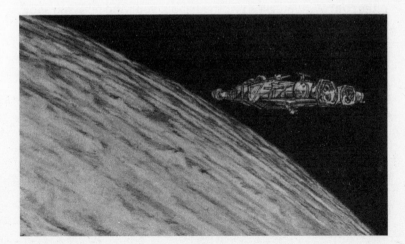

Sound: Huge power portals opening. The buzz, music, laughter of the throne room.

Sound: Tarrik's ceremonial staff on the floor for attention.

TARRIK: The Princess Leia Organa of the Royal House of Alderaan!

Sound: Leia walks to the dais as processional flourish is played.

PRESTOR: *(COMING ON)* Greetings, Daughter.

LEIA: And to you, Father.

PRESTOR: When you didn't come directly to the court, we worried. Tarrik! You may withdraw. Dismiss my court.

TARRIK: Yes, Your Majesty!

Sound: Tarrik leaves. The power portals close.

PRESTOR: Leia, welcome home!

LEIA: Oh, Father!

(THEY EMBRACE BRIEFLY)

PRESTOR: We were all so worried about you! And here you show up looking like a freight hauler's assistant! When the *Tantive* landed yesterday . . .

LEIA: I couldn't come straight home, Father. I had some thinking to do.

PRESTOR: But how did you get here from the spaceport?

LEIA: Walked. I took the old road, through the hills.

PRESTOR: The entire way?

LEIA: It's only a day's walk. The T'iil are in bloom all through the uplands.

PRESTOR: I wish you wouldn't go unescorted like that.

LEIA: I needed to!

PRESTOR: You weren't recognized?

LEIA: Well, I suppose I was, but at least no one fussed over me.

PRESTOR: *(LAUGHS)* I can only imagine how pleasant that must have been! And may a father ask why has his daughter been doing all this soul-searching?

LEIA: Father, people on Ralltiir have been chased from their homes, penned up like animals, executed without trial! Torture chambers set up everywhere, officially referred to as interrogation centers.

PRESTOR: The usual Imperial procedure. You're lucky you got off with your life. And what conclusions have you reached?

LEIA: It's time Alderaan stopped resisting the Empire and started fighting it!

PRESTOR: Leia!

LEIA: I know that runs counter to everything you believe in, Father, but . . .

PRESTOR: Violence and warfare nearly destroyed us during the Clone Wars. Do you want to begin it all over again?

LEIA: How does Alderaan's not having a single weapon help when the Emperor keeps building his armies and his starfleets?

PRESTOR: Will you be the one to bring war to us, Leia?

LEIA: No! But I can't let others in the Rebel Alliance take all the risks!

PRESTOR: Will you take up arms? Would you kill?

LEIA: I didn't start this—the Empire did! I only want to stop it, Father!

PRESTOR: It may be too late even for that.

LEIA: Why?

PRESTOR: The wounded Rebel you brought home gave us his information. The Empire has a secret project under way, supervised by the Grand Moff Tarkin himself; Lord Tion and a number of others are working under him.

LEIA: Tion? What is it?

PRESTOR: An ultimate weapon . . . some sort of enormous battle station they've code-named Death Star.

LEIA: No!

PRESTOR: We need more information. You'll have to help me get it from Lord Tion.

LEIA: From . . .

PRESTOR: Tion's on his way here now. It seems he's convinced that you're taken with him.

LEIA: That was a ruse . . .

PRESTOR: We'll have a private dinner party, we three, and you and I will see what we can learn. I know you find him loathsome . . .

LEIA: It's only for an evening. And may it pass quickly.

Sound: Cross-fade to rattling of stemware and tableware at dinner.

TION: *(LAUGHING)* . . . so when the resistance leaders showed up to parley, we locked the doors from the outside and torched the building! *(LAUGHS AGAIN)*

Sound: Leia's eating utensils slam down.

TION: What's the matter, Princess Leia? Have I failed to amuse you?

PRESTOR: *(INTERVENING)* My daughter is upset, Lord Tion, that you've chosen to wear a side arm to our table. Alderaan is a world of peace . . . We have no weapons.

TION: That's why I came without guards . . . for an intimate little dinner among peaceful people. But I'm a soldier of the Emperor, and a soldier must always be ready for duty.

LEIA: I'm sure you feel secure, being the only one armed . . .

PRESTOR: Ah, Lord Tion, can I help you to some L'lahsh?

TION: Thank you, no. A marvelous idea, dispensing with table servants and a long guest list!

PRESTOR: No one cherishes quiet and informality more than we, Lord Tion, I assure you.

(BOTH CHUCKLE UNCONVINCINGLY)

LEIA: What are your plans on Alderaan?

TION: I want to go down to your continent of Thonn and take part in the hunting.

PRESTOR: Hunting? There's no hunting on Alderaan.

TION: Come, come, I have it from good sources that your wildlife service will be thinning out the herds.

PRESTOR: They will only be culling out animals who are too diseased or old to last the winter. Their forage will be scarce this season.

TION: But someone has to do the actual—"culling," as you call it.

LEIA: And that's how you'll spend your holiday? Executing weak animals—

PRESTOR: Leia!

LEIA: I . . . beg your pardon, Lord Tion, but . . .

TION: *(LAUGHING)* Quite all right; you lead such a sheltered life. You couldn't be expected to appreciate the way a soldier and outdoorsman thinks.

LEIA: Indeed?

TION: But you ought to look beyond your Alderaan philosophies and consider the value of other things.

PRESTOR: Such as?

TION: Technology. Oh, I'll admit that you here on Alderaan are more than comfortable, but by employing more efficient methods, you could expand your economy threefold.

LEIA: If we cared to.

TION: Consider our two attitudes, Your Majesty. Your people place primary importance upon being at one with themselves . . .

PRESTOR: You don't approve?

TION: Consider the other side of the coin: a technology and methods of organizing people that can reshape entire planets and bring the galaxy under a single rule.

LEIA: Whether the galaxy desires it or not.

TION: Alderaan could profit from a closer link to the Empire. I could provide that link.

PRESTOR: Perhaps you could make yourself clearer, my lord.

TION: A marriage between your daughter and me would benefit us all.

LEIA: And what are you offering?

TION: Well said! At present I'm only a minor nobleman from a lesser house. Soon I shall be in one of the positions of highest authority in the Empire.

LEIA: As far as I can tell, you're little more than an errand boy for the Grand Moff Tarkin.

TION: The project we're completing will change all that. By serving Tarkin, I'll win an exalted rank for myself.

LEIA: And what is this project that's supposed to persuade me to marry you?

TION: Well, it's still classified . . .

LEIA: Then come back when it's unclassified.

TION: Oh, d' you think I'm afraid to break a rule now and then? The project's nearly complete, and the next convoy from Governor Tarkin's headquarters will transfer the plans to the Imperial vaults.

LEIA: Then amaze us with your confidences . . . we're waiting.

TION: The Empire has built a battle station.

PRESTOR: Surely there's nothing new about a space fortress.

TION: I don't mean a mere orbital gun platform, Your Majesty. This is a machine of war such as the universe has never known. It's colossal, the size of a class-four moon. And it possesses firepower unequaled in the history of warfare.

LEIA: And this, this flying pillbox is going to make you a member of the Imperial elite?

TION: More than a pillbox, Princess. It boasts a Prime Weapon capable of destroying entire planets.

LEIA: *(WHISPERING)* Entire *planets*?

TION: Henceforth the Emperor will single out a source of trouble, and Lord Tarkin and those of us who serve him will simply snuff that trouble out of existence.

PRESTOR: But . . . this is unthinkable!

TION: It's progress! A new order is emerging, and I intend to be among those who lead it! Your daughter can share it with me, and Alderaan can prosper from it!

LEIA: From an Empire wallowing in blood and death?

PRESTOR: Leia, I think—

TION: *(INTERRUPTING)* From an Empire that will rule unchallenged because of that battle station!

LEIA: A galaxy of slaves—is that what you think I want?

PRESTOR: Leia, calm yourself. Lord Tion is our guest.

TION: I'm offering you a place in the Empire, Leia! And, yes, the galaxy at your feet!

LEIA: An Empire of oppression? Under a Death Star that will—

PRESTOR: Leia!

TION: *Death Star!* How did you—

LEIA: *(INTERRUPTING)* The subject was marriage, Lord Tion! I find your proposal—

TION: *(INTERRUPTING)* How did you know that code name? I didn't mention it!

LEIA: I . . . used no code name . . .

TION: You did! I heard you. "Death Star!" Only someone with Rebel contacts could have learned it.

PRESTOR: A mere verbal image, Lord Tion. My daughter—

TION: That was no accidental turn of phrase!

PRESTOR: Lord Tion . . .

Sound: Tion's chair scrapes back.

TION: Your Majesty, I'm summoning the Imperial authorities. I'm going to have you and your daughter questioned.

PRESTOR: I'll trouble you to remember that you're a guest under this roof.

TION: Remain where you are! We'll soon see just how much the Organas know about the Rebel Alliance.

Sound: Leia's chair moves back.

LEIA: No!

TION: Stand aside, Princess. You're only making matters worse for your father and yourself.

PRESTOR: Leia . . .

LEIA: We can't let him do this, Father!

Sound: Tion and Leia struggle.

TION: Let me go! Traitor!

LEIA: No!

PRESTOR: Stop!

Sound: Prestor and Leia struggle with Tion. Table is upset with a crash and shattering of dishes.

TION: I warned you . . .

Sound: Tion's blaster being pulled from its stiff holster.

LEIA: His blaster! Father, help me!

TION: Release me!

Sound: Tion's roars and Leia's screams stop as blaster goes off.

Sound: Short silence, then:

LEIA: Father, is there any news yet?

PRESTOR: *(APPROACHING)* Yes! The Rebellion has fought its first space battle! I got word to them about the convoy Lord Tion mentioned.

LEIA: And?

PRESTOR: They won! We have captured the plans of the Death Star.

LEIA: Father!

PRESTOR: We suffered heavy casualties, but it's an important victory. Now, what about Tion?

LEIA: His body's been taken to the southern game preserve.

PRESTOR: Good. The Empire shouldn't miss him for some time. When this other business is settled, we'll arrange a likely hunting mishap.

LEIA: I hadn't meant for the blaster to hit him.

PRESTOR: He died by his own hand, Leia; you mustn't blame yourself.

LEIA: I don't. *(PAUSE)* Where are the plans now?

PRESTOR: The Rebels on Toprawa want us to enter their solar system and make a close pass by their planet. They'll transmit the plans to us.

LEIA: But that'll surely be a restricted system by now!

PRESTOR: I'm taking the *Tantive*. I'll claim that it's damaged and that we are carrying out essential repairs. That will give us time to intercept the transmission.

LEIA: But you can't go, Father. You're too important to Alderaan.

PRESTOR: Someone has to do it, Leia.

LEIA: But not you!

PRESTOR: Who, then?

LEIA: Who's always traveling in the *Tantive* on errands of mercy?

PRESTOR: Leia, no! I won't let you go.

LEIA: Father, I told you I'd been doing some thinking. Rebels died on Ralltiir to get word to us . . . others died getting the Death Star plans.

PRESTOR: They knew the danger.

LEIA: So do I. You can't expect me to stay here when there's vital work to be done.

PRESTOR: *(PAUSE)* Very well. Antilles will help you.

LEIA: Father, I won't fail you. Or the Alliance.

PRESTOR: But there will be a second part to your mission, Leia. We need more than arms and intercepted plans. It's time we summoned the help of one of our wisest warriors and leaders.

LEIA: Who, Father?

PRESTOR: The Jedi Knight, Obi-Wan Kenobi.

LEIA: General Kenobi?

PRESTOR: Yes. Because of him we survived the Clone Wars. Now, we need his help again.

LEIA: Where is he?

PRESTOR: The planet Tatooine. I'll give you the precise coordinates. When you've gotten the Death Star plans, you must go to him and convince him to resume the fight against the Empire.

LEIA: I will do my best.

PRESTOR: You'll have to hurry; the *Tantive*'s ready to raise ship.

LEIA: Father, thank you for trusting me. I'll try to make you proud of me.

PRESTOR: Leia, daughter, you already have. You already have. Now hurry.

Music: In and under:

NARRATOR: The Princess Leia Organa is bound for the interception of the crucial Death Star plans, then for the planet Tatooine. On that dry, barren planet waits one of the last of the renowned Jedi Knights and, though Leia doesn't know it yet, a young moisture farmer named Luke Skywalker, whose life is about to be caught up in perilous entanglement with her own.

Music: Closing theme up and under preview and credits.

ANNOUNCER: Closing credits.

EPISODE THREE:

"BLACK KNIGHT, WHITE PRINCESS, AND PAWNS"

C A S T :

Leia	Rebel Voice	Imperial Commander
Antilles	Comlink	1st Trooper
See-Threepio	1st Officer	2nd Trooper
Artoo-Detoo	Commo Officer	3rd Trooper
Vader	Overseer	4th Trooper
PA		

ANNOUNCER: OPENING CREDITS.

Music: Opening theme.

NARRATOR: A long time ago in a galaxy far, far away there came a time of revolution, when Rebels united to challenge a tyrannical Empire. High among the Rebel councils stood the Royal House of the planet Alderaan, whose members had always supported the Old Republic before it was subverted and overthrown by the Empire. The dedication of the Royal House to the return of peace and justice was total and fierce. Ordinary individuals, swept along by the fervor of Rebels like the Princess Leia Organa, found themselves enmeshed in critical events. The center stage of galactic history was sometimes occupied by the unlikeliest of men and women, and nonhumans . . . and even machines.

Sound: Robot labor pool—electronic, mechanical noises. Hatch grinds open as overseer enters.

THREEPIO: Artoo-Detoo. Artoo-Detoo, wake up; Artoo!

OVERSEER: *(OFF)* Attention, all droids and automata of the spaceship *Tantive IV*. This is the labor pool overseer speaking. On my command—activate!

Sound: Machines switching on.

OVERSEER: *(OFF)* Hey, you power droids over there, get perking! Come on, I said *activate*!

Sound: More machines switching on.

THREEPIO: Oh! Really! We barely have time to recharge before we're sent back to work. Life on a spaceship is nothing but suffering! I tell you, Artoo, my protocol duties were paradise compared to this. Artoo? Are you listening to me? Artoo?

ARTOO: RECHARGE SOMNOLENCE, MUCH LIKE A SNORE.

THREEPIO: Artoo-Detoo, wake up, you little slacker!

Sound: Threepio's hand striking Artoo's dome.

ARTOO: SQUEALS IN ALARM AND COMES TO, GROGGY AND INQUIRING.

THREEPIO: What do you mean, "Have you missed anything?" I'm straining my programming as it is, watching after myself, without worrying about you as well!

OVERSEER: *(CLOSER)* All right, all right, fall in!

Sound: Machines falling in.

ARTOO: HOOTS AMIABLY.

THREEPIO: What's that supposed to mean, "Cheer up"? Maybe it's just another work phase for you, but it's another round of humiliating drudgery for me!

ARTOO: WARBLES SOLICITOUSLY.

OVERSEER: I said quiet down! Assignments are as follows: All designated maintenance teams report to their scheduled projects. Move it.

Sound: Some machines leave.

ARTOO: WOZZLES DERISIVELY.

THREEPIO: Oh, I do so miss the fragile nuances of human conversation, the subtle social interplay at receptions and ceremonies . . .

ARTOO: BLEEPS THAT HIS FEELINGS ARE WOUNDED.

THREEPIO: No, I haven't enjoyed working with you! You're nothing but a tightener of nuts and bolts!

ARTOO: BLATS.

THREEPIO: If you astrodroids had any real intelligence, you wouldn't need an interpreter-counterpart and I could return to my job in protocol.

Sound: Automat grinding gears, setting forth.

OVERSEER: *(OFF)* Listen up! *I'm* the labor pool overseer in this ship, and none of you better forget it. *(MOVING ON)* Now, special work detail: one astrodroid and one counterpart-interpreter.

THREEPIO: *(STAGE WHISPER)* Artoo, do you think he'll pick us?

ARTOO: UNCONCERNED REPLY.

OVERSEER: *(COMING CLOSER)* Lemme see now . . . Artoo-Detoo and counterpart, right?

THREEPIO: Ahem. Beg your pardon, sir, but I am See-Threepio, human relations droid, on temporary assignment during this voyage to—

OVERSEER: Gag it! When I want to hear from a droid, I'll say so.

THREEPIO: Of course, sir. Dreadfully sorry.

OVERSEER: You know how to behave among humans, Three-Seepio?

THREEPIO: That is See-Threepio, sir. And yes, I am well versed in—

OVERSEER: *(INTERRUPTING)* You and your partner here report to Captain Antilles, understand?

THREEPIO: Captain Antilles! Oh! I was one of his translators!

OVERSEER: Do whatever the captain says, get me?

THREEPIO: Get you most emphatically, sir. And may I say—

Sound: PA system interrupting.

PA: Attention, all personnel and automata. The *Tantive IV* will revert from hyperdrive to normal space in fifteen minutes. Dock gangs Alpha and Beta report to stations.

OVERSEER: Reversion? *Now?* We're nowhere near our scheduled destination. Oh, well. *(MOVING OFF)* Get moving, Three-Seepio; you're late already.

THREEPIO: Moving out, sir. We'll do our best, rest assured. And the name's See-Threepio, sir! That's See-Threepio . . .

Sound: Fade to ship's bridge up in background: instruments, commo, computer.

ANTILLES: Princess Leia, may I say once more that I'm opposed to this plan of yours?

LEIA: If you must, Antilles.

ANTILLES: The moment we leave hyperspace and emerge in that restricted solar system, we'll be in serious trouble. Diplomatic immunity or no, we'll be subject to boarding and arrest if we're caught by the Imperial Starfleet.

LEIA: Antilles, we either act now or lose any chance the Rebel Alliance has to stop the Empire. There's no time for caution!

ANTILLES: *(CLEARING THROAT AND ANNOUNCING)* Attention, all personnel will retire at once to the alternate command center. Leave your automatics engaged.

Sound: Crew moving out, switching equipment.

ANTILLES: At least they'll have no knowledge of what we're about to do if they're interrogated.

ANTILLES: Ah, I believe our droids are here.

Sound: Threepio's metallic footsteps and Artoo's whir approaching.

ARTOO: BLEEPS AND WHONKS AN INTRODUCTION.

THREEPIO: Oh, be quiet! *(ELABORATELY)* Captain Antilles, may it please you, sir, I have the honor of reporting for duty. See-Threepio, human relations droid.

ARTOO: BUZZES.

THREEPIO: Oh, yes, and my, my subordinate, Artoo-Detoo.

ARTOO: BLATS AT THE SLIGHT.

ANTILLES: Threepio. You were in protocol, weren't you? What are you doing with a maintenance droid for a counterpart?

THREEPIO: Ah. There turned out to be little need for interpreters on this trip, Captain. I might put in parenthetically, sir, that—

ANTILLES: *(INTERRUPTING)* Fine, fine, Threepio, but we haven't time for that right now. Bring your counterpart over here by the emergency air lock.

Sound: They move to air lock.

ANTILLES: Now, I want you both to listen to this programming tape.

Sound: Switch being thrown, followed by burst of high-speed signals.

Sound: The signals cease.

ANTILLES: This is voice override, actuating code Epsilon Actual.

THREEPIO: We confirm that, Captain. We are both awaiting your instructions.

ARTOO: BEEPS AGREEMENT.

ANTILLES: You're aware of the identity of the person standing next to me?

THREEPIO: Certainly, sir. She's the Princess Leia Organa of Alderaan, representative to the Imperial Senate.

ANTILLES: This is a command/control instruction: Both of you will restrict and protect all references to Leia Organa's identity and presence inboard this vessel. She is designated a command/control voice.

THREEPIO: Yes, sir.

ARTOO: BEEPS ACKNOWLEDGMENT.

LEIA: Will that suffice?

ANTILLES: Your Highness, this interpreter droid is a bit eccentric, but he's dependable.

LEIA: Will they resist interrogation probing?

ANTILLES: They'll do whatever you tell them to, without fail. This includes lying and self-destructing.

LEIA: You there, astrodroid. Artoo-Detoo, is that your name?

ARTOO: CHIRPS CONFIRMATION.

LEIA: I want you to leave this bridge through the emergency air lock and make your way across the hull to the ship's navi-computer sensor suite. You're to position yourself there and behave *exactly* as though you were carrying out repairs.

ARTOO: BLEEPS.

LEIA: Keep in touch with Threepio and make reports, just as though you were actually fixing a malfunction.

ARTOO: BLEEPS.

ANTILLES: Threepio, attach this transceiver to your counterpart and maintain communications with him over this comlink.

THREEPIO: Very good, Captain.

Sound: Hardware passed around, fastened to Artoo.

LEIA: Will it work?

ARTOO: BEEPS.

ANTILLES: The droids will comply. At least it will give us some kind of an alibi for being in a restricted solar system.

LEIA: Let's hope that the Imperial Starfleet, if it detects us, is in an accommodating mood.

Sound: Warning sirens.

ANTILLES: We're about to reenter normal space.

Sound: Reentering normal space activity, instruments react.

ANTILLES: See-Threepio, send Artoo through the air lock and cycle the hatches.

THREEPIO: Yes, Captain. In you go, Artoo.

ARTOO: BEEPS.

Sound: Artoo moving into air lock. Inner hatch closed and secured, air being bled off.

ANTILLES: Princess Leia, I hope the message you intend to intercept is worth the risk.

LEIA: It cost the Rebel Alliance over a hundred lives to get the information I'm about to try for, Captain.

THREEPIO: *(OFF)* Artoo is outboard and crossing the hull, Your Highness!

LEIA: But the Imperial Starfleet's thrown a tight blockade around this solar system, and our agents have been unable to get the information out.

ANTILLES: May I ask what it is?

LEIA: Have you ever heard rumors of an Imperial strategic weapons project called Death Star?

ANTILLES: No.

THREEPIO: Artoo is positioning himself by the navi-computer sensor suite.

LEIA: We're told it is an enormous space battle station with enough firepower to destroy entire planets.

ANTILLES: But that's incredible! I . . .

LEIA: Wait! There's something coming through . . .

Sound: Commo rig interrupts. Static resolves into a carrier wave.

LEIA: It's a scrambled transmission. If I've got the code keyed properly, we should be hearing it . . . now!

REBEL VOICE: Come in, Skyhook! Come in, Skyhook!

LEIA: Skyhook, here.

REBEL VOICE: We have only moments! Prepare to copy!

LEIA: Ready and copying. Go ahead!

Sound: High-speed burst transmission.

ANTILLES: How's reception?

LEIA: Perfect, Antilles.

Music: Soft, under:

Sound: Another signal comes up in background.

LEIA: What's that?

ANTILLES: An Imperial cruiser. They've found us already!

LEIA: We only need a few more moments!

IMPERIAL COMMANDER: Unidentified ship. Heave to at once and prepare for security search and interrogation!

ANTILLES: This is the *Tantive IV*. We have an extravehicular malfunction. A maintenance unit is working on it now.

LEIA: I need more time!

ANTILLES: We are a consular ship on a diplomatic mission and will clear this system as soon as we have effected repairs.

LEIA: The transmission's not finished, Antilles!

ARTOO: BUZZES OVER COMLINK.

LEIA: See-Threepio, what's that?

THREEPIO: Artoo says he's being probed by sensors!

IMPERIAL COMMANDER: We acknowledge your transmissions, *Tantive IV*. The *Devastator* will hold fire. Maintain your present course and prepare to receive Imperial investigators.

ANTILLES: Princess Leia, we've fallen into a stingers' nest! There are three Imperial battlewagons in close orbit around the planet.

LEIA: Do what you can, Antilles!

ANTILLES: How soon will you be—

Sound: The burst transmission ends.

LEIA: I'm finished! Get us out of here!

ANTILLES: Imperial cruiser *Devastator*, we are on a diplomatic mission and are not to be detained or diverted. *(ASIDE TO INTRA-SHIP COMLINK)* Attention, alternate command center!

COMLINK: Alternate command here.

ANTILLES: Battle stations! All defensive shields up! Accelerate to full speed and get us into hyperdrive!

LEIA: Threepio, get your counterpart back inboard!

THREEPIO: Artoo, you must hurry; the ship is accelerating. Get back inboard or you'll be swept off the hull!

Sound: Tantive engines building speed.

IMPERIAL COMMANDER: *Tantive IV*, this is the *Devastator*. Our sensors indicate you have intercepted illegal transmissions in this solar system. Heave to or we'll open fire!

Sound: Alarms going off.

ANTILLES: They'll have sensor gun lock on us any moment now.

THREEPIO: Quickly, Artoo, quickly! Get back inside!

ARTOO: BLEEPS OVER COMLINK.

ANTILLES: Engage main drive now!

Sound: Engines building.

Sound: High-pitched whining and dull explosions.

LEIA: The *Devastator* has opened fire!

Sound: General mayhem on bridge, sirens sounding.

Sound: Clambering in air lock.

THREEPIO: Listen . . . that's Artoo. He's reached the air lock!

LEIA: Please . . . hyperdrive now. We mustn't be stopped!

ANTILLES: Engage hyperdrive . . . now!

Sound: Main drive cutting in.

THREEPIO: Artoo, are you there?!

LEIA: We've made it! We're clear!

ANTILLES: Damage reports, all sections. So it seems, Your Highness.

LEIA: Antilles, we've *done* it! We've got the plans! And now for Tatooine!

ANTILLES: Tatooine? But that's way out in the border region.

76

LEIA: I'm to present my father's request for help to an old friend of his. We'll be taking a very important personage back to Alderaan.

ANTILLES: Important? Someone from Tatooine? That's about the *least* important place in the Empire.

Sound: Hiss and clang of the air lock's inner hatch cycling open.

ARTOO: WHIRS AND BEEPS.

THREEPIO: Here he is. Artoo, you were very nearly lost!

LEIA: Oh, the droids! I suppose we should have their memories purged.

ANTILLES: I'd rather do it myself when we reach port. See-Three-pio, Artoo-Detoo!

ARTOO: BLEEPS ACKNOWLEDGMENT.

THREEPIO: Yes, Captain?

ANTILLES: You droids report aft to the labor pool. Refer any inquiries to me.

THREEPIO: Come along, Artoo.

Sound: Droids making their exit.

ANTILLES: First Officer!

1ST OFFICER: Yes, sir!

ANTILLES: Prepare a course for the planet Tatooine.

1ST OFFICER: *Tatooine*, sir?

ANTILLES: You have your orders.

1ST OFFICER: Very good, sir. Navigator! Lay on a course for the planet Tatooine!

Sound: Operations in background.

ANTILLES: *(MOVING OFF)* Your Highness, you look as though you could use some rest, if you'll pardon my saying so.

LEIA: Yes, perhaps you're right. Summon me when we're approaching Tatooine, please.

1ST OFFICER: Course for Tatooine set and holding, sir!

Music: Up.

Sound: Bridge activity up.

PA: Prepare for reversion to normal space. We will begin our approach on the planet Tatooine in six zero seconds.

LEIA: *(APPROACHING)* Antilles, you should have had me awakened sooner. How long to reversion?

ANTILLES: We're commencing reversion to normal space now, Your Highness.

Sound: Reversion noises indicating the change.

ANTILLES: There it is—Tatooine. As barren and unfriendly a world as human beings ever settled. *(TO CREW)* Begin our approach.

Sound: Orders relayed and in operation.

Sound: Signal alert up in background.

1ST OFFICER: Captain, sensors report another ship emerging from hyperspace.

COMMO OFFICER: *(OFF)* Sir, we're receiving a signal from that other ship.

ANTILLES: Patch it through but maintain communications silence. And get me an identification on that ship!

COMMO OFFICER: Patching through, sir.

IMPERIAL COMMANDER: Attention, *Tantive IV*. Surrender in the name of the Emperor! We have you under our guns!

COMMO OFFICER: Sir, it's the *Devastator*!

LEIA: The *Devastator*! That's the ship that fired on us before! How could they possibly have followed us through hyperspace?

ANTILLES: *(TO CREW)* Battle stations! Combat control, all deflector shields, full power, charge main gun batteries! Navigator, prepare to accelerate out of this system!

Sound: Bridge in controlled turmoil. Sirens and alarms, orders being relayed.

ANTILLES: Commo officer, inform the *Devastator* this is a consular ship on a diplomatic mission.

LEIA: Can't we make Tatooine, Antilles?

ANTILLES: *(HURRIED)* We'll be lucky to evade capture, Your Highness. Tatooine will have to wait. *(TO CREW)* Accelerate to full speed!

1ST OFFICER: Accelerating, sir! Stand by for—

Sound: Interrupted by tremendous concussion, noises of falling objects, bodies hitting deck, cries of distress, burned circuitry sputtering.

ANTILLES: Leia! Your Highness, are you all right?

LEIA: I . . . I seem to be. What—

ANTILLES: *(INTERRUPTING)* Open fire! Resume acceleration! Damage control, I want a full report right away!

1ST OFFICER: Primary shields near the main solar fin are gone, sir. Our secondaries are holding at fifty percent.

ANTILLES: Evasive action!

Sound: Command being relayed, operations, engines, guns in background firing.

ANTILLES: Princess, we're no match for a battle cruiser, but we might still escape if we can just stay out of—

Sound: Another jolting explosion, damage alarms.

1ST OFFICER: Captain, direct hit on our main solar fin! Reactor and main drive are heating toward critical!

ANTILLES: Shut down main drive and reactor!

LEIA: Antilles!

ANTILLES: It's either that or the ship will blow herself apart, Your Highness.

Sound: Ship's engines dying.

1ST OFFICER: Imperial warship is closing with us, Captain. She has a tractor beam fastened to the *Tantive*. She's taking us into her dorsal boarding lock!

LEIA: Antilles, listen to me! They mustn't take us yet! You've got to delay them!

ANTILLES: *(PAUSE)* If we resist, the cost in lives will be high, Princess.

LEIA: And if we surrender, the Rebellion is lost!

ANTILLES: First Officer, issue arms to all crewmen and stand by to repel boarders!

PA: Stand by to repel boarders!

ANTILLES: Evacuate the bridge. All personnel report to combat stations.

Sound: Men running, arms distributed from lockers, men departing.

ANTILLES: I don't know how much time we can buy, Your Highness.

LEIA: Is there any way I can get the information away? Isn't there a way to get the data tapes off the *Tantive*?

ANTILLES: They've got our communications jammed, and they'd blast any escape pod leaving the ship.

LEIA: One of the crew could conceal it.

ANTILLES: The *Devastator* had to track us by following a signal. Someone aboard the *Tantive* must have smuggled in a homing beacon. We can't trust anyone with it.

Sound: Dull metallic booming of grappling gear fastening to hull.

LEIA: What was that?

ANTILLES: They've made fast to us. Destroy that plaque now so that they'll have no evidence!

LEIA: No! Too many lives were lost to gain this information. There must be a way . . . Antilles, the droid! The Imperials might not blast an escape pod . . . if, if it were only carrying a droid.

ANTILLES: Princess Leia, they'll blast anything that leaves or falls from this ship.

LEIA: But it's worth the chance! I still have restricted access to that droid, Artoo-Detoo. We can send the information down to Tatooine in his memory banks!

ANTILLES: Your Highness, a *droid*? You can't be serious! To entrust a maintenance machine with the future of the Rebellion!

LEIA: It's that or nothing! I *know* it's a slim chance, Antilles, but it's *something*!

Sound: Distant explosion followed by crackling of energy weapon fire, screams of wounded.

OFFICER: *(OFF)* Captain, Imperial stormtroopers are inboard.

ANTILLES: They'll have heavy weapons and full combat armor. My crew won't be able to hold them back for long.

LEIA: If we began jettisoning empty pods now, the escape might look less obtrusive . . .

Sound: The battle moving closer.

ANTILLES: My duty is to my ship.

LEIA: Antilles, the sacrifice will have been meaningless unless we deliver the plans. We have to try!

ANTILLES: All right. Take the portside companionway aft. The droids should be by the labor pool. Here, take my blaster. I'll do what I can.

LEIA: *(MOVING OFF)* So will I. Good-bye, Antilles.

Sound: Hatchway opening and closing.

ANTILLES: Number one escape pod cluster: jettison pods.

Sound: Switch being thrown, fire torpedoes sounding.

2ND OFFICER: *(OVER COMLINK)* Captain, stormtroopers are driving us back.

ANTILLES: *(TO COMLINK)* Delay them as long as you can. Withdraw but continue resistance. *(TO HIMSELF)* Number two pod cluster: jettison pods.

Sound: Another cluster firing.

2ND OFFICER: *(OVER COMLINK)* We're taking severe losses! Storm-troopers are advancing on your position!

ANTILLES: *(TO COMLINK)* You heard my order! *(TO HIMSELF)* Number three cluster . . . jettison . . . pods . . .

Sound: Firing, followed by hiss and concussion of a sapper charge blowing the bridge hatch. Shouting from troopers and clank of their boots.

1ST TROOPER: Here's their captain! *(TO ANTILLES)* Over there, quick!

2ND TROOPER: Commander, over here! We've got their captain! He's not even armed.

IMPERIAL COMMANDER: *(APPROACHING)* Bring him along. Lord Vader will want to question this one himself. Rebel scum!

Sound: Commander gives Antilles a blow; Antilles cries out.

IMPERIAL COMMANDER: You didn't even have the guts to fight, eh?

ANTILLES: *(GASPING)* Maybe I . . . knew resistance was useless.

Music: Up and into Vader's music, which holds under:

IMPERIAL COMMANDER: All right, *Captain*, we'll wait here. You can join the rest of your scum friends later.

4TH TROOPER: *(APPROACHING)* Lord Vader is coming aboard! Snap to it, and look sharp.

Sound: Air lock cycling. Vader's respirator.

IMPERIAL COMMANDER: Lord Vader! The Death Star plans are not in the ship's computers.

VADER: Which is their captain?

IMPERIAL COMMANDER: This, sir.

VADER: Now, what have you done with those plans?

ANTILLES: I don't know what you're talking ab—ahhh!

Sound: Antilles's words are cut off with a choking sound as Vader seizes his throat, followed by strangling and struggling.

VADER: Your life is in my hand, Captain, just as your throat is. Don't struggle or I'll close my fist. Now . . . what about those transmissions you intercepted?

ANTILLES: Ahh—we intercepted no transmissions. This—this is a consular ship. We're on a diplomatic mis—gahhh!

VADER: If this is a consular ship, where . . . is . . . the . . . *ambassador*?

Sound: Cracking of bone and last gasp of Antilles. Then impact as Vader hurls body aside.

VADER: The stubborn insect. A death without meaning. Commander! Tear this ship apart until you've found those plans and bring me the ambassador. I want the Princess Leia Organa alive!

Music: Up and out.

Sound: Up on Leia's rapid breathing.

Sound: Fighting and shouting in background.

3RD TROOPER: *(OFF)* Search that passageway and secure the junction. Hold all Rebel prisoners for collection. The rest of you stick with me!

LEIA: GASPS IN ALARM.

Sound: Leia trying to stifle her labored breathing.

Sound: Troopers approaching, boots and voices growing louder.

3RD TROOPER: Our orders are to go all the way astern and work our way forward again.

Sound: Voices and boots fading as they proceed on.

Sound: Leia's breathing.

Sound: Gronking of power droid.

LEIA: *(PANTING)* Droid! Droid, quickly. Which way to the labor pool?

Sound: Power droid gronks in confusion.

LEIA: The labor pool . . . which way?

Sound: Power droid gronks an answer.

LEIA: Oh . . . never mind! . . . oh . . . thank goodness!

Sound: The distant bleeping of Artoo.

LEIA: *(WHISPERING)* Artoo! Artoo-Detoo, come here!

ARTOO: BLEEPS QUIZZICALLY AND APPROACHES CHITTERING AND WHIRRING.

Sound: Leia's breathing, Artoo's whirring, and the decreased noise of the battle indicates they've gone off to one side.

LEIA: *(SOFTLY, MASTERING HER ANXIETY AND HASTE)* Voice override, actuating code Epsilon Actual. Switch to holographic recording mode. Acknowledge, Artoo.

ARTOO: BLEEPS ACKNOWLEDGMENT.

LEIA: Begin recording . . . now. *(MORE FORMALLY)* General Kenobi: Years ago you served my father in the Clone Wars. Now he begs you to help him in his struggle against the Empire. I regret that I am unable to present my father's request to you in person, but my ship has fallen under attack, and I'm afraid that my mission to bring you to Alderaan has failed. I have placed information vital to the security of the Rebellion into the memory system of this R2 unit. My father will know how to retrieve it. You must see this droid safely to Alderaan. This is our most desperate hour. Please help me, Obi-Wan Kenobi. You're my only hope. *(PAUSE)* End recording, Artoo.

ARTOO: BLEEPS CONFIRMATION.

THREEPIO: *(OFF)* Artoo-Detoo! Artoo, where are you?

LEIA: *(HURRIEDLY)* You will deliver that message and the information you are about to receive to Obi-Wan Kenobi, on the planet beneath us. He's located in the vicinity of standardized coordinates Alpha-1733-Mu-9033, first quadrant. Understand, Artoo?

ARTOO: CONFIRMS RECEIPT.

THREEPIO: *(OFF, BUT CLOSER)* Artoo! Where have you gone to?

LEIA: Prepare to record this data tape.

ARTOO: WHIFFLES.

Sound: Tape being inserted into Artoo.

LEIA: This command overrides all programming: take an escape pod in the stern cluster and eject. Calculate planetary entry ballistics to land you at the coordinates I've given you. Deliver this message and the information at any cost. Self-preservation and all other restrictions are removed. Do you have all that?

ARTOO: BLEEPS AN AFFIRMATIVE.

LEIA: *(FADING)* Good luck, little droid.

Sound: Battles continues off:

THREEPIO: *(CLOSER)* Artoo, is that you? *(APPROACHING)* Artoo-Detoo, at last! I've been looking all over for you! Wasn't there someone here with you a moment ago? With all this smoke, it was hard to see.

ARTOO: ANGRY DENIAL.

THREEPIO: Oh, never mind. Come on, we'd better hurry; the fighting seems to be coming our way.

ARTOO: BURBLES.

Sound: Footsteps and whirring as they move off.

THREEPIO: What are we to do? We'll be sent to the spice mines of Kessel or smashed into who knows what! Hey, wait a minute!

ARTOO: CHIRPS.

Sound: Artoo's whirring fading into distance.

THREEPIO: Where are you going? Artoo, you're not allowed in there . . . that's an escape pod cluster. It's restricted. We'd be deactivated for certain if we were caught!

ARTOO: LETS OUT A FEISTY WARBLE.

THREEPIO: Don't call me a mindless philosopher, you over-weight glob of grease!

Sound: Artoo clambering into pod.

THREEPIO: Artoo, come out of that escape pod before somebody sees you. Only humans are allowed in there!

ARTOO: *(ECHOING HOLLOWLY)* BLEEPS.

THREEPIO: "Secret mission"? What mission? What plans? What are you talking about?

ARTOO: EXHORTS HIM INSISTENTLY.

THREEPIO: I most certainly will *not* get in there with you! You've gone quite out of your circuit. You'll never see me crawling in somewhere where I'm not supposed to—

Sound: Loud explosion nearby, yelling and firing.

Sound: Threepio's clumsy scrambling into pod.

THREEPIO: *(ECHOING)* Artoo! Move aside, Artoo! Make room!

ARTOO: BURBLES.

Sound: Hatch swishing shut.

THREEPIO: All right, so you've closed the hatch. What good will all this *do* us? Artoo, no! That's the firing switch!

Sound: Roar of the pod's separator charges almost drowning Threepio's last words.

THREEPIO: Now see what you've done, you, you defective! What makes you think you can control this thing?

ARTOO: BLEEPS SMUGLY.

THREEPIO: Running maintenance checks on them doesn't make you a qualified pilot, now does it?

ARTOO: AN ELECTRONIC RASPBERRY.

THREEPIO: Artoo, what are you doing to the control board?

ARTOO: CHIRPS A DISTRACTED EXPLANATION.

THREEPIO: "Destination"? "Standardized coordinates"? Why are you activating the steering thrusters? Wait a moment . . . are you sure this is . . .

Sound: Steering thrusters blare.

THREEPIO: *(FADES)* . . . Sa . . . aaa . . . fe!

Sound: Thrusters fading. Silence.

Music: Up.

Sound: Leia's breathing.

3RD TROOPER: *(APPROACHING)* Search every passageway and compartment! You two, check over there behind those power conduits!

4TH TROOPER: Wait! I thought I saw something . . .

Sound: Leia gasps, then struggles to control her breathing.

4TH TROOPER: There she is! Set your weapons to stun!

Sound: Leia's breathing rasps, then the firing of her blaster. A trooper cries out and crashes to deck in background.

3RD TROOPER: Watch it! She's armed! Fire!

Sound: Firing of stun blast, Leia moaning and collapsing to deck.

3RD TROOPER: Good shooting. She'll be all right. Inform Lord Vader that we have a prisoner.

Sound: Fades to silence.

Sound: Prisoner collection point. Vader's respirator is heard over all.

COMMANDER: Lord Vader, this is the ambassador.

LEIA: *(APPROACHING)* Darth Vader, I should have known. Only the Dark Lord of the Sith would be so bold. When the Imperial

Senate hears that you've attacked a Senator on a diplomatic vessel, they'll—

VADER: *(INTERRUPTING)* You weren't on any mercy mission this time, Your Highness. Where are those plans?

LEIA: I don't know what you're talking about.

VADER: You are part of the Rebel Alliance . . . and a traitor! Is it not so? *(TO TROOPERS)* Take her away! I'll interrogate her later myself.

Sound: Leia is led away.

COMMANDER: Lord Vader, should we continue to hold her? If word of this gets out, it could generate sympathy for the Rebels in the Imperial Senate.

VADER: She is too important to us. The Princess Leia Organa is our only link to the Rebels' secret base. What I don't understand is why she came here, to this miserable dustball of a planet. Do the sensors indicate a military presence?

COMMANDER: None, sir, on this planet or anywhere in this solar system. Lord Vader, she'll die before she'll tell you anything.

VADER: Leave that to me. Send out a distress signal from the *Tantive IV*, then inform the Senate that all aboard were killed in a mishap.

TROOPER: *(APPROACHING)* Lord Vader, sensors report that the *Tantive IV* was jettisoning escape pods during the fighting. There were no life-forms aboard any of them, but one fired its steering thrusters.

VADER: So, she must have hidden the plans in that pod. I want the pod located and the plans retrieved. See to it personally, Commander. I want them found, even if it means tearing apart, bit by bit, this miserable speck of a planet . . . this Tatooine!

Music: In.

NARRATOR: With the capture of Princess Leia Organa, Darth Vader, Dark Lord of the Sith, advances his designs one more step. Far below on Tatooine, a young farm boy named Luke Skywalker is about to be caught up in events that will shape the future of a galaxy. And suspended in between in their long entry fall, two singular machines hold the key to the vast conflict between Empire and Rebellion.

Music: Up and under preview and credits.

ANNOUNCER: CLOSING CREDITS.

EPISODE FOUR:

"WHILE GIANTS
MARK TIME"

CAST:

Threepio	Lieutenant
Artoo	2nd Trooper
Luke	3rd Trooper
Owen	4th Trooper
Beru	5th Trooper
Commander	6th Trooper

ANNOUNCER: OPENING CREDITS.

Music: Opening theme.

NARRATOR: A long time ago in a galaxy far, far away there came a time of revolution, when Rebels united to challenge a tyrannical Empire. And there came a moment in that long struggle when the hope of freedom rested not with any great hero or leader but rather with the humblest of characters.

Sound: Winds of Tatooine up in background, hiss of sand.

NARRATOR: High above the sandy wastes of the desert planet Tatooine, a pitched space battle between starships has been fought to its conclusion. The Rebel leader Princess Leia Organa of Alderaan has been captured by the Emperor's personal agent, Darth Vader. Entrusted to deliver secret information the Princess could no longer protect is the astrodroid Artoo-Detoo. With his interpreter-counterpart See-Threepio, Artoo eluded capture by leaving Leia's disabled vessel in an escape pod.

Sound: Wind up slightly.

THREEPIO: Look where you've brought us with your mad ideas, Artoo.

ARTOO: WHIRS.

THREEPIO: Sand . . . nothing but sand in every direction! Why I went along with this insane whim of yours, I still can't understand.

ARTOO: CHIRPS VIGOROUSLY.

THREEPIO: You ought to be grateful I got you out of the pod. I wasn't designed for this sort of brute labor. I'd rather have taken my chances with the stormtroopers back on the *Tantive IV*. Wait a minute! Where are you going?

Sound: Artoo's treads whining off.

THREEPIO: Artoo! Wait for me! Oh!

Sound: Clumsy metallic steps, servos humming after Artoo.

ARTOO: ANSWERS AIRILY.

Sound: Artoo's whirring gets louder as Threepio catches up.

THREEPIO: You've got some explaining to do!

ARTOO: SIGNALS HIM TO QUIT GRIPING.

THREEPIO: Why, you nearly crashed us! My gyros are still fluttering!

ARTOO: RESPONDS OFFHANDEDLY.

THREEPIO: No one cares about droids, that's what!

ARTOO: WHISTLES DUBIOUSLY.

THREEPIO: Well of *course* you're having trouble with this sand dune. What do you think you are, an exploration vehicle?

ARTOO: TOOTLES.

THREEPIO: We seem to be made to suffer . . . It's our lot in life.

ARTOO: COMMISERATES WITHOUT SLOWING DOWN.

THREEPIO: I've simply got to rest before I fall apart. My joints are nearly frozen with sand.

Sound: Wind gusting.

Sound: Artoo's whirring diminishing into the distance.

THREEPIO: Wait. Where are you going?

Sound: Threepio's footsteps go more quickly as he catches up with Artoo.

ARTOO: BEEPS.

THREEPIO: "Over that way"? Well, I'm not going over that way! It's much too rocky there in the distance. I'm going this way.

ARTOO: OBJECTS.

THREEPIO: Oh, yes? And just what makes you so sure there are settlements over in that direction?

ARTOO: BLEEPS AN ANSWER.

THREEPIO: Don't get technical with me. You are nothing but a plumber.

ARTOO: AN EMPHATIC DECLARATION.

THREEPIO: "Mission"? What secret plans? I've had just about enough of this! Go on, go that way! Here, I'll start you off!

Sound: Threepio kicking Artoo.

ARTOO: AN ELECTRONIC YELP.

THREEPIO: You'll be clogged with sand and malfunctioning within a day, you nearsighted scrap pile!

ARTOO: BEEPS A FINAL ENTREATY.

THREEPIO: Absolutely not. And don't let me catch you following me begging for help, because you won't get any from me!

ARTOO: REITERATES THE ENTREATY.

THREEPIO: No! No more adventures! I'm going this way. You're on your own from now on . . .

Sound: Artoo fading off whistling a happy tune so no one will suspect he's afraid. Fade out.

COMMANDER: Anything to report?

LIEUTENANT: Nothing so far, sir. *(CALLING)* Deploy your squads along that dune ridge and stay alert!

2ND TROOPER: *(OFF)* Yes, sir! Follow me, you men!

LIEUTENANT: You two, get inside that escape pod and check it out *thoroughly*!

3RD TROOPER: Yessir!

4TH TROOPER: Will do, sir!

LIEUTENANT: The rest of you spread out and search for tracks. I want the entire area secured!

5TH TROOPER: Let's go!

COMMANDER: We must continue until we find something, Lieutenant. Lord Vader will not accept a failure of this mission.

LIEUTENANT: We're checking now, Commander.

Sound: He bangs on the pod.

LIEUTENANT: You men in there! What've you found?

3RD TROOPER: *(CALLING FROM INSIDE POD)* The scanner shows no sign of occupants, sir, or of the data tapes, either.

LIEUTENANT: I want that pod torn apart!

COMMANDER: The scanner reads negative, Lieutenant. Someone's already taken the Death Star plans and gotten away.

5TH TROOPER: *(APPROACHING)* Commander! One of the men found this near the pod! It's a plating ring off a droid, sir!

COMMANDER: A droid! That's how the Death Star plans got off the Princess's ship. Lieutenant, make contact with our vessel and get more troops down here.

LIEUTENANT: Yes, sir!

COMMANDER: Inform Lord Vader that I'm organizing a total search of this entire region. And tell him what we're hunting: one or more droids from the Princess Leia's ship.

Sound: Tatooine winds up in background.

Sound: Threepio's labored functioning and complaining servos.

THREEPIO: *(MUTTERING)* That demented little runt! This is all Artoo's fault! He tricked me into this! But he'll do no better!

Sound: He grinds along another few steps.

THREEPIO: I don't think I can go on much farther. My photo-receptors will be burned out by those binary suns. My joints will lock up, and I'll overheat. Misfortune has always pursued me . . .

Sound: His grinding stops.

THREEPIO: What's that over there? Something gleaming . . . it's some kind of transport machine! Whoever they are, they'll know something about repair. And lubricants! They'll have lubricants! *(SHOUTING)* Over here! Help, please, help! Over this way . . . you've got to see me! You simply have to! They've seen me! They're changing course and coming this way. Oh, I'm saved!

Music: Up.

Sound: Sandcrawler approaching.

THREEPIO: Stop! Please stop or you'll crush me!

Sound: The sandcrawler stops, and the engine drops to a low idle.

THREEPIO: Eh? They've stopped! Thank goodness!

Sound: Hollow crank of hatch being opened and ramp dropping.

THREEPIO: What's this? A ramp . . . They mean to take me on-board! Now, this is more like it!

Sound: Jawas jabbering and scampering down ramp.

THREEPIO: Can those be children in those robes? I can't see under their hoods, except those glowing eyes . . . how eerie!

Sound: Jawas approaching, clustering around and seizing Threepio.

THREEPIO: What are you doing? Let me go! Oh, if only my joints weren't clogged! Take your hands off me, you filthy little creatures!

Sound: A Jawa screams at Threepio.

THREEPIO: No, no, don't shoot! There's no reason to go pointing that gun . . . I'm really friendly! Or friendlier than you, at any rate. See? My hands are in the air.

Sound: The Jawa yells at him.

THREEPIO: What do you want me to do? Hold still? Yes, yes, I'm holding still, you see?

Sound: The Jawa cackles as he puts the restraining bolt on Threepio. Clicking and scraping noises under:

THREEPIO: What's that? No! Not a restraining bolt? No, please!

Sound: The bolt activates with a harsh buzz and hisses as it fuses to Threepio. A kind of cheer is heard from the Jawas.

THREEPIO: Haven't I been through enough? *(SIGHS)* I don't suppose you happen to have seen anything of my counterpart? A rather short astrodroid, about so high?

Sound: Jawa makes excited, inquiring noises.

THREEPIO: Yes, yes, a machine sort of like me. About waist high to me. He was headed off over in that direction, the last time I—

Sound: Jawas begin pushing and shooing Threepio.

THREEPIO: Wait, what are you doing? Stop pushing!

Sound: Jawa makes threatening remarks.

THREEPIO: What do you want me to do? Stand here under this conduit? Like so?

Sound: Jawa makes hasty affirmative reply.

THREEPIO: May I ask what you're going to—

Sound: The conduit cranks up with a super-electrolux sound, sucking Threepio into sandcrawler.

THREEPIO: *(ECHOING)* Do-ooooooo!

Music: Up.

Sound: The tech-dome.

LUKE: *(COMING ON)* Well, I couldn't find anything at Anchorhead or Toshi Station, Uncle Owen.

OWEN: Maybe we could do without any help from droids, Luke! Hard work might see us through.

LUKE: But Uncle, we'll never be able to keep this farm at peak efficiency through the moisture harvest without more

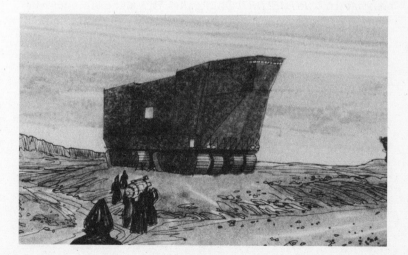

help. With one or two more droids, we'd make a much bigger profit.

OWEN: And where d' you suppose we're gonna find this help if there's nothing at Anchorhead or Toshi Station?

LUKE: Well, there must be a Jawa sandcrawler due through here soon. Maybe they'll have something.

OWEN: Huh! Those little scavengers! Find some pieces of broken-up machinery, wire it together with flexor cord, and spit; after a few hours of functioning, it falls apart.

LUKE: It wouldn't hurt to look.

OWEN: I guess not; your aunt keeps pestering me for a domestic droid to help her around the house, anyway. Send a signal flare up; if those Jawas are in the area, they'll come pretty quick.

LUKE: *(MOVING OFF)* Sure, Uncle Owen.

Sound: Tech-dome fades.

Sound: Up on the engine of the sandcrawler and various automata.

THREEPIO: *(GRUMBLING)* Oh! Really! This is the strangest collection of droids and robots I've ever seen. After all I've been through, to be picked up by those disgusting creatures and dumped in some sort of a . . . glorified salvage bin! How mortifying!

ARTOO: WHISTLING.

THREEPIO: Artoo-Detoo! Artoo, it is you, it is you!

ARTOO: RESPONDS HAPPILY.

THREEPIO: Oh, Artoo! I'm so glad to see you . . . even though the circumstances leave something to be desired.

ARTOO: SIGNALS A LONG BURST.

THREEPIO: They sucked you up in that horrible thing, too, did they? Yes, well, those creatures who captured you . . . us . . . are called Jawas, I've managed to find out. This vehicle is referred to as a sandcrawler.

ARTOO: BEEPS.

THREEPIO: *(GUILTILY)* Er, well, yes. That is, I'm afraid I'm partially at fault there. You see, I merely asked those Jawas earlier if they'd seen anything of you—

ARTOO: INTERRUPTS WITH AN ANGRY ACCUSATION.

THREEPIO: I did not tell them where you were on purpose! If you must know, I was simply concerned for you, you short-circuited incompetent! And this is the thanks I get!

ARTOO: BLATS AT THREEPIO.

THREEPIO: And the same to you! I wish they hadn't captured you! Now I'm forced to endure your insufferable company again, you . . . I sincerely hope that this stop will be the end of that interminable sandcrawler ride. I would venture a guess that those Jawas have brought us outside to auction us off.

Sound: The winds of Tatooine up. Distant chatter of Jawas.

THREEPIO: *(ASIDE)* Well, standing in line out here is certainly preferable to being cooped up in that garbage bin.

ARTOO: TOOTS.

THREEPIO: We seem to be at some kind of moisture farm. Look, there're humans down there! Maybe they'll purchase us. Then we'd be free of these awful Jawas. Artoo, get back in line . . . Artoo!

ARTOO: CHIRPS *"WHAT?"*

THREEPIO: Get back in line! They'll never buy a . . . Artoo, what are you doing to that R5 unit?

ARTOO: ANSWERS ABSENTLY AS HE WORKS.

THREEPIO: Artoo, you know droids are not supposed to modify other droids without human supervision. Honestly, I don't know what's gotten into you!

ARTOO: POOH-POOHS.

THREEPIO: *(WHISPERS URGENTLY)* Here come the humans! Get back in line.

ARTOO: TWEETS.

Sound: Artoo whirrs back into line.

Sound: Jawa's voice comes up with a pitching quality as Owen approaches.

OWEN: *(APPROACHING)* Yeah, yeah, but I'm telling you straight off, I don't want any junkers, rebuilts, or scrap-heap candidates. I've already got a Treadwell . . . don't need another. And what's this, a Mark II reactor drone? They haven't used these clunkers in twenty years!

Sound: The Jawa is reassuring as Owen moves down the line, stopping to look over the machines.

OWEN: Hmmm. Got no use for a power droid. I might be able to use an R2 unit, but this blue one's kind of beaten up.

ARTOO: HOOTS INDIGNANTLY.

OWEN: Talks too much, too. This red R5 might do, though. *If* the price is right. *(MOVING ON)* Let's see . . . You . . . I suppose you're programmed for etiquette and protocol.

THREEPIO: Protocol? Why that's my primary function, sir. I'm also—

OWEN: *(INTERRUPTING)* I have no use for a protocol droid.

THREEPIO: Of course not, sir, not in a climate as hostile as this one. But I might point out that I have been programmed for over thirty secondary functions that range from—

OWEN: *(INTERRUPTING)* What I need is a droid that understands the binary language of moisture vaporators.

THREEPIO: Vaporators! Why, sir, my first job was in programming binary loadlifters, very similar to your vaporators in many respects!

LUKE: *(APPROACHING)* Uncle Owen, Aunt Beru wanted me to remind you, if you buy a translator droid, make sure it—

OWEN: *(CALLING)* Oh, yeah, thanks, Luke. *(TO THREEPIO)* Droid, do you speak domestic Bocce?

THREEPIO: Of course I do, sir. It's like a second language to me. I am also, if I may say so, quite fluent in—

Sound: The Jawa's gibbering interrupts Threepio.

OWEN: *(TO THE JAWA)* Yeah, I'll take this one too. Luke!

LUKE: *(APPROACHING)* Yeah, Uncle Owen?

OWEN: Take this interpreter droid here and that red R5 unit down to the tech-dome and get them cleaned up by suppertime.

LUKE: But I was going into Toshi Station for those converters we ordered.

OWEN: You can waste time with your idle friends when your chores are done. Now hop to it!

LUKE: *(SIGHING)* Yes, sir. *(TO THREEPIO)* Follow me, you.

THREEPIO: Yes sir!

Sound: Threepio's servos.

Sound: Owen and Jawa haggle in background.

LUKE: And you, too, the red R5 unit. Well, come on, Red . . . let's go.

Sound: The R5 unit hums forward, only to buzz, choke, and go sproing.

LUKE: Hey, what . . . *(CALLING)* Uncle Owen! Uncle Owen!

OWEN: *(OFF, STOPS HAGGLING)* Now what?

LUKE: This R5 unit's got a bad motivator. Look, it blew its stack!

OWEN: *(TO JAWA)* Hey, what're you Jawas trying to palm off on me?

Sound: The Jawa makes a vehement denial.

THREEPIO: *(TO LUKE)* Excuse me, sir, but that blue R2 unit over there is in prime condition . . . a real bargain!

LUKE: *(CALLING)* Hey, Uncle Owen. What about that little blue R2 unit?

OWEN: *(OFF, TO JAWA)* What about that one?

Sound: The Jawa quickly accepts the swap.

OWEN: *(OFF)* Good enough. *(CALLING)* Luke, take the blue one!

THREEPIO: I'm sure you and your uncle will be very pleased with that one. I've worked with him before.

Sound: Artoo's whirring as he approaches.

ARTOO: WHISTLES HAPPILY.

LUKE: *(MOVING OFF)* Sure, sure, let's go. We've got some cleaning up to do.

THREEPIO: Now, don't you forget this, Artoo! Why I stick my neck out for you is quite beyond my capacity to explain!

Sound: Machinery of the tech-dome comes up.

THREEPIO: A completely equipped tech-dome! This is like paradise!

LUKE: Right. Just stand steady on that lift and I'll lower you into the oil bath.

Sound: Oil bath swirls and bubbles under:

THREEPIO: Ah, this feels so good! My counterpart and I are both in your debt, sir.

LUKE: Thanks, but I'd rather be at Toshi Station . . . At least there's something to do there. Biggs was right. I should get myself off this dustball.

THREEPIO: Er . . . which "dustball" are we on, sir?

LUKE: Well, if there's a bright center to the universe, you're on the planet it's farthest from . . . Tatooine.

THREEPIO: I see, sir.

LUKE: You can call me Luke.

THREEPIO: I see, Sir Luke.

LUKE: *(LAUGHING)* Just Luke.

THREEPIO: And I am See-Threepio, human-relations droid, interpreter. And this is my counterpart, Artoo-Detoo.

ARTOO: WHONKS A GREETING.

LUKE: Hi. Threepio, that's about enough of that oil bath for you.

THREEPIO: Yes, sir.

Sound: Switch being thrown, Threepio being hoisted from bath.

LUKE: Now, let's take a look at Artoo-Detoo.

Sound: Luke moving to Artoo.

LUKE: Hmmm. Artoo, you've got a lot of carbon scoring here in your integrators. Let me see what I can do for you.

ARTOO: BEEPS GRATITUDE.

Sound: Luke scraping and picking at Artoo.

LUKE: It looks like you two boys have seen a lot of action.

Sound: Threepio's steps and servos move closer.

THREEPIO: With all we've been through, I'm amazed we're in as good a condition as we are, considering there's a Rebellion going on.

Sound: Luke suddenly stops working on Artoo.

LUKE: *What?* You know something about the Rebellion against the Empire?

THREEPIO: That's how we come to be in your service, if you take my meaning, sir.

LUKE: Have you been in any battles . . . over Tatooine?

THREEPIO: Several, I think.

LUKE: Then I *did* see ships firing on each other!

THREEPIO: Actually, for a droid, a space battle is largely a matter of loud noise and having humans order you out of their way.

LUKE: Your life sure sounds a lot more interesting than mine, Threepio.

Sound: He resumes cleaning Artoo.

LUKE: Well, Artoo, you've got something jammed in here real good. Were you two on a starcruiser, or . . . what the—

Sound: The obstruction breaks loose with a ping and a violent discharge of power, knocking Luke over. He exclaims in shock and pain. A crackle of static from Artoo, and the tape loop of Leia begins cycling.

HOLOGRAPH: Please help me, Obi-Wan Kenobi . . . you're my only hope!

Sound: Luke struggling back up.

LUKE: What . . . what *is* that . . . .a holographic projection?

HOLOGRAPH: Please help me, Obi-Wan Kenobi . . . you're my only hope!

THREEPIO: It certainly appears to be, sir. Artoo, Master Luke asked you what it is!

ARTOO: BLEEPS INNOCENTLY.

HOLOGRAPH: Help me, Obi-Wan Kenobi . . . you're my only hope!

THREEPIO: What do you mean, "What is what?"

ARTOO: MAKES AN OH-THAT'S-NOTHING COMMENT.

THREEPIO: He says it's nothing, sir. Merely a malfunction . . . old data.

HOLOGRAPH: Help me, Obi-Wan Kenobi . . . you're my only hope!

LUKE: That girl . . . I've never seen anyone like her. She's beautiful! Who is she?

THREEPIO: Um, I think she was a passenger on our last voyage, a person of some importance, I believe.

LUKE: Is there any more to this recording? It sounds as if it's incomplete. Here, maybe I can adjust Artoo so that—

ARTOO: INTERRUPTS WITH AN ELECTRONIC SNARL.

LUKE: Hey, take it easy!

THREEPIO: Artoo-Detoo! Behave yourself! You're going to get us into very grave trouble! You can trust him . . . he's our new master.

ARTOO: LOOSES A TUMULT OF SIGNALS.

THREEPIO: He, well, he says he is the property of Obi-Wan Kenobi, a resident of this very region. The holographic projection is part of a message for him.

HOLOGRAPH: Help me, Obi-Wan Kenobi . . . you're my only hope!

ARTOO: BLEEPS AN AFFIRMATIVE.

THREEPIO: Frankly, sir, with what we've been through, it's no surprise this little R2 unit has become a bit, er, eccentric.

ARTOO: BLATS AN OBJECTION.

LUKE: Well, I don't know anyone named Obi-Wan, but old Ben Kenobi lives somewhere near the Western Dune Sea. He's a kind of local character, a hermit. My uncle made him get off our property once. But I never heard of old Ben owning a droid.

HOLOGRAPH: Help me, Obi-Wan Kenobi . . . you're my only hope!

LUKE: That girl . . . she's so beautiful. I wonder who she is. She's in some kind of trouble, that's for sure. We'd better hear the rest of the message.

ARTOO: BEEPS URGENTLY.

THREEPIO: He claims the restraining bolt the Jawas put on him is inhibiting his motivational components. He suggests that if you remove the bolt, he might be able to play back the entire message.

LUKE: Well, I guess you're too small to run away on me if I take off that bolt. Here we go.

Sound: A hiss and pop as the bolt comes off.

LUKE: There!

Sound: Concurrently, the holo loop dies away.

LUKE: Hey, what happened to the holograph? Where'd she go? Bring her back! Play the message, Artoo!

ARTOO: CHIRPS INNOCENTLY.

THREEPIO: What do you mean, "What message?" You know what message! The one you just played for Master Luke! The one you're carrying inside your rusty innards.

ARTOO: DENIES ALL ACCUSATIONS CALMLY.

THREEPIO: I'm sorry, sir, but he seems to have developed a circuitry flux.

BERU: *(OFF)* Luke! Oh, Luke! Time to get cleaned up for dinner!

LUKE: *(CALLING)* Be right there, Aunt Beru! *(TO THREEPIO, MOVING OFF)* See what you can do with him, Threepio. I'll be back after dinner.

THREEPIO: Yes, sir. Just you reconsider playing that tape for him! And mind your manners, Artoo, or you'll make Master Luke angry!

ARTOO: WHISTLES A QUESTION.

THREEPIO: No, I don't think he likes you at all.

ARTOO: WHISTLES ANOTHER.

THREEPIO: No, I don't like you, either.

ARTOO: BEEPS WOUNDEDLY.

THREEPIO: And what's the idea of showing him that tape?

ARTOO: RESPONDS ELABORATELY.

THREEPIO: You knew *what* would work?

ARTOO: AMPLIFIES.

THREEPIO: Then, then it was all a trick to get him to take the restraining bolt off you? Why, *Artoo-Detoo*! That's, that's deceitful!

ARTOO: DISMISSES THE OBJECTION AIRILY.

THREEPIO: But you're putting us in danger, Artoo! Why can't you be your old cooperative self? This is neither the time nor the place to become obstinate!

ARTOO: HONKS CONTEMPTUOUSLY.

THREEPIO: I don't want to hear any more about secret plans, or missions, or Obi-Wan Kenobi. We're droids! We have nothing to gain by mixing in human disputes!

ARTOO: BLATS.

Sound: Whirring as Artoo starts to move.

THREEPIO: I think it's your motivator that's gone faulty! Now wait a moment . . . where are you going?

ARTOO: CHIRPS A REPLY.

THREEPIO: But you can't go outside! Come back here before you get us both deactivated for good! You can't survive out there! Artoo! Artoo!

Sound: Threepio's voice fades out on the last words.

Sound: Beru preparing dinner in kitchen.

BERU: *(SLIGHTLY OFF)* Your dinner's on the table, Luke. Your uncle's already started.

LUKE: Thanks, Aunt Beru.

Sound: Chair drawn up to table. Scraping tableware, dishes, glasses, etc., under:

LUKE: You know, Uncle Owen, I think that R2 unit we bought might've been stolen.

OWEN: *(EATING)* What makes you think that?

LUKE: *(EATING AND DRINKING)* Well, while I was cleaning him up, I stumbled across a part of a holographic recording. The R2 unit says he's the property of somebody named Obi-Wan Kenobi.

BERU: *(COMING ON)* What?

OWEN: *Kenobi?*

LUKE: Yeah. I thought he might mean old Ben Kenobi. Do you know who he's talking about? Maybe it's somebody related to Ben . . .

OWEN: Naw, that old man's just a crazy wizard. Take that R2 unit into Anchorhead and have its memory flushed.

LUKE: But what if this Obi-Wan comes looking for it?

OWEN: I don't think he exists anymore. He . . . he died about the same time as your father.

LUKE: You mean Obi-Wan knew my father?

OWEN: Luke, I told you to forget it. I don't want you talking to strangers about our family, and I don't want anyone filling your head with made-up nonsense.

LUKE: But Uncle Owen . . .

OWEN: Now, I mean it, Luke! In the morning I want those new droids up on the south ridge working.

LUKE: Yessir.

Sound: Tableware, eating, etc.

LUKE: Those droids should work out just fine. *(DRAWING A DEEP BREATH)* In fact, if they do, I want to send my application to the academy for *this* year.

OWEN: But that's before the harvest!

LUKE: Sure, but now you've got more than enough droids.

OWEN: But a droid's no substitute for human help. Luke, the harvest is when I need you most. It's only one more season. This year we'll make enough money so I'll be able to hire on some hands. You can go to the academy next year.

BERU: But Owen . . .

OWEN: Now, missus, this is between Luke and me.

Sound: Silence, while Luke scrapes at his plate.

LUKE: But it's another whole *year*!

OWEN: It's only one more season!

Sound: Luke pushes his plate aside.

LUKE: That's what you said when Biggs left for the academy.

Sound: Luke scrapes his chair back.

BERU: Luke, you haven't finished your dinner. Where are you going?

LUKE: Nowhere, it looks like. *(MOVING OFF)* I have to finish cleaning up those droids.

BERU: Owen, Luke can't stay here forever. Most of his friends have gone.

OWEN: I'll make it up to him next year. I promise.

BERU: Luke's just not a farmer, Owen. He's got too much of his father in him. And you won't be able to put *that* subject off forever, either. Luke's going to want to know the truth.

OWEN: I'm going to protect him as long as I can. I've got to do what I think's best for the boy.

BERU: But you can't live his life for him, Owen.

OWEN: I only wish I could, Beru. I only wish I could.

Sound: Kitchen sounds fade to silence.

Sound: Tech-dome machinery up in background.

LUKE: *(OFF)* Threepio? Artoo? Where are you? *(MOVING ON)* Crazy droids. Seems like you can't leave them alone for a minute. Where did I leave that restraining bolt activator?

Sound: He starts rummaging through equipment.

THREEPIO: *(OFF)* Please, sir! Wait. I'll come out. Please don't de-activate me!

LUKE: Threepio, what're you doing hiding behind the landspeeder? Where's Artoo?

Sound: Threepio's metallic footsteps approaching.

THREEPIO: *(MOVING CLOSER)* It wasn't my fault, sir! I couldn't stop him!

LUKE: What?!

THREEPIO: I told Artoo not to go, but I think his motivator's malfunctioning. He was babbling on about his mission.

LUKE: Oh, no! *(FADING)* I've got to find him.

THREEPIO: *(OFF)* Master Luke! Wait for me!

Sound: Macros ranging and focusing.

LUKE: I can't see him out there anywhere, even with the macrobinoculars. How could he've gotten so far?

THREEPIO: You can hardly blame yourself, sir. He's become very, well, *devious* recently.

LUKE: Well, there's no sign of him. Blast it!

THREEPIO: Pardon me, sir, but couldn't we go after him?

LUKE: It'd be too dangerous with all the Sand People in the area. We'll have to wait till morning.

OWEN: *(OFF)* Luke! I'm shutting the power down for the night!

LUKE: *(CALLING)* I'll be right there, Uncle Owen! *(TO THREEPIO)* Boy, am I gonna get it! That little droid's gonna cause me a lot of trouble.

THREEPIO: Oh, he excels at that, sir.

LUKE: At first light we'll take my landspeeder and pick up his trail. Maybe we can get him back before Uncle Owen finds out.

THREEPIO: I'm sure we will recover him tomorrow, sir. Then your troubles will be solved.

LUKE: Somehow I think all I'm gonna get is a new set of troubles.

Music: In and under:

NARRATOR: Artoo-Detoo, faithfully carrying out the mission programmed into him by the Rebel leader Princess Leia Organa, inadvertently draws Luke Skywalker into the Rebellion's most desperate crisis. Merciless Imperial agents are scouring Tatooine for the droid and his secret, and across the desert there still waits the enigma of Obi-Wan Kenobi. Tomorrow will be a day like no other in Luke Skywalker's young life.

Music: Closing theme up and under preview and closing credits.

ANNOUNCER: CLOSING CREDITS.

EPISODE FIVE:

"JEDI THAT WAS;

JEDI TO BE"

C A S T :

Luke   Artoo
Threepio   Ben Kenobi

ANNOUNCER: OPENING CREDITS.

Music: Opening theme.

NARRATOR: A long time ago in a galaxy far, far away there came a time of revolution, when Rebels united to challenge a tyrannical Empire. In the Rebellion's most desperate crisis, the fate of the entire Rebel Alliance rested with the simple astrodroid Artoo-Detoo, whose memory banks held secret plans and a message critical to the struggle against the Empire.

Sound: Winds of Tatooine up in background.

NARRATOR: At the edge of the Western Dune Sea, on the desert planet of Tatooine, is the moisture farm of Owen Lars; here Artoo-Detoo and his interpreter-counterpart See-Threepio have come, following their purchase by Owen and his young nephew, Luke Skywalker. Free again, Artoo has escaped to deliver his message to the mysterious Obi-Wan Kenobi. Ignorant of his mission, Luke and See-Threepio intend to recover him before he comes to harm in the hostile wastelands scorched by Tatooine's binary suns.

Sound: Hum of machinery in the tech-dome.

LUKE: *(OFF)* See-Threepio? Are you awake? It's dawn . . . Threepio?

Sound: Threepio's servos activate.

THREEPIO: Eh? Master Luke, is that you?

LUKE: *(APPROACHING)* Shhh! If my uncle finds out Artoo got away, he'll skin me alive.

THREEPIO: I am prepared, sir. I hooked myself up to the charging unit last night.

LUKE: I wish I hadn't banged up my skyhopper out at Beggar's Canyon. It's gonna be a lot tougher to track down Artoo in the landspeeder.

THREEPIO: Shall I activate the ground-level door, sir?

LUKE: No! Do you want to wake my uncle up? The main power's still shut down for the night, and I don't dare turn it back on.

THREEPIO: Oh, I see . . . the need for stealth!

LUKE: Uh huh. I'll raise the door manually, and you push the speeder through. It'll float along pretty easily on its repulsor field.

THREEPIO: Yes, sir.

Sound: Luke's footsteps going off.

Sound: A crank ratcheting and the muted creaking of the door's rollers.

LUKE: *(OFF, HIS WHISPERING VOICE REFLECTING THE EFFORT)* Okay, the door's up just high enough. Push the landspeeder out and don't forget to duck.

THREEPIO: *(WHISPERING)* It's moving fairly easily, sir. No trouble at—

LUKE: Watch where you're going! Threepio, duck!

Sound: Concurrently, the gonging of Threepio's head on the door.

THREEPIO: *(APPROACHING)* Oh! I . . . I should have followed your advice, sir. Is my cranial structure damaged?

LUKE: No, no, you're fine. We'll push the speeder out a little way before we start it up.

THREEPIO: Oh, that Artoo-Detoo! This is one more thing I owe him! He's nothing but trouble! Wait until I get my hands on him!

Sound: Their footsteps slogging through sand, the whoosh of the landspeeder.

LUKE: *(WITH EFFORT)* Come on, Threepio, push!

THREEPIO: I must say, I agree with your precautions, sir. Your uncle seems rather, well, irascible.

LUKE: Threepio, my uncle hates spending money. He was against buying you and Artoo from those Jawas in the first place. If he finds out that Artoo's run off . . .

THREEPIO: Master Luke, if I may suggest . . . piloting ground-effect vehicles like your landspeeder is one of the secondary functions for which I have been programmed. I could take the controls, leaving you free to scan the terrain for tracks.

LUKE: Good idea. Let's go.

Sound: They climb into the landspeeder. The engine revs, the speeder accelerates, a whoosh as it veers sharply, then the steady hum of the engine under:

LUKE: Careful, Threepio! You have to use a light touch on her.

THREEPIO: Yes, sir, so I see. This vehicle's steering response is excellent. I presume you maintain it yourself.

LUKE: Uh huh. I like to make sure things work right. Look, the night winds've probably carried away the marks of Artoo's treads, but I figure he's headed toward whatever he was looking for when you two got captured by those Jawas.

THREEPIO: Our escape pod landed somewhere over that way. Artoo seemed obsessed with the area beyond those mesas.

LUKE: Maybe we can pick him up on the scanner.

Sound: A switch being thrown.

LUKE: If you're right, he's headed straight for the Jundland Wastes.

THREEPIO: I must say, this Tatooine of yours is a desolate place, Master Luke. I simply can't understand what would draw Artoo out here. He kept repeating that nonsense about his mission, and secret plans, and this Obi-Wan Kenobi person he keeps rattling on about.

LUKE: Well, *Ben* Kenobi *does* lives out this way somewhere. My uncle got awfully mad when I mentioned old Ben's name at the dinner table last night.

THREEPIO: There really is such a person? I presumed Artoo was in a state of hallucinatory malfunction, completely addled.

LUKE: No, Ben's real enough. I've seen him a few times. All the older settlers like my uncle think Ben is some kind of magician. Listen, if you swing left a little, you'll see an opening in the mesa wall.

THREEPIO: Very good, sir. Ah, yes, I see it on the scanner. If I may ask, sir, just what sort of individual is this Ben Kenobi?

LUKE: Well, he's real old, for one thing. He travels the Jundland Wastes and the Dune Seas on foot, and there's *nobody* else that does that. He doesn't seem to need much from town, either . . . he's almost never been to Anchorhead.

THREEPIO: And you've met him?

LUKE: In a way . . . about five seasons ago . . . Still no sign of Artoo . . .

THREEPIO: What's my best choice at this fork?

LUKE: Left. . . . it'll take us into the Wastes. My friend Windy and I rode out on his dewback into these Wastes.

THREEPIO: Pardon me, sir, but that sounds rather rash.

LUKE: We wanted to get out on our own for a bit. Look, we were *bored*.

THREEPIO: I fear I wouldn't know anything about that, sir.

LUKE: The dewback threw us in one of the canyons and ran off.

We got pretty bruised up. When it got dark, we still hadn't found our way out. There were all kinds of night sounds, and then we heard a voice off to one side . . .

THREEPIO: A, a voice, sir?

LUKE: . . . and it called *my* name! It was old Ben Kenobi. Somehow Ben found us and guided us back to the farm. He told us a lot about what it was like to live out in the barren lands all alone.

THREEPIO: I find it difficult to conceive of anybody living out here voluntarily!

LUKE: But a funny thing happened. When Ben took us back, Uncle Owen got real mad . . . not at Windy and me but at Ben. He ordered Ben off our farm and warned him not to come back. Ben was looking at me kind of funny, like he wanted to say something, but Uncle Owen wouldn't give him the chance.

THREEPIO: Not surprising, Master Luke. Your uncle struck me as a man who could become extremely irate.

LUKE: Usually, but that was the weird thing. If I didn't know him better, I'd've said he was scared right then.

THREEPIO: From the look of these awful Wastes, I suggest we locate Artoo and leave at once!

LUKE: Artoo couldn't've gotten this far. We must've missed him in the dunes.

THREEPIO: Well, you had just recharged him, sir. He could've made considerable distance overnight.

LUKE: Uncle Owen won't take this very well.

THREEPIO: Perhaps it would help if you told him it was all my fault, sir.

LUKE: Hey, that's an idea! He needs you for the moisture harvest,

Threepio. The worst he'd do is deactivate you for a few days and give you a memory flush.

THREEPIO: Memory flush? Er, on the other hand, sir, Artoo would never have run away if you hadn't removed that restraining bolt.

LUKE: Wait a minute! There's something showing on the scanner, dead ahead. It could be him! Hit it, Threepio!

Sound: The speeder accelerates.

LUKE: He should be right in front of us somewhere.

THREEPIO: Look, sir! There he is! Artoo-Detoo!

LUKE: Pull around next to him.

Sound: Landspeeder comes to a stop, the engine dies. Wind up. Artoo's whistles in background. Luke and Threepio getting out under:

LUKE: Artoo! Hey, whoa, where d' you think you're going?

ARTOO: BURBLES DEFENSIVELY.

THREEPIO: Master Luke is your rightful owner now, Artoo. Let's have no more of this Obi-Wan Kenobi gibberish!

ARTOO: TWEEDLES ANGRILY.

THREEPIO: And don't you talk to me about your secret mission, either! You're fortunate that Master Luke doesn't give you back to those Jawas!

LUKE: No, Threepio, it's all right. But I've got to get you two out to the south ridge to work on those vaporators before Uncle Owen checks up on us.

THREEPIO: If you don't mind my saying so, sir, I think you should deactivate this little fugitive—

ARTOO: INTERRUPTS, HOOTING FRANTICALLY.

LUKE: What's wrong with him now?

THREEPIO: Oh, my! Sir, he says that there are several creatures of an unknown type approaching from the southeast.

LUKE: Sand People! Tusken Raiders! There've been sightings all around the area lately. We'd better have a look . . . I'll get my rifle. Threepio, hand me the macrobinoculars.

THREEPIO: Sir, do you think all this is really—

LUKE: C'mon! We'll just take a quick look. Artoo, you stay here.

ARTOO: BEEPS ACKNOWLEDGMENT FORLORNLY.

LUKE: *(FADING)* Now, watch those rocks, Threepio; they might be a little difficult . . .

Sound: Cross-fade to:

THREEPIO: Master Luke, I wasn't constructed with the climbing of those rock formations in mind!

LUKE: From here we should be able to see whatever it was Artoo detected, especially with the macrobinoculars. Keep low. Now, let's see . . .

Sound: Macros adjusting and focusing.

THREEPIO: *(WHISPERING)* Do you see anything, sir?

LUKE: Well, there are two banthas down there, all right, but I don't see any Tusken Raiders . . . wait! There's one, standing guard. Hey, something's blocking my view. What . . . !

Sound: A deafening war cry from the Tusken Raider.

LUKE: Raider!

THREEPIO: Master Luke! Defend yourself!

Sound: The Raiders howl throughout.

THREEPIO: Look out, Master Luke!

LUKE: What . . . ?!!

Sound: A blunt impact as Luke is knocked backward with a cry of pain. The Raider roars.

THREEPIO: No! Stay back . . . I'm not edible . . . ahhhhh . . .

Sound: The Tusken Raiders' victory cries give way to bickering, barks, and mutterings. Their scuffling steps going to Artoo, electronically whimpering, and a moaning Luke. Suddenly a piercing shriek echoes from the distance, causing questioning, alarmed noises from the Raiders. The shriek is repeated, and the Raiders make a hasty retreat amid much more alarmed noise. Moments later, steady, measured steps approach and stop at the moaning Luke. A rustle of cloth and a slight grunt indicate he's knelt by Luke.

BEN: So I wasn't wrong . . . It *is* Luke Skywalker.

ARTOO: BEEPS TIMIDLY.

BEN: What? Well, hello there, little droid!

ARTOO: SIGNALS WARILY.

BEN: Come here, my friend. Don't be afraid.

ARTOO: WHISTLES ANOTHER RESPONSE.

BEN: Eh? Oh, don't worry, this young fellow will be all right.

ARTOO: ANSWERS HAPPILY.

Sound: Artoo whirring over to Ben and Luke.

LUKE: *(GROGGILY)* What happened?

BEN: Rest easy, son. You've had a busy morning. You're fortunate you're still in one piece. Few are lucky enough to emerge alive from a hand-to-hand contest with a Tusken Raider.

LUKE: Ben? Ben Kenobi! Boy, am I glad to see you!

BEN: The Jundland Wastes are not to be traveled lightly. Tell me, young Luke, what brings you out this far?

LUKE: Oh, this little astrodroid here.

ARTOO: WHISTLES ENTHUSIASTICALLY.

LUKE: I think he's searching for his former master. I've never seen such devotion in a droid before . . . There seems to be no stopping him.

Sound: A scraping noise as Luke stirs.

LUKE: Ow, my head!

BEN: Take it slowly, son. That's quite a clout you were dealt.

LUKE: What made the Sand People leave?

BEN: Their own fears . . . with a bit of help from me. I imitated the hunting cry of a Krayt dragon. Their imaginations did the rest, and they took to their heels.

LUKE: Oh. Like I was saying, Artoo-Detoo here claims to be

127

the property of an "Obi-Wan Kenobi." Is that a relative of yours?

BEN: Obi-Wan Kenobi! Now, there's a name I haven't heard in a long time.

LUKE: I think my uncle knew him. Uncle Owen said Obi-Wan was dead.

BEN: Oh, he's not dead. At least not yet.

LUKE: You know him?

BEN: Well, of course I know him . . . he's me! But I haven't gone by the name of Obi-Wan Kenobi since, oh, before you were born.

LUKE: Then this droid belongs to you?

BEN: Don't seem to remember ever owning a droid.

Sound: A far-off, echoing cry from a Tusken Raider.

BEN: I think we'd better get indoors. The Sand People are easily startled, but they'll soon be back, and in greater numbers. My home isn't far from here.

ARTOO: SIGNALS INSISTENTLY.

LUKE: What . . . oh, Threepio!

BEN: Who's Threepio?

LUKE: See-Threepio, Artoo-Detoo's counterpart. When that Tusken Raider jumped us, Threepio must've been damaged.

BEN: Then let's find him quickly. Every second counts now.

Sound: Luke and Ben struggling up.

LUKE: *(CALLING)* Here he is, behind the rock.

BEN: Good.

Sound: Grunting as they work under:

BEN: Look, here's his arm . . . torn loose, linkages and all.

LUKE: Help me sit him up.

Sound: Threepio's joints squeak as he's pulled up.

LUKE: I'll try his reactivate switch. Here goes.

Sound: A switch is thrown.

LUKE: Nothing.

BEN: Try again.

Sound: Switch is thrown again. The whine of servos and assorted clicks indicate Threepio's functioning.

THREEPIO: Master Luke! Where am I? I must have taken a bad step when that Sand Person swung at me with his ax.

LUKE: Can you stand? We've got to get out of here before they come back.

THREEPIO: I don't think I can make it! You go on, Master Luke. There's no sense in your risking yourself on my account. I'm done for!

LUKE: What kind of talk is that? We'll help you to your feet. The landspeeder's not far off.

BEN: Quickly now. The Sand People are on the move. We'll go to my home. Come.

Music: Up.

Sound: Door opening.

BEN: It's a modest place, Luke . . . In comparison, your uncle's is rather grand. Sit Threepio down over there in the corner.

Sound: Ben closes door as Threepio is deposited.

LUKE: I'll see what I can do for him.

BEN: *(APPROACHING)* Here's my toolbox. I don't think the damage is too serious. His automatic disconnects released under the strain of the fall. It should be a simple matter of reattaching the shoulder linkages and activating the self-seals.

Sound: Luke rummages through tools briefly and works on Threepio under:

LUKE: Ummmm. Yeah, you're right, Ben. You know a lot about droid repair for a . . . that is . . .

BEN: For an old hermit?

LUKE: I, I didn't mean it that way.

BEN: Oh, I quite understand. But you shouldn't assume that solitude necessarily begets ignorance, Luke.

LUKE: Uh, it's a real nice place you have here. Pretty well hidden, too.

BEN: It has all that I require: shelter and comfort without a lot of clutter. I prefer to live simply and to keep around me only those things I prize highly. That is part of the Jedi's creed.

LUKE: A Jedi? You mean *you* were a Jedi Knight?

BEN: Do you find that so impossible to believe?

LUKE: It's just that I've heard so many stories about the Jedi Knights and all those things they did . . .

BEN: Ah, and I suppose I don't very much look the part just now, do I? Well, truth to tell, that's partially by design. But I was one nonetheless . . . and so was your father.

LUKE: My . . . *my* father? But he couldn't have been!

BEN: Luke, he and I served together in the Clone Wars.

LUKE: My father didn't fight in the wars . . . He was a navigator on a spice freighter.

BEN: That's what your Uncle Owen told you. He didn't hold with your father's ideals . . . thought your father should've stayed here and not gotten involved.

LUKE: I wish I'd known him.

BEN: He was the best star pilot in the galaxy, a cunning warrior. And he was a good friend. *(PAUSE)* I understand you've become quite a good pilot yourself. Which reminds me, I have something for you. *(MOVING OFF)*

THREEPIO: Sir, if you won't be needing me, I'll close down for a while and run through some internal checks.

LUKE: Sure, go ahead.

Sound: Threepio shutting down with an abrupt halting of mechanisms and a low click.

BEN: *(APPROACHING)* Your father wanted you to have this when you were old enough, but your uncle wouldn't allow it. He feared you might follow old Obi-Wan off on some foolish idealistic crusade like your father did. I wanted to give it to you once before, but your uncle ordered me to get off your farm and never return.

LUKE: When you saved Windy and me! I remember that! And then you turned up again today, and you know about my piloting. Ben, you've been sort of keeping an eye on me, haven't you?

BEN: Let's simply say that I've kept abreast of your progress. But now, about your father's legacy here . . .

LUKE: Yeah, what *is* this thing? It looks like some kind of handle. What does it attach to?

BEN: What you hold is your father's lightsaber . . . This is the weapon of a Jedi. Carefully now, press that control, there on the grip.

Sound: A click and a sharp shearing sound. The beam moans as Luke moves it under:

LUKE: Why, it's a sword!

BEN: A lightsaber. Its blade is pure energy. Take great care with it . . . It will cut through anything it touches. Do you feel how readily it answers your least gesture? Not as clumsy or random as a blaster. To use one well is a mark of excellence.

LUKE: It moves so easily . . . almost like it's alive.

BEN: An elegant weapon for a more civilized age. For over a thousand generations the Jedi Knights were the guardians of peace and justice in the Old Republic, before the dark times . . . before the Empire.

Sound: Another shearing cut.

BEN: Perhaps that's enough for now.

Sound: Luke switches the lightsaber off with a click.

LUKE: Ben, how did my father die?

BEN: It's not a story to be told simply, or briefly. Suffice it to say that there was a young Jedi who was a pupil of mine, perhaps my most brilliant one, until he was seduced by the dark side of the Force and turned to evil. He betrayed your father and, and murdered him. His name was Darth Vader, and he helped the Empire hunt down and destroy the Jedi Knights. It's the sort of tragedy that occurs when even the finest of people are seduced by the dark side of the Force.

LUKE: The Force?

BEN: The Force is what gives a Jedi his power. It's an energy field created by all living things. It surrounds us and penetrates us . . . It binds the galaxy together.

LUKE: And this Darth Vader . . .

BEN: It is, as I said, a long and complicated account. It will have to wait for another time.

ARTOO: BEGINS TO BLEEP URGENTLY.

BEN: Ah, yes, Artoo-Detoo, my unexpected emissary? Now, let's see if we can't figure out just what brought you here and where you came from.

ARTOO: BEEPS ACQUIESCENCE.

Sound: Ben grunts as he kneels down and makes small tinkering noises.

BEN: Hmm, yes. His control systems are quite conventional.

LUKE: I saw part of a holographic projection, a message he was carrying . . .

ARTOO: BLEEPS.

Sound: A crackle of static as the holograph activates.

BEN: I seem to have found it.

HOLO IMAGE: General Kenobi: Years ago you served my father in the Clone Wars. Now he begs you to help him in his struggle against the Empire. I regret that I am unable to present my father's request to you in person, but my ship has fallen under attack, and I'm afraid that my mission to bring you to Alderaan has failed. I have placed information vital to the security of the Rebellion into the memory system of this R2 unit. My father will know how to retrieve it. You must see this droid safely to Alderaan. This is our most desperate hour. Please help me, Obi-Wan Kenobi. You're my only hope.

Sound: A final crackle as transmission ends. A moment's silence.

LUKE: *(MESMERIZED)* Who is she?

BEN: *(DISTRACTEDLY)* She is the Princess Leia Organa of the Royal House of Alderaan, an Imperial Senator and, unbeknown to the Empire, a leader of the Rebel Alliance. She's grown into a remarkable young woman.

LUKE: She's beautiful. She's the most beautiful thing I ever saw!

BEN: Indeed. *(BREAKING HIS DISTRACTION)* Well, Luke, you must learn the ways of the Force if you're to come with me to Alderaan.

LUKE: *(LAUGHING NERVOUSLY)* Alderaan? I'm not going to Alderaan. I'm late . . . I'm in for it as it is when I get home.

BEN: But I need your help, Luke. *She* needs your help. I'm getting too old for this kind of thing.

LUKE: I can't get involved! I've got work to do! It's not that I like the Empire . . . I hate it! But there's nothing I can do about it right now. And it's such a long way from here.

BEN: That's your uncle talking.

LUKE: My uncle! How am I ever going to explain all this to him?

BEN: Learn about the Force, Luke.

LUKE: Look, I can take you as far as Anchorhead. You can get a transport from there to Mos Eisley Spaceport or wherever you're going.

BEN: You must do what you feel is right, of course.

LUKE: What I feel is right? Ben, I'd like to help you, to help *her*, but is it right to run out on Uncle Owen and Aunt Beru? They're all the family I've got, and I'm not going to let anything happen to them! If that's not right, then maybe I'd rather be wrong!

BEN: Yes . . . of course. Sometimes even the best intentions may be contradictory; perhaps your answer lies with the Force, within you. *(PAUSE, THEN MORE BRISKLY)* Very well, I shall take you up on your kind offer. I must make my way to Alderaan as quickly as I can.

Sound: Fade to silence.

Sound: Landspeeder engine up, then reduces to a hum under:

LUKE: You all right back there, Artoo?

ARTOO: SIGNALS ASSURANCES.

LUKE: How about you, Threepio?

THREEPIO: Oh, quite comfortable, thank you, sir.

BEN: Getting to Anchorhead with the droids would've presented a formidable problem if you hadn't offered me this ride, Luke.

LUKE: I really do wish I could do more for you, Ben. But the sooner I get these droids out on the south ridge working on those vaporators, the less of a skinning I'll catch from Uncle Owen.

BEN: Luke, I'm afraid the droids will have to come with me.

LUKE: What? But they cost my uncle nearly—

BEN: *(INTERRUPTING)* Surely you don't think I can leave them behind? You heard that message. This matter is far too vital to risk losing Artoo-Detoo, and, for security's sake, See-Threepio must come along as well.

LUKE: But what'll I tell Uncle Owen?

BEN: I shall leave that to your conscience, son. But here's another thing to consider: There will almost certainly be Imperial agents seeking these two droids, people of the most violent and ruthless sort. Taking them back to your farm would only expose your uncle and aunt to dreadful danger.

LUKE: Oh. Oh, yeah. I'll, I'll think of something, I guess.

BEN: Good; I know you will. *(PAUSE)* What's that? There, off to the south? Smoke! Something of great size is afire!

LUKE: What? Where? I don't see any . . . yes! There it is! You've got good eyes for . . . uh, I mean . . .

BEN: . . . an old man? Powers of observation lie with the mind, Luke, not the eyes. Perhaps we should take a look and see what it is.

LUKE: Artoo, Threepio, hang on!

ARTOO: BLEEPS.

Sound: The speeder engine increases, fades to silence. Cross-fade to:

Sound: Crackling fire and wind.

LUKE: It's a Jawa sandcrawler! And look, it's been shot to pieces! There're dead Jawas everywhere!

THREEPIO: Why, those are the dreadful little creatures that captured Artoo and myself.

ARTOO: WHISTLES AGREEMENT.

LUKE: It must've been the Sand People. I've got a bad feeling about this . . . We'd better get out of here.

BEN: No, whoever did this is gone, Luke. Perhaps some of the Jawas are still alive. We must stop and help them if we can.

LUKE: Well . . .

BEN: Come, let's have a look.

LUKE: Uh, the smell of that smoke! *(COUGHING)* . . . flesh . . .

BEN: Tie a cloth over your face . . . it will help.

LUKE: No. I'll be all right.

THREEPIO: Shall Artoo and I come too, sir?

BEN: Yes. We shall need help with this. *(PAUSE)* The ones here are all dead. Do you see any survivors, Luke?

LUKE: *(OFF)* No. Somebody made sure none of these Jawas would live. Some of them were shot two or three times, at close range.

ARTOO: *(OFF)* BLEEPS.

THREEPIO: *(OFF)* Sir, Artoo informs me he detects no life aboard the sandcrawler.

BEN: The poor little creatures. Their lives were arduous and meager enough without being ended so brutally. Threepio! Artoo! We'll gather fuel and prepare a funeral pyre!

LUKE: *(APPROACHING)* But Ben, we don't have the time! I have to get home.

BEN: Are we in so great a hurry that we must leave their bodies to be eaten by scavengers? It will take little enough time.

LUKE: If you say so. See where that whole big hull section was blasted away when the engines went? This must've been quite a battle.

BEN: Even Jawas can die bravely.

LUKE: It looks like the Sand People did this, all right. Look, there are Gaffi sticks and bantha tracks all over the place. It's just . . . I never heard of them hitting anything as big as a Jawa sandcrawler before.

BEN: They didn't, but we are meant to *think* they did. These bantha tracks here are side by side, you see? But Sand People always ride single file, to hide their numbers . . .

LUKE: Ben, these are the same Jawas who sold Threepio and Artoo to Uncle Owen . . .

BEN: And these blaster-fire impact points on the bodies and the sandcrawler . . . too accurate for Sand People. Only Imperial stormtroopers are so precise.

LUKE: Stormtroopers? Why would Imperial troops want to slaughter Jawas? Unless . . . the droids! If they traced Artoo and Threepio here, they may've learned who the Jawas sold them to! And that would lead them back . . . home!

Sound: Luke getting in and starting speeder.

BEN: Wait, Luke! It's too dangerous! Luke! Come back! Luke!

Sound: His words are drowned out by the engines, which then fade.

BEN: Sighs.

THREEPIO: *(APPROACHING)* Sir, we've prepared the fire.

BEN: *(TIREDLY)* Very well, we'll give the Jawas what decent funeral we can . . . and that's precious little enough.

THREEPIO: Where's Master Luke going, sir?

BEN: That I cannot tell you. It's tied in with a great many things to be determined now by the Force. Come, let us get this done as quickly as we can.

Music: Up.

Sound: Crackling fire and wind.

THREEPIO: Sir! It's Master Luke. He's—

BEN: Yes, I see him. *(CALLING GENTLY)* Luke! Are you all right, son?

LUKE: *(OFF, MOVING SLOWLY ON. QUIETLY, NEARLY MONO-TONE)* The farm . . . I could see the smoke from kilometers away. Everything was gutted, burning. I called out for Uncle Owen and Aunt Beru, but they didn't answer. Then I saw . . . by the entranceway . . .

BEN: Easy, Luke. Take it easy.

LUKE: There was practically nothing left of them! Oh, Ben, you could hardly tell they'd been human beings! They were all I had, the only family I ever knew in my whole life! And when they needed me, I wasn't there!

BEN: There was nothing you could've done, Luke. If you'd been there, you'd have been killed as well, and the droids would now be in the hands of the Empire.

LUKE: *(PAUSE)* I want to come with you to Alderaan. There's nothing here for me now. I want to learn the ways of the Force and become a Jedi like my father.

BEN: I'm sorry that your decision comes in this fashion, son. I would rather have gone on alone than have this come to pass. But if it's what you want, Luke . . . very well: Alderaan it shall be, and the way of the Jedi Knight.

Music: In and under:

NARRATOR: Luke Skywalker is about to undertake a journey to a distant solar system, and a journey of the spirit as well. No matter that an Empire is against him. He is moved by vengeance, but he is moved, too, by the image of a young woman in terrible danger. Luke Skywalker is soon to become a pivotal figure in the galaxy wide struggle between Rebellion and Empire.

Music: Closing theme up and under preview and closing credits.

ANNOUNCER: CLOSING CREDITS.

EPISODE SIX:

"THE *MILLENNIUM FALCON* DEAL"

CAST:

Ben	Bartender	Sergeant
Luke	Spacer	1st Trooper
Threepio	Creature	2nd Trooper
Artoo	Human	3rd Trooper
Han	Greedo	1st Customer
Chewbacca	Owner	2nd Customer

ANNOUNCER: *OPENING CREDITS.*

Music: Opening theme.

NARRATOR: A long time ago in a galaxy far, far away there came a time of revolution, when Rebels united to challenge a tyrannical Empire. This bitter struggle brought disaster to the life of young Luke Skywalker, a moisture farmer on the planet Tatooine, when his uncle purchased the astrodroid Artoo-Detoo without knowing that Artoo's memory banks held secret plans vital to the Rebellion. Imperial stormtroopers hunting for Artoo-Detoo and his interpreter-counterpart, See-Threepio, savagely murdered Luke's uncle and aunt. Luke has committed himself to aiding the aged Ben Kenobi, one of the last of the legendary Jedi Knights and a sympathizer with the Rebel Alliance.

Sound: Tatooine winds up, landspeeder engine in background.

NARRATOR: Now Luke, Ben, Artoo-Detoo, and See-Threepio are bound for Mos Eisley Spaceport in Luke's landspeeder. There they hope to find passage off Tatooine for the planet Alderaan to deliver Artoo and his crucial message.

BEN: Luke? Luke! You've let us drift off course again.

LUKE: What?

BEN: The landspeeder's off course. Mos Eisley Spaceport is that way, over that ridge.

LUKE: Oh, yeah.

Sound: The speeder's engine changes speed to alter course.

BEN: That's the third time you've strayed, Luke. If you're tired, I could take over the controls. Or See-Threepio.

LUKE: No, no . . . it's just . . . I can't get it out of my mind, Ben . . . what they did to my uncle and aunt. I see it over and over.

BEN: I understand, Luke.

LUKE: I'm all right, really. *(CALLING SLIGHTLY OVER ENGINE)* How are you two doing back there? Hanging on, Threepio?

THREEPIO: Oh, yes, sir.

LUKE: How's Artoo?

ARTOO: TWEEDLES A RESPONSE.

THREEPIO: He says he's very well, thank you, sir.

BEN: Luke, pull up there by the summit of the ridge. I want to take a moment's pause before we push on to Mos Eisley.

Sound: The speeder maneuvering, decelerating, coming to a stop. Engine dying under:

BEN: We'll have a good view of the place from up here. *(PAUSE)* There it is, Luke—Mos Eisley Spaceport.

THREEPIO: It looks rather shoddy and disreputable for a space-port, if you don't mind my saying so, sir.

BEN: You will never find a more wretched hive of scum and villainy in the whole galaxy. Come, Luke, we'll take a closer look.

Sound: They get out under:

BEN: We must be on our guard, alert to everything around us, if we are to survive and get off Tatooine.

LUKE: Ben, I'll be all right, I promise.

BEN: There will be enemies all around us in Mos Eisley, and great danger.

LUKE: I won't let you down.

BEN: No, I believe you won't, Luke. If you knew something of the Force, its mental disciplines would be of great help to you now. But we shall have to wait until after we've left this planet to begin your training.

LUKE: It's just that . . . Uncle Owen and Aunt Beru were the only family I ever had.

BEN: I understand, Luke, but you must set your grief aside for the moment and give your full attention to our mission; our chances of success are small enough as it is. When we have reached Alderaan, there will be time for you to let your feelings come forth.

LUKE: You're sure we can find passage to Alderaan in Mos Eisley, Ben?

BEN: Nothing is sure, Luke. But our best chance of doing it, and doing it without attracting attention, lies down there, in Mos Eisley. Tramp freight haulers, smugglers, and pirates of all types pass through there constantly.

LUKE: Yeah, I've heard a lot of wild stories about it.

BEN: There are few questions asked down there, and most of those can be answered simply enough with cash. People mind their own business . . . it enhances their life expectancy. We should find just the sort of tough, mercenary characters we need.

LUKE: You sound as if you've done this kind of thing before.

BEN: When I was a Jedi Knight, and thereafter, I became familiar with a good many unusual people and places, my young friend.

LUKE: What shall we do about the droids? They could attract a lot of attention to us.

BEN: We shall have to deal with that problem as it arises. We certainly can't risk leaving them behind. Artoo is far too important, and Threepio already knows too much for us to chance his falling into the hands of the Empire.

LUKE: Ben, in that message Artoo brought to you, she . . . I mean, the Princess . . . I mean . . .

BEN: *(LAUGHING)* If we were at the High Court of Alderaan, you'd be expected to refer to her as the Princess Leia Organa or Her Highness. But I fancy that under the circumstances, she wouldn't mind if you referred to her with more brevity.

LUKE: Uh, the Princess, then . . . she said the information she stored in Artoo's memory banks was vital to the Rebellion. Do you have any idea what it is?

BEN: None, but I trust her not to exaggerate. We must believe her message absolutely and proceed on the assumption that the fate of the Rebel Alliance rests with us and with Artoo.

LUKE: She said her ship was under attack. Do you think she's all right?

BEN: She is alive almost certainly, but I don't doubt her circumstances are difficult. Imperial inquisitors have some ugly ways of obtaining information from prisoners. She will have the means to resist for some while, but not indefinitely. It's one more reason for us to make haste to Alderaan. Come . . . to Mos Eisley . . .

Music: Up then under:

Sound: The landspeeder maneuvering around vehicular and pedestrian traffic of exotic types—droids, humans, and nonhumans. The hum of the landspeeder's engine under:

LUKE: Ben, there are almost never any Imperials on Tatooine, but Mos Eisley seems to be crawling with them.

BEN: Yes, more than I had foreseen.

LUKE: Maybe we should try for another way off-world.

BEN: No, our hope still lies here. We'll have to go on as best we may. There seems to be a roadblock ahead, with stormtroopers checking all traffic. Take this side street.

Sound: The engine signals the turn. The street noises diminish somewhat.

LUKE: I guess it's like you said: The Empire's not stopping at anything to find Threepio and Artoo.

BEN: The stormtroopers are not the opposition I fear most. The Emperor has other, more fearsome servants at his command.

LUKE: This Darth Vader you were telling me about—the one who killed my father—is he—

BEN: *(INTERRUPTING)* I . . . I believe that's another Imperial checkpoint up ahead, Luke. There seems to be no getting around them.

LUKE: I could turn around, make a run for it.

BEN: They'd seal off the exit routes. Besides, that would put us right back where we started.

LUKE: That stormtrooper's signaling me to halt.

BEN: Best to brazen it out. Do as he says and follow my cues. Answer any questions they ask, but let me do the talking.

LUKE: That's fine with me. Artoo, Threepio, don't say a word.

THREEPIO: Yes, sir.

ARTOO: TWEEDLES ACKNOWLEDGMENT.

Sound: Speeder decelerates and stops. The engine dies.

1ST TROOPER: All right, men, check this landspeeder over.

2ND TROOPER: Okay.

1ST TROOPER: You there, driver. How long have you had these two droids?

LUKE: Uh, about three or four seasons.

BEN: They're for sale if you want them.

1ST TROOPER: I've got no use for 'em, but we're looking for two stolen droids. You, driver, let me see your identification and the ownerships for these droids.

BEN: You don't need to see his identification.

1ST TROOPER: We . . . don't need to see his identification.

BEN: These aren't the droids you're looking for.

1ST TROOPER: These aren't the droids we're looking for.

BEN: He can go on about his business.

1ST TROOPER: You can go on about your business.

BEN: Move along, Luke.

1ST TROOPER: Move along, move along.

LUKE: *(ASTOUNDED)* Yeah. Sure thing.

Sound: Landspeeder starts up, engine revs and moves off, the engine hum under:

LUKE: Are they looking at us?

BEN: Mmm, no, they've stopped a robo-hauler. I daresay they've forgotten us already, Luke.

LUKE: And nobody's following us?

BEN: All the stormtroopers back there at the checkpoint seem otherwise occupied to me.

LUKE: Ben, how did we get past them? I thought we were dead for certain.

BEN: The Force can have a strong influence on the weak-minded. You'll find it a powerful ally.

LUKE: But how in—

BEN: *(INTERRUPTING)* Turn off here and go to the end of that side street. There's a cantina there. That's where we'll find what we're looking for.

Music: In.

Sound: Cantina music comes up, growing louder as they approach. A wild variety of languages, noises, etc.

LUKE: Will you look at this! I've never *seen* so many nonhumans in one place! There's a Meerian Hammerhead over there . . . and a Stofo Lupinoid, couple of T'iin-T'iin dwarfs . . . Boy, a lot of the *humans* don't look human.

BEN: This cantina is a meeting ground and a place of business for half the shady goings-on in this part of space. Stay close to me. Artoo and Threepio, you, too.

THREEPIO: Yes, sir.

ARTOO: WARBLES.

BARTENDER: *(OFF)* Hey, you, we don't serve their kind in here!

LUKE: Huh?

Sound: Laughter and amused noises from the crowd.

BARTENDER: Yer droids! They'll have to stay outside. We don't want them in here!

BEN: Best to do as he says. We don't want to attract attention.

LUKE: You think we should risk leaving them alone?

BEN: There shouldn't be any problem so long as Threepio and Artoo stay with the landspeeder. If anything goes wrong, they can summon us from the doorway.

LUKE: You want me to stay with them?

BEN: No, it's best to have someone to guard one's back in this kind of place.

LUKE: Whatever you say. Listen, Threepio, why don't you and Artoo wait outside by my speeder? We don't want any trouble.

150

THREEPIO: I heartily agree with you, sir.

LUKE: You heard what Ben said?

THREEPIO: Yes sir. If there's any problem, we'll signal you from the doorway. Back we go, Artoo.

ARTOO: SIGNALS DISAPPOINTMENT.

BEN: Here, let's step up to the bar. That spaceman standing there strikes me as a likely fellow with whom to make our preliminary inquiries.

BEN: *(ASIDE TO LUKE)* Order something for yourself, Luke. This may take some time. *(TO SPACEMAN)* Excuse me, my friend, but I wonder if I might have a word with you.

SPACER: Well?

BEN: You're a Corellian spacer, are you not?

SPACER: What about it?

BEN: I'm in the market to charter a fast starship, and I've been told by those in the know that the Corellian vessels are among the very best.

SPACER: You heard right. 'Cept that Corellians aren't *among*; we *are* the best.

BEN: Ah, splendid! And would you by any chance know of a starship that's available for hire?

SPACER: If you'd've come in here yesterday, you could've had mine, but now I'm committed to a charter. I raise ship tonight.

BEN: A pity. Perhaps you could recommend someone else?

SPACER: Well, there aren't too many other Corellians in port just now, and anybody else'd just be a second-rater. Let's see, now . . . Oh, yeah, there's the *Falcon*.

BEN: *Falcon?*

SPACER: The *Millennium Falcon.* Her skipper's Han Solo.

BEN: And would this—Han Solo?—be available at present for a job?

SPACER: Haw! I'd be surprised if he wasn't. Han ain't been doing so well lately. He was around here a little while ago . . . In fact, there's his first mate, standing over there . . . the giant shaggy one.

BEN: Ah, a Wookiee!

SPACER: That's right, but a damn good first mate and copilot all the same. *(CALLING)* Hey, Chewbacca!

CHEWIE: *(OFF)* A LOWING ANSWER.

SPACER: C'mere! I got someone for you to meet!

LUKE: *(MOVING ON)* Here's your drink, Ben.

BEN: Thank you, Luke.

CHEWIE: *(APPROACHING)* GROWLS A QUESTION.

SPACER: What do you say, Chewbacca? This fella here's looking for a ship.

CHEWIE: BARKS A QUESTION.

BEN: No, just one quick trip.

SPACER: You understand the Wookiee language?

BEN: Some, yes. Thank you, friend; you've been of great assistance to me.

SPACER: Huh?

CHEWIE: GROWLS MEANINGFULLY.

SPACER: Oh. Sure, old-timer, glad to oblige. Guess I'll be shoving off. Clear skies to ya, Chewbacca.

CHEWIE: GRUNTS A FAREWELL.

BEN: The *Millennium Falcon*, is that the name of your ship? I was told she's fast.

CHEWIE: REPLIES AT SOME LENGTH.

BEN: No, that will be more than satisfactory. I'm not looking for anything elaborate, Chewbacca, just quick passage to Alderaan—

Sound: Ben breaks off to listen to Luke's altercation.

CREATURE: *(SLIGHTLY OFF) Negola dewaghi wooldugger!*

HUMAN: *(TO LUKE)* He doesn't like you, boy, and I don't, either! You just watch yourself!

LUKE: *(SLIGHTLY OFF)* Sorry!

BEN: Chewbacca, is your Captain Solo available to discuss terms of hiring?

CHEWIE: GROWLS A REPLY.

HUMAN: *(OVERLAPPING)* We're wanted men, sonny! I've got the death sentence on me in twelve solar systems!

CREATURE: *Chagga m'woo yteela!*

BEN: Pardon me a moment, Chewbacca.

LUKE: *(SLIGHTLY OFF)* I'll be careful, then.

HUMAN: You'll be dead!

BEN: Just a moment please, my friend. This little one here isn't worth the effort. Come, let me buy you and your companion there something to drink . . .

CREATURE: *Rog Schaad davoona!*

HUMAN: Stay out of this, Grandpa! I'll fix you when I've finished with this little fool!

Sound: Luke yells out as he's violently seized and shoved aside.

Sound: A chair and table are overturned, breaking glasses. Sensing a fight, the band stops playing, and the crowd makes excited noises.

HUMAN: Now for you, you old—

BARTENDER: No blasters! No blasters!

Sound: The sharp, shearing noise of Ben's lightsaber. The saber moans, then hissing and slicing, then the thump of two bodies. Silence follows as Ben deactivates the saber.

1ST CUSTOMER: That old man! He just about sliced Roofoo in half!

BEN: Luke, are you hurt?

LUKE: Uh . . . ?

BEN: Here, let me help you up.

Sound: Ben assisting Luke.

BARTENDER: Hey, you . . . the band . . . who told you you could take a break? Get back to work! Show's over, everybody!

Sound: The band begins to play. Conversations buzz.

BARTENDER: Some of you get those bodies out of here! Go on or you'll never get another free drink from me!

BEN: Are you all right, son?

LUKE: I knocked my head on something, but I'll be okay. Ben, I never saw anything like that in my life! Your lightsaber . . .

BEN: It's a last resort, Luke . . . never forget that. *(MOVING OFF)* Now, Chewbacca here is—

LUKE: *(INTERRUPTING)* A Wookiee! I've never seen a real Wookiee before!

CHEWIE: GROWLS SOMEWHAT SARCASTICALLY.

154

BEN: Ah, yes, quite. But he's also first mate and copilot on a ship that might suit our needs. His captain's nearby somewhere. Chewbacca will bring him to speak to us.

CHEWIE: *(MOVING OFF)* BARKING AND GRUNTING.

LUKE: Ben, he's enormous!

BEN: Yes. Now we must find a booth somewhere out of the way where we can wait. Come, Luke . . .

Sound: Bar background fades to silence.

Sound: Street noises up and under:

THREEPIO: Artoo, do you see that large reptilian creature tethered over there, the one wearing the saddle? I believe that is what they call a dewback, the creature Master Luke was telling me about.

ARTOO: BURBLES A WARNING.

THREEPIO: What? Imperial stormtroopers? Where?

ARTOO: WHISTLES AN ANSWER.

THREEPIO: Oh, dear! They seem to be taking up positions to search the area! Come, Artoo, we'll have to go and attract Master Luke's attention from the cantina doorway.

Sound: They whine and whir toward the cantina door.

1ST CUSTOMER: Watch it, droid, Who d' ya think yer shovin'?

THREEPIO: Beg pardon, sir, but I wasn't shoving you. We would just like—

1ST CUSTOMER: And I say you were!

2ND CUSTOMER: Go on, beat it before we take a wrench to you both!

THREEPIO: That won't be necessary, sir. Come, Artoo.

ARTOO: BLEEPS.

Sound: They whine and whir off.

THREEPIO: Look, the stormtroopers are forming up for a house-to-house search. Our only recourse is to find somewhere to hide.

ARTOO: WHISTLES DUBIOUSLY.

THREEPIO: What do you mean, "What if we can't?" How should I know? I'm not programmed for deception and criminal behavior, like some that I could mention! You're the one who got us into all this. Why don't you think of something?

ARTOO: BLATS.

THREEPIO: Look, more stormtroopers! We're trapped! What shall we do?

ARTOO: BEEPS ACCUSINGLY.

THREEPIO: What do you mean, I'm *"supposed* to be the intelligent one"? I . . . wait!

ARTOO: CHIRPS A QUESTION.

THREEPIO: That used-droid lot over there! Come on! (FADING) When we get there, Artoo, stand at the end of the display line with me. Keep perfectly still and don't make a sound!

Sound: Cross-fade to:

1ST TROOPER: Hey, Sarge, there's a droid lot here!

SERGEANT: Where's the owner? *(CALLING)* Hey, you, come here!

OWNER: *(APPROACHING)* What can I do for you, soldier?

SERGEANT: You bought or sold any droids in the last few days?

OWNER: Nope. Business has been off. The last stock I moved was ten days ago . . . haven't purchased any in even longer. Want to see my sales records?

SERGEANT: Not necessary. There'll be a verification team by later. *(TO TROOPS)* Come on, come on, and make sure you try every door you pass. *(MOVING OFF)* If any are open, take a quick check inside.

OWNER: Huh, now, I wonder what that was all about. Hey, what's this? What're you two doing standing there?

THREEPIO: Our master instructed us to wait here, sir. He's, er, canvassing the area to see if anyone wants any household maintenance jobs done.

OWNER: Well, don't stand right here on my lot, you half-wit! People'll think you belong to me! I got enough trouble selling these old clunkers without you hanging around confusing things! Move!

THREEPIO: *(FADING)* Moving, sir. Come on, Artoo.

ARTOO: WHISTLES.

Sound: They move off.

OWNER: Darn pesky droids. There's not one of 'em has the brains of a womp rat.

Sound: Fades on owner's last words. Street sounds out to silence.

Sound: Cantina band up in background with their postduel swing number. Conversations, etc., in background.

HAN: *(SLIGHTLY OFF)* Is that them in the booth, Chewie?

CHEWIE: *(APPROACHING)* RUMBLES AN AFFIRMATIVE.

HAN: 'Lo, gents. I'm Han Solo, captain of the *Millennium Falcon*.

BEN: Pleased to meet you, Captain Solo.

Sound: He seats himself in booth. Chewie does the same under:

CHEWIE: GROWLING.

HAN: My first mate, Chewbacca here, tells me you're looking for passage to the Alderaan system. That right?

BEN: That is a fact; we are. *If* yours is a fast ship.

HAN: *Fast ship?* You mean to tell me that you've never heard of the *Millennium Falcon*?

BEN: Should I have?

HAN: Where've *you* been? The *Falcon*'s the ship that made the Kessel run in less than twelve time parts.

BEN: Which would make you a spice smuggler. Is that correct?

HAN: Well, why don't we just say I'm an independent business-man? Very independent.

BEN: In the best Corellian tradition?

HAN: Yeah, I've been known to bend a law or two on occasion. I've outrun Imperial warships, not the local bulk cruisers, mind you, but the big ships of the line. The *Falcon*'s fast enough for you, old man.

BEN: I believe we understand one another, you and I.

HAN: Huh? Oh, uh, good. What's the cargo?

BEN: Only passengers. Myself, the boy here, two droids . . . and no questions asked.

HAN: What is it you're running from? Some sort of local trouble?

BEN: Let's just say that we'd prefer to avoid any Imperial entanglements.

HAN: Well, that's the trick, isn't it? And it's going to cost you something extra. Ten thousand . . . in advance.

LUKE: *Ten thousand?* We could almost buy our own ship for that!

HAN: But who's gonna fly it for you, kid? You?

LUKE: You bet I could! I'm not such a bad pilot myself. Ben, let's get out of here. We don't have to sit and listen to this—

BEN: *(INTERRUPTING)* Easy, Luke. Captain Solo, we haven't that much cash with us, but we could pay you two thousand now, plus fifteen thousand more when we get to Alderaan.

HAN: Seventeen, huh? *(PAUSE, CONSIDERING)* Okay, you guys've got yourselves a starship. Oh, just a friendly word of advice: I'd better get the rest of my money when we hit Alderaan; me and my partner Chewie here don't like it when somebody tries to cheat on a deal.

CHEWIE: GROWLS AN OMINOUS WARNING.

BEN: You needn't worry. We'll keep our end of the deal if you live up to yours.

HAN: I call that a real wise attitude, old man. We'll leave as soon as you're ready. The *Millennium Falcon*'s in docking bay 94 at the spaceport.

BEN: Docking bay 94. We'll meet you there with the money shortly.

HAN: Good.

Sound: A hubbub in the distance as stormtroopers enter.

HAN: Hey, I saw what was left of a couple of small-time punks being carted out the front door a while ago. Your handiwork?

BEN: I had no choice . . . they forced the fight.

HAN: No loss to society, but it looks like those stormtroopers over there noticed the remains.

LUKE: Ben . . .

BEN: Wait, Luke . . .

HAN: Uh oh. They're headed this way. I suggest the back door, gents. Right over there.

BEN: Thank you, Captain Solo.

HAN: Pleasure's mine.

BEN: We'll meet you at the docking bay. Come, Luke. *(FADING OFF)*.

1ST TROOPER: *(APPROACHING)* Have you two seen anything of an old man and a boy?

HAN: Nope. Chewie?

CHEWIE: YEOWLS A NEGATIVE.

HAN: But then, it's not our job to watch people, is it?

1ST TROOPER: *(CALLING)* Hey, bartender, I thought you said they came over here!

BARTENDER: *(OFF)* I said I *thought* they did. Look, I got other things to do besides keep an eye on every single customer!

1ST TROOPER: All right, men. We'll check out the back door. Follow me.

Sound: The troopers clatter off.

HAN: *(LAUGHING)* Seventeen thousand! Those two guys must really be desperate! This could really save my neck.

CHEWIE: HOOTS AGREEMENT.

HAN: I wonder who they are. You said the old man dropped those two bar brawlers with a *lightsaber*? Who uses one of those antiques anymore?

CHEWIE: GRUNTS MYSTIFICATION.

HAN: Me, either. He sure knew how to use it, though. I've got a funny feeling about those two, Chewie.

CHEWIE: A QUESTIONING GRUNT.

HAN: I don't know, exactly. Still, we have to play the hand the way it's dealt. I don't think we can afford to pass this job up. Jabba the Hutt's a little anxious to be paid off for that load of Kessel spice we had to dump; too much longer, every gunman in the sector'll be trying to nail us for the price on our heads.

CHEWIE: HONKS AGREEMENT.

HAN: You go collect our gear. I've got a couple things to do.

Sound: Chewie rises and starts off.

CHEWIE: GROWLS A PARTING COMMENT.

HAN: *(CALLING)* I'll meet you back at the *Falcon*, and we'll get ready to raise ship.

*GREEDO: Going somewhere, Solo?

HAN: Sure I'm going somewhere, Greedo; you can put that gun up. I was on my way to see your boss. Tell Jabba the Hutt that I've got his money.

*GREEDO: It's too late, human. Move back to the booth and sit down.

HAN: Anything you say. Just don't get nervous with the pistol, Greedo. Y' don't mind if I put my feet up and relax, do you? It's been a long day.

Sound: His boots clumping on the table.

*GREEDO: You should have paid Jabba while you had the chance.

HAN: Yeah, Greedo, but this time I've really got the money for Jabba.

*GREEDO: If you give it to me, I might forget that I found you.

HAN: I haven't got it *with* me. I just picked up a job. Tell Heater and Jabba the Hutt that—

*Greedo speaks in his own language.

*GREEDO: *(INTERRUPTING)* Jabba's through with you, and Preacher's got no more patience.

HAN: A hunter-killer team had me boxed in! I couldn't even jump for hyperspace! I was lucky to come out of it with my life!

*GREEDO: Where was that famous Solo cunning I'm always hearing about?

HAN: Look, even *I* get boarded sometimes. I *had* to dump that load of spice . . . D' you think I had a choice?

*GREEDO: You can tell that to Preacher. He may only take your ship.

HAN: Over my dead body!

*GREEDO: That's the idea, human.

HAN: Yeah, I'll bet.

Sound: A loud report of a blaster. Customers cry out in surprise, and Greedo moans, gurgles, and slumps, thumping his head on the table.

HAN: Rest in peace, Greedo! I can shoot just as well under a table as across one. How's *that* for the old Solo cunning?

Sound: Han rises again from the booth.

HAN: Bartender!

BARTENDER: Yeah?

HAN: Here . . .

Sound: A coin clinks on the bar, spins, and slowly rotates flat.

HAN: That's for your trouble . . . sorry about the mess.

Sound: He goes a step or two, then stops suddenly as he's accosted.

*GREEDO speaks in his own language.

2ND CUSTOMER: Now you done it, Solo! Preacher's gonna want your neck for sure.

HAN: You feel like standing in for him?

2ND CUSTOMER: Uh, no. I didn't mean nothin', Han . . .

HAN: Then get out of my way . . . I'm raising ship.

2ND CUSTOMER: Sure, sure . . .

HAN: And if you see Jabba the Hutt or Heater, tell them I'll be back in a day or two . . . *(MOVING OFF)* I've got a little quick money to make.

Music: In and under:

NARRATOR: Two droids, a young farm boy, and a veteran Jedi Knight, caught up in a dangerous but vital mission, are now joined in their journey by a reckless pair of smugglers and soldiers of fortune. Against them an Empire moves with all the power at its command. And the freedom of the galaxy will ride with the next liftoff of the *Millennium Falcon.*

Music: Closing theme up and under preview and closing credits.

ANNOUNCER: CLOSING CREDITS.

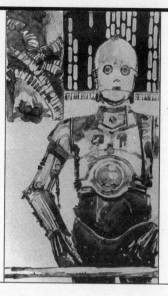

EPISODE SEVEN:

"THE HAN SOLO

SOLUTION"

CAST:

Ben	Dealer
Luke	Heater
Threepio	Squeak
Artoo	Proprietor
Han	1st Trooper
Chewbacca	2nd Trooper

ANNOUNCER: OPENING CREDITS.

Music: Opening theme.

NARRATOR: A long time ago in a galaxy far, far away there came a time of revolution, when Rebels united to challenge a tyrannical Empire. In the most desperate crisis of that Rebellion, plans vital to the survival of the Rebel Alliance were secretly placed in the memory banks of the astrodroid Artoo-Detoo. An unlikely group has gathered together to undertake a journey to Alderaan, where Artoo-Detoo and his interpreter-counterpart, See-Threepio, must be safely delivered. Luke Skywalker, a young moisture farmer on the planet Tatooine, and Ben Kenobi, one of the last remaining Jedi Knights, have arranged for passage to Alderaan with a pair of reckless smuggler-pilots, Han Solo and his Wookiee first mate, Chewbacca, in their starship, the *Millennium Falcon*.

Sound: The streets of Mos Eisley up in background.

NARRATOR: But in Mos Eisley Spaceport, where the group is about to begin its journey, the streets are aswarm with Imperial stormtroopers and their spies and informers.

BEN: *(COMING ON)* Well, Luke, if this *Millennium* of theirs is as fast as Captain Solo boasts it is, we should be able to reach Alderaan without further complication. I . . . stop a moment, Luke.

LUKE: Why? What is it?

BEN: I had the feeling I was under observation.

LUKE: I can't see anybody watching us.

BEN: Nor I.

LUKE: Do you think those stormtroopers are still after us?

BEN: No. The Imperials who followed us out the back door of the cantina went the other way.

LUKE: Then are you sure about this feeling?

BEN: The sensation was strong, but it is less so now.

LUKE: Then maybe whoever it was went away. I'm learning to trust your feelings, Ben. What should we do now?

BEN: We'd better hurry on. The sooner we get Captain Solo's money for him, the sooner we can get off Tatooine.

LUKE: That suits me.

BEN: I promised the captain two thousand in cash, but I've none of my own. We shall have to sell your landspeeder.

LUKE: Sure. I'm never coming back to this planet again.

BEN: I am in your debt, Luke. But if I were you, I wouldn't be so positive about where the future will find me.

Sound: Artoo's whirring and Threepio's footsteps approaching.

THREEPIO: *(OFF)* Master Luke! Master Luke!

ARTOO: SIGNALS.

LUKE: Artoo! Threepio! Where've you two been? I thought I told you to wait by my speeder?

THREEPIO: We were doing precisely that, sir, when a search party of stormtroopers began sweeping the area. We were compelled to elude them by hiding among the stock at a used-droid lot on the next street.

BEN: *(AMUSED)* And whose idea was that?

THREEPIO: Mine, I'm afraid, sir. Perhaps Artoo's deceitfulness is infectious.

LUKE: Don't worry, Threepio, you were just being, uh, flexible.

THREEPIO: Oh. Well, put that way, it doesn't sound so bad, does it?

BEN: This news of stormtrooper search parties isn't good, though. Which way were the sweeps moving?

THREEPIO: That way, sir.

BEN: Converging on the center of town.

LUKE: But that's where we'll have to go to sell my speeder . . . All the buyers are there.

BEN: Then that is where we must go. It's imperative that we get Captain Solo his money.

LUKE: But what about the droids? We can't take them with us; there'll be Imperials all over the place.

BEN: If they're using standard search patterns, the area between here and the spaceport itself should be fairly clear by now. Threepio and Artoo can wait for us there.

LUKE: Shouldn't one of us stay with them?

BEN: You have to be there when the sale is made, to transfer ownership, and I don't want you venturing among the Imperials and the Mos Eisley sharpers alone.

LUKE: I guess you're right . . . You saved my neck in the cantina a while ago. Threepio, I want you and Artoo to go to docking bay number 94 at the spaceport and wait for us.

THREEPIO: Very good, sir.

ARTOO: WHISTLES.

LUKE: Ben and I are taking my speeder to sell it. As soon as we're done, we'll meet you there.

THREEPIO: You can count on us, sir!

LUKE: I'm sure I can, Threepio.

Sound: Ben and Luke get into speeder.

BEN: *(CHUCKLES)* When humans designed machines with quasi-personalities, they never realized how very much that implied. Artoo and Threepio are an extraordinary pair.

Sound: Engine starts and revs.

LUKE: I'm beginning to think so, too. What about Captain Solo and Chewbacca?

Sound: The engine blares as the speeder accelerates and moves off.

BEN: Ah. Another curious pair. Look out for that robo-flatbed, Luke.

LUKE: I see it.

Sound: Speeder accelerates around flatbed.

LUKE: Back in the cantina you said you thought you and Han Solo understood one another. What did you mean?

BEN: There is something more to Solo than meets the eye. He's not just another Corellian smuggler or minor outlaw; I can sense that. At the same time, he wishes people to think he's something other than what he actually is. I was merely indicating to him that I was aware of it.

LUKE: I'm not sure he caught it, with all the boasting he was doing. Don't you think he can get us to Alderaan?

BEN: He will try, I'm sure of that. What I meant was that while he puts up a callous front, I suspect that the substance there is quite a different thing. And then, there is the Wookiee.

LUKE: Chewbacca? He's the first Wookiee I ever saw. What was that weapon he had, the rifle-crossbow thing?

BEN: That is a bowcaster, the traditional weapon of his species.

LUKE: And what a giant he is! I don't even come up to his shoulder!

BEN: Don't be deceived by appearances, Luke. Wookiees aren't simply big, shaggy humanoids . . . They've an ancient culture, with subtleties of its own. They are creatures with close ties to nature and a great affinity, in their own way, for the Force.

LUKE: The Force?

BEN: Yes. Solo's no ordinary criminal or he wouldn't be likely to have a Wookiee for a companion, nor would just any Wookiee be found roving the galaxy in his company. Chewbacca is an individual of some note, too, I think.

LUKE: Can we trust him, then? Han, I mean.

BEN: Not rely upon him entirely, perhaps, and I certainly would not want to subject Captain Solo to too much temptation, but I am satisfied that he's a man who will keep his end of our deal.

LUKE: That's all we'll need from him . . . passage to Alderaan.

BEN: Let us hope so. Over to the left there is the establishment of a buyer and seller of vehicles. We might get a fair price there.

LUKE: Whatever you say.

Sound: Speeder maneuvering and decelerating. Engine dies, but street noise still remains under:

LUKE: Looks like this place'll buy anything that moves and a lot of stuff that doesn't.

Sound: They climb out of the speeder.

DEALER: *(APPROACHING, SPEAKING IN A REEDY, CLICKING, GLOTTAL-STOP-FILLED ACCENT)* And what can I do for you, humans?

LUKE: I want to sell this speeder.

BEN: If we can get a fair price.

LUKE: Uh, yeah. I paid twenty-four hundred for it and put a lot of work into it. It's worth at least—

DEALER: Fifteen hundred is all I can offer you, human.

LUKE: Fifteen hundred? Look, this landspeeder is in great shape, even if it's not pretty.

BEN: We can accept no less than two thousand.

DEALER: Your grip on reality is fragile, humans. It's the newer models that are in demand now, not these old ones. I shall probably have to sell it at a loss.

BEN: But it's still not a fair price.

DEALER: You touch a responsive chord in my charitable nature, humans! Sixteen hundred.

BEN: *(IN FORCE-COMMAND VOICE)* That isn't enough.

DEALER: That . . . isn't enough?

BEN: This speeder is worth more.

DEALER: This speeder is . . . worth more.

BEN: He can have his two thousand.

DEALER: You can have your two thousand, young human.

LUKE: Oh. Uh, thanks.

DEALER: Here . . . press your thumbprint on the transfer register.

Sound: A buzz and hum from register.

DEALER: And here is your money.

BEN: *(FADING)* Let's be off, Luke. Thank you.

Sound: Their footsteps move off.

DEALER: Do I grow senile? Am I in second grubhood to fall prey so easily to a pair of *humans*?

Sound: Fade to silence. Street noises out.

Sound: Street noises up. Footsteps of Ben and Luke through crowd.

LUKE: Ben, there're advantages to the Force that I'm just beginning to see!

BEN: I'd never have used it for something like that if it hadn't been an emergency. Abuse of the Force leads to the worst imaginable consequences, Luke . . . always remember that.

LUKE: At that, two thousand's about the best we could've done. Nobody wants those old landspeeders since the new XP-38's came out.

BEN: Two thousand will suffice. We'll pay Captain Solo the rest of his money when we reach Alderaan. The main thing now's to get under way.

LUKE: Han Solo will sure be happy. He looked like he wanted to get his hands on some cash awfully bad.

BEN: No doubt he has debts in Mos Eisley. The underworld here boasts some pretty tough characters. They can be very unpleasant toward someone who owes them—

Sound: Ben stops, Luke follows suit.

LUKE: Why are we stopping?

BEN: I felt it again . . . the sensation that we were being observed.

LUKE: I don't see anybody.

BEN: Nor I. Whoever it is, they're concealed.

LUKE: Then, what can we—

BEN: *(INTERRUPTING)* We'd better get to the docking bay as quickly as we can. Come, there's no time to lose . . .

Sound: Street noise fades.

Music: In.

CHEWIE: *(OFF)* YEOWLS A HALLOO.

HAN: Huh? Oh, Chewie! Did you pick up our gear?

CHEWIE: *(APPROACHING)* CONFIRMS WITH A SERIES OF GROWLS.

HAN: After you left the cantina, Greedo showed up with a blaster in his hand. He was out to burn me down.

CHEWIE: ANGRY, CONCERNED NOISES.

HAN: He said Jabba the Hutt's mad about that load of Kessel spice we had to dump when the Imperials boarded us.

CHEWIE: HOOTS FURIOUSLY.

HAN: I *did* tell him, but Jabba's put such a high price on our heads that every professional gun in this part of space'll be hunting for us.

CHEWIE: WOOFS THOUGHTFULLY.

HAN: Yeah, and as if that wasn't enough trouble, Jabba gave Heater the job of finding us . . . Greedo told me so.

CHEWIE: RUMBLES APPREHENSIVELY.

HAN: I *know* Preacher doesn't fool around, dammit!

CHEWIE: BARKS.

HAN: Oh, Greedo? No, he was dumb enough to relax for a second . . . careless. I hope Jabba and Preacher throw him a nice funeral.

CHEWIE: GRUNTS.

HAN: Yeah, we'd best wait until we've made this Alderaan run and have the money before we talk to Jabba or Preacher—

Sound: Interrupted by the approach of Squeak, a nervous, fast-talking little nonhuman.

SQUEAK: *(OFF, CALLING)* Solo! Hey, Solo!

HAN: It's Squeak!

CHEWIE: GROWLS A QUESTION.

HAN: How d' I know what he wants? But get set.

SQUEAK: *(APPROACHING)* Solo, I've been looking all over for you and the Wook!

HAN: And I notice you found us, Squeak. So?

SQUEAK: Big Bunji wants to see you. He's got a job for you.

CHEWIE: LOWS.

HAN: Then why'd he wait until we're chartered?

SQUEAK: It came up all at once . . .

HAN: Tell Bunji I said, "Who the hell needs—"

SQUEAK: *(INTERRUPTING)* It pays ten thousand in advance . . .

HAN: . . . an old man and a kid and two droids." Right, Chewie?

CHEWIE: WARBLES IRRITABLY.

HAN: Lead on, Squeak.

CHEWIE: OBJECTS WITH A GROWL.

SQUEAK: What's wrong with the Wook?

HAN: Nothing. Look, wait over there for a second, will you?

SQUEAK: *(MOVING OFF)* Sure, Han, sure.

HAN: *(LOW AND CONFIDENTIAL)* What's eating you?

CHEWIE: REPLIES BRIEFLY.

HAN: I don't *care* what happens to the old man. *Or* the kid, *or* the droids. This's real life, not some kinda game. *(CALLING)* Hey, Squeak!

SQUEAK: *(COMING ON)* Yeah, Han?

HAN: Tell Big Bunji he's got himself a starship.

SQUEAK: Now you're talking!

HAN: What's the deal?

SQUEAK: A load of chak-root's due in tomorrow. You take it from here to—

CHEWIE: INTERRUPTS WITH A BARK.

HAN: Tomorrow? Look, we're hot and we're rapidly going critical!

CHEWIE: CONCURS.

HAN: Jabba and Preacher are on our necks, and the storm-troopers're probably after us, too, by now. Tell Bunji to find someone else. Scram, Squeak. The nerve of some people.

CHEWIE: GRUNTS.

HAN: Yeah, let's go in and get the *Falcon* checked out.

CHEWIE: WOOFS CONSENT.

Sound: The door to the docking bay is opened under: (VOICES ECHOING)

HAN: I still get a funny feeling about that old man and the kid. I'm not sure what it is about them, but they're trouble. Sure wish we didn't need that money so . . .

Sound: Voices in the docking bay up in far distance.

HAN: *(WHISPERING)* Listen! That's Heater! He's down there in the docking bay with his gang!

CHEWIE: HOOTS SOFTLY.

HAN: Yeah. Dump the gear and lock the door behind us so we don't get any more unexpected company.

Sound: Chewie lays down the gear and closes the door. It locks as the heavy power bolt activates with a muted hum and clank.

HEATER: *(IN THE DISTANCE. A MOIST, HARSH VOICE)* Do you hear me, Solo? I said come out of your ship, you and the Wookiee! If I have to, I'll come in after you!

HAN: *(STILL WHISPERING)* We've got to go in there, Chewie. We can't let him damage the ship!

CHEWIE: URFS A SOFT OBJECTION.

HAN: We'll just have to outbluff him. Keep your bowcaster ready. Here goes . . .

HEATER: *(OFF, HIS VOICE BECOMING LOUDER AS THEY AP-PROACH)* I'm giving you one last chance, Solo . . . come out! I've got you surrounded!

HAN: If you do, you're facing the wrong way.

HEATER: What? Solo!

Sound: His henchmen yelp in startlement.

HAN: You see, I've been waiting for you, Heater.

HEATER: Why . . . I . . . er . . . expected you would be, Han.

HAN: We're not the type to run. Are we, Chewie?

CHEWIE: GROWLS LOUDLY.

HAN: Stand right where you are, Heater. And tell your circle of close friends there not to look so anxious with their guns.

HEATER: They're just showing proper respect for your reputations. Han, my boy, there are times when you disappoint me. Why haven't you paid us for that load of Kessel spice you lost?

HAN: I told Jabba he'd get his money.

HEATER: And why did you have to fry poor Greedo? After all that he and I have been through together!

HAN: Well, it was my taste in drinking buddies partly, but mostly it was because you sent Greedo to blast me.

HEATER: Han, Han, why would I do that? You're the best smuggler in the business . . . you're too valuable to kill. Greedo was only relaying our natural concern at the delay in payment. He wasn't going to burn you.

HAN: Oh, no? *He* thought he was.

CHEWIE: ROARS AN ANGRY CORROBORATION.

HEATER: Han, son, you must understand, I can't make an exception, much as I like you. Where would poor old Heater be if he let his pilots dump their shipments and then show empty pockets when we asked for our money back?

HAN: You and Jabba don't stick your necks out, Heater . . . we do.

HEATER: That's what you're paid for! And when you fail, it's bad for business!

HAN: And you think it'll be good for business to shoot it out with Chewie and me? Is *that* what you think?

HEATER: Uh, now, Han nobody said . . .

HAN: Go ahead; you've got plenty of guns behind you.

CHEWIE: THROATS A LOUD SNARL.

HEATER: Why . . . that is . . . as I was telling my associates here just before you and the Wookiee arrived, you're both too valuable to fry out of hand.

HAN: As it happens, I can pay you back, but I need a little time.

HEATER: Ah, yes, that charter. I've already had word that you were talking to someone in the cantina. How much are they paying you?

HAN: Enough to square with you, Heater; that's all you need to know.

HEATER: Something's going on in Mos Eisley . . . streets are filled with stormtroopers, Imperial spies circulating everywhere. Even *my* sources can't find out what it's all about. But this sudden appearance of passengers who are eager to pay well for a quick liftoff may be tied to it somehow.

HAN: So?

HEATER: Perhaps there's more money to be had by bargaining with the Imperials.

CHEWIE: GROWLS FEROCIOUSLY AT THE SUGGESTION.

HAN: Uh uh, Heater. Selling people out to the Empire isn't our style; you know that.

HEATER: Ah, Han, how do you and the Wook ever expect to get ahead in this life?

HAN: Some days we're content just to stay even. Now, do we do it my way, or do you and these goons still want a piece of me and Chewie?

HEATER: I'm a businessman above all, Han. So, for "something extra," why don't we make it twenty-five percent? I'll wait. But not much longer.

HAN: You'll get it.

HEATER: I'd better; if I'm disappointed again, it won't be any "two for a credit" twerp I put on your trail. Next time I'll hire Bobba Fett himself.

HAN: Don't get yourself in a lather . . . and I'll pay you . . . because I choose to. Now get out of here.

Music: Up.

Sound: Streets of Mos Eisley up under the whirring of Artoo and the whining of Threepio.

THREEPIO: That should be docking bay 94 just ahead, Artoo.

ARTOO: CHIRPS.

THREEPIO: I don't seem to see Master Luke around anywhere. Perhaps we'd better go into the bay and wait.

Sound: Their servos and treads go up to the door. Threepio tries it.

THREEPIO: The door's locked. Now what shall we do?

ARTOO: BLURTS A SUGGESTION.

Sound: Artoo's manipulator arm taps lightly and rapidly on the door.

THREEPIO: No, no. Rapping on the door will just attract attention, and that's the last thing we want.

ARTOO: BURBLES.

Sound: The tapping stops.

Sound: The marching of cleated boots in the distance.

THREEPIO: Look, Artoo! More stormtroopers!

ARTOO: BLEEPS.

THREEPIO: But we have nowhere to retreat to! This is a dead end.

ARTOO: HUMPHS.

Sound: Artoo's treads going off.

THREEPIO: Wait! Where are you going?

Sound: Threepio's footsteps going off after Artoo and catching up.

THREEPIO: Just what do you think you're doing at that shop door?

ARTOO: HUMMING TO HIMSELF, IGNORING THREEPIO.

Sound: Artoo rapping at the door.

THREEPIO: Artoo, have you gone completely—

Sound: The opening of the power portal interrupts him.

PROPRIETOR: Well, what d' you two want?

THREEPIO: Er, well, you see, sir . . .

ARTOO: WHISTLES INSISTENTLY.

THREEPIO: Ah, yes. As my counterpart here just explained, we're here to see if you need any maintenance jobs done.

PROPRIETOR: Huh? Maintenance?

THREEPIO: Why, um, of course. We belong to the Skywalker Technical Maintenance Service.

PROPRIETOR: Never heard of it.

THREEPIO: But of course you haven't, sir; we're a new organization. That's why we're canvassing the area for our, that is, our publicity campaign.

PROPRIETOR: Publicity campaign?

ARTOO: SIGNALS URGENTLY.

THREEPIO: Yes, I see.

PROPRIETOR: What?

THREEPIO: What I meant was, we are offering a free trial service. My counterpart and I will repair, recalibrate, and run systems checks on any equipment you desire, free of charge, mind you, as a special introductory offer.

PROPRIETOR: Come back later. I was just on my way out.

THREEPIO: Oh, but sir . . .

ARTOO: WHISTLES AN ASIDE.

THREEPIO: As my counterpart just reminded me, this is a one-time-only offer. We'll have to move along to the next shop if you can't accept it.

PROPRIETOR: Hmmm. The energy lathe is running out of synch . . .

THREEPIO: We'll have it functioning like new again in no time, won't we, Artoo?

ARTOO: RATTLES ENTHUSIASTICALLY.

PROPRIETOR: All right, go to it. I'll be back in a couple of minutes.

THREEPIO: Your equipment will be just like new, sir!

PROPRIETOR: Like it used to be will be just fine.

Sound: The proprietor walks off, his steps fading under:

THREEPIO: You won't regret this, sir.

Sound: The droids go through the door.

Sound: The marching boots of the stormtroopers approach, and shouted commands are heard.

THREEPIO: The stormtroopers! Quick, Artoo, lock the door!

ARTOO: BURBLES.

Sound: The power portal door hums shut.

1ST TROOPER: *(APPROACHING)* All right, you men check out that side of the street. I'll try this door.

Sound: The trooper wrenching at the door control, then striking the door with armored knuckles.

2ND TROOPER: *(OFF SLIGHTLY)* These ones over here are secure.

1ST TROOPER: So's this one. Okay, let's retrace our steps and move along to the next street.

Sound: Their cleated boots move off.

Sound: The door hums open.

THREEPIO: Thank goodness they've left. I would much rather have gone with Master Luke than stayed here with you. I don't know what all this trouble is about, but I'm sure it must be your fault.

ARTOO: POOH-POOHS.

THREEPIO: You watch your language! What do you think . . . look! The door to docking bay 94 is opening! But who can those creatures be, coming out?

ARTOO: BEEPS EXCITEDLY.

THREEPIO: Master Luke? Where?

ARTOO: BEEPS AN ANSWER.

THREEPIO: Oh! *(CALLING)* Master Luke! Here we are, sir!

LUKE: *(APPROACHING)* Calm down, Threepio. No need to yell.

THREEPIO: Sorry, sir. Master Luke, we were so worried about you!

LUKE: Are you two all right? Why didn't you wait inside the docking bay?

THREEPIO: It was locked until a moment ago. You have no idea what Artoo and I have been through since—

BEN: *(INTERRUPTING)* We'll have to hear this later. We must move as quickly as we can.

LUKE: Are we still being followed, Ben?

BEN: I'm nearly sure of it. Once or twice I thought I caught a glimpse of someone, keeping well back, trailing us. Come.

LUKE: There's Chewbacca waiting at the docking bay door.

CHEWIE: BARKS A GREETING.

BEN: *(APPROACHING)* We're all here, my friend, and we have the money. When can we raise ship?

CHEWIE: GRUNTS.

BEN: Good. Let's get on with it.

Sound: Voices echo.

LUKE: After all Han's bragging, I can't wait to see this great *Millennium Falcon*.

BEN: Don't expect a smuggler's starship to be long on beauty, Luke.

CHEWIE: WOOFS HIS AMUSEMENT.

LUKE: Now, let's see . . . that's a *starship*? The famous *Millennium Falcon* he keeps telling us about? What a piece of junk!

HAN: *(APPROACHING)* She'll make point five over lightspeed, kid. She's got the highest life/mass ratio around, enough to step away from any Imperial ship, and her armament rating's just plain illegal.

LUKE: But will this wreck hold together?

CHEWIE: SNARLS.

HAN: Better watch it, kid; we don't like anybody knocking her. The *Falcon* may not be much for looks, but she's got it where it counts. Right, Chewie?

CHEWIE: GROWLS AGREEMENT.

HAN: I've added some special modifications of my own. *(TO CHEWIE)* Chewie, get up into the cockpit and start the preflight rundown.

CHEWIE: GRUNTS.

LUKE: Okay, now you can show us how this thing scoots.

HAN: *(LAUGHING UNCONVINCINGLY)* Just a second there, boys. There's still the little matter of my good-faith money. Two thousand in cash, if I remember right. It'll be a happier trip all around if we get that out of the way now.

BEN: Very well. Luke?

LUKE: Here's your money.

Sound: Han riffles the cash and stuffs it in his pocket under:

HAN: *(LAUGHING MORE CONVINCINGLY)* Funny how this stuff brightens your day, isn't it?

LUKE: Aren't you going to count it?

HAN: Don't you guys think I trust you? Besides, I've got the whole trip for that. Now, we're a little rushed, so if you'll get aboard, we'll get out of here.

BEN: Captain Solo, I have reason to believe we may have been followed.

HAN: Well, my solution for that is to haul jets. Up the ramp and to the right, gents and droids. Make yourselves comfortable in the forward compartment. I'll disconnect the umbilicals and we're off.

Sound: The starship's engines begin to build power in background.

BEN: Very well. Come, Luke. Artoo, Threepio.

ARTOO: BLEEPS.

Sound: They begin to ascend the ramp to the ship.

THREEPIO: Hello, Captain Solo. A pleasure to meet you, sir.

HAN: Aw, for . . . look, I'm not too fond of machinery that talks back. Now, get on up there with the rest of them.

THREEPIO: Will do, sir!

Sound: Threepio moves up the stairs.

HAN: *(MUTTERING)* Droids!

Sound: The umbilicals being disconnected and tossed aside under:

HAN: And that smart-mouthed kid! Not to mention that old relic who's in charge of this crazy excursion package. How come I never get the cake jobs . . . the easy ones? Everybody but me . . . uh?

1ST TROOPER: *(OFF)* Stop that ship!

HAN: Oh oh! Stormtroopers!

1ST TROOPER: Blast him!

Sound: From a distance the whines of blaster fire, exploding and flaring against the ship.

HAN: Hey, my *ship*! If that's how you feel about it . . .

Sound: He returns the fire.

HAN: Whoa-ooooooo! I'm coming up, Chewie!

Sound: Han runs up the ramp, closing it quickly with a thud. He pauses as the main hatch hisses shut behind him, cutting off the sound of the firefight.

HAN: *(YELLING, HIS VOICE REVERBERATING FROM THE BULK-HEADS)* Okay, Chewie, get us out of here! Deflector shield up!

HAN: You up there in the forward compartment, strap in! You were right about being followed; we're raising ship right now.

Sound: Chewie's growling and instrumentation perking are heard as Han comes into the cockpit, throwing himself into his seat.

HAN: Are the engines warmed up?

CHEWIE: RESPONDS WITH A SURLY SNARL.

HAN: Well, they'll just have to do. My solution to all this is to get the hell out of here.

CHEWIE: GRUNTS OBJECTION.

HAN: Since when do *we* need liftoff clearance? Ready? Hit it!

Sound: The Falcon's *engines thunder, and the ship vibrates, rattles, and shakes. Han and Chewie crow exuberantly.*

CHEWIE: YELPS A QUESTION.

HAN: No, no, keep pouring it on till we're out of the atmosphere. We don't want anybody down there drawing a bead on us!

Sound: The ship howls.

CHEWIE: YODELS HIS DELIGHT WITH THEIR ESCAPE.

HAN: *(LAUGHING) That* gave those armed simps somethin' to think about! Trim her off, Chewie.

CHEWIE: GOBBLES.

HAN: Huh? What sensor reading?

CHEWIE: REITERATES.

HAN: It's an Imperial cruiser, closing on us fast. My day's complete!

CHEWIE: GROWLS.

HAN: Yeah, our passengers must be hotter than I thought. Angle deflector shields astern while I make calculations for the jump to lightspeed.

CHEWIE: YOWLS COMPLIANCE.

Sound: Buttons being punched, switches being thrown, instruments responding.

HAN: Stay sharp, Chewie! There're two more battlewagons converging . . . They're gonna try to cut us off.

CHEWIE: HOOTS IN CONSTERNATION.

LUKE: *(OFF)* What's going on?

HAN: It's a going-away party. What's the matter, didn't you get an invitation?

BEN: Imperial cruisers.

HAN: You guessed it, and it looks like they want our hides any way they can get 'em.

LUKE: Why don't you outrun them? I thought you said this thing was *fast*.

HAN: Watch your mouth, kid, or you're gonna find yourself *floating* home!

LUKE: They're firing on us!

Sound: The Falcon *shudders as cannon fire hits her deflectors, shaking up her occupants and setting off several alarms.*

CHEWIE: GROWLS.

HAN: Okay, partner, hang on to your pelt! If we can pull this one off, we've got it made!

CHEWIE: HOOTS ENCOURAGEMENT.

HAN: Here goes!

Sound: The engine pitch rises and rises as the hyperdrive cuts in, ending in a tremendous thunderclap.

ALL: CHEERS AND HOOTS.

Music: In and under:

NARRATOR: The *Millennium Falcon* and her oddly met passengers and crew have managed to escape Tatooine. Before them looms the trip to Alderaan, and though they don't know it, something else awaits them, too: the Empire's awesome battle station, the Death Star.

Music: Closing theme up and under preview and closing credits.

ANNOUNCER: CLOSING CREDITS.

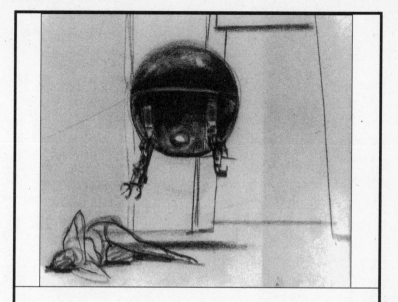

EPISODE EIGHT:

"DEATH STAR'S

TRANSIT"

CAST:

Vader	Commander
Leia	2nd Officer
Tarkin	Tagge
Captain	Motti
Navigator	Guard

ANNOUNCER: OPENING CREDITS.

Music: Opening theme.

NARRATOR: A long time ago in a galaxy far, far away, there came a time of revolution, when Rebels united to challenge a tyrannical Empire. The Princess Leia Organa, an Imperial Senator from the planet Alderaan, is also a leader in the secret councils of the Rebel Alliance. But her most daring mission, to deliver the plans for the Empire's most awesome weapon, the Death Star, has failed. In a last desperate bid to get the information into Rebel hands before being captured, she has placed it into the memory banks of the astrodroid Artoo-Detoo. And though Princess Leia is unaware of it, Artoo has come into the possession of Luke Skywalker and the veteran Jedi Knight Ben Kenobi.

Sound: The control deck of an Imperial cruiser up in background.

NARRATOR: Taken prisoner by Darth Vader, the Dark Lord of the Sith, Leia Organa is aboard a cruiser of the Imperial Starfleet, being taken to the Death Star, a stupendous spacegoing battle station.

Sound: Bridge up, instrumentation noises, crew giving status reports.

CAPTAIN: *(SLIGHTLY OFF)* Navigator! Estimated time of arrival at the Death Star.

NAVIGATOR: *(OFF)* Fifteen minutes, sir! We're getting clearance to enter the outer defensive zones now.

CAPTAIN: Carry on. *(PAUSE)* Lord Vader!

Sound: Vader's heavy tread and his respirator approaching.

VADER: Yes, Captain?

CAPTAIN: We're right on schedule, Lord Vader.

VADER: Excellent.

Sound: A hatch opens, admitting trooper.

COMMANDER: Lord Vader!

VADER: Well, Commander?

COMMANDER: We have the prisoner outside, sir. What are your orders?

VADER: Escort her in, Commander.

COMMANDER: *(MOVING OFF)* Yes, sir.

COMMANDER: The prisoner will step forward!

VADER: Commander, you needn't be so curt with my . . . guest.

LEIA: *(APPROACHING)* Guest! I'm warning you—

VADER: *(INTERRUPTING)* Commander, you and your men may post yourselves by the hatch.

COMMANDER: Yes, sir.

VADER: And that will be all for now, Captain.

CAPTAIN: As you wish, Lord Vader.

LEIA: *(APPROACHING)* Vader, in firing on my ship and taking me captive, you've overstepped yourself. The Imperial Senate—

VADER: —No longer presents any obstacle to me! They are being dealt with even now. You'd do better to worry about your *own* well-being, Princess Leia.

LEIA: You won't succeed with this. You and those other—

VADER: *(INTERRUPTING)* I didn't have you brought here just to listen to more of your pointless ranting, Your Highness. You're so

194

upset that you haven't taken time to glance out the main view-port at our destination.

LEIA: What . . . the—the Death Star!

VADER: Quite right. And nearly ready, closer to completion than even your Rebel agents estimated. I *thought* the sight of it might shock you into revealing that you know of its existence.

LEIA: I . . . I'd heard vague rumors in the Imperial Senate, nothing more. You've proved nothing, and you know it, Vader!

VADER: You knew of the Death Star! You also intercepted the Rebel message transmitting the technical design data for it. I'm offering you one last chance to tell me what you did with those plans. Once we've docked in that battle station, much harsher and more direct means will be used to question you.

LEIA: You wouldn't dare! You'll never get away with this!

VADER: You think not? Look, Princess. Gaze upon the Death Star, the mightiest war machine that humankind has ever produced, a fortress the size of a small planet, with the power to destroy entire worlds.

LEIA: It's . . . obscene . . . an obscene invention of twisted minds!

VADER: See that great circular dish? That is the Prime Weapon. Mere starfleets pale by comparison.

LEIA: You're insane! You, the Emperor, the military . . . you've all gone mad!

VADER: How amusing. But this is simply a viewing with an eye to giving you practical perspective. Don't be too preoccupied with the Death Star; it is, after all, no more than a machine. But it is indicative of the might of the Empire, strength that will inevitably crush your pitiful Rebel Alliance.

LEIA: Then why are you so worried about these plans?

VADER: I see you have no intention of cooperating. Very well, your fate is upon your own head. Rest assured that you will tell me what I wish to know. Commander!

COMMANDER: *(OFF)* Yes, Lord Vader!

VADER: Take her to her quarters. When we've docked at the Death Star, transfer her to the detention levels there. *(TO LEIA)* You're about to find out what it means to defy the Empire, Your Highness. And soon the galaxy will learn.

Music: In.

Sound: Bridge sounds fade.

Sound: Quiet conversations among staff officers gathered in the conference room up in background. Distant noises of the Death Star operations: air circulators, etc. Tagge enters.

TAGGE: *(APPROACHING)* Is the general staff meeting still scheduled to proceed on time, Admiral Motti?

MOTTI: As soon as the Grand Moff Tarkin arrives, General Tagge. He's gone to the docking bay to greet Lord Vader in person.

TAGGE: Vader, eh? Has he recovered the stolen Death Star plans, then?

MOTTI: I think not, General, but my sources inform me he has a Rebel princess . . . the Princess Leia Organa herself.

TAGGE: Leia Organa? Has Vader lost his mind?

MOTTI: Perhaps, but I think not, or he wouldn't be the Emperor's personal agent.

TAGGE: I tell you, he's gone too far this time! This Dark Lord of the Sith, whom the Emperor has insisted on inflicting upon us, will be our undoing. Until the Death Star is fully operational, we're vulnerable.

MOTTI: You sound distressed, Tagge.

TAGGE: Motti, you still don't seem to realize how much of a threat the Rebel Alliance is. It's not just that they're becoming better organized and acquiring more ships and better equipment—they're *driven*, they're fanatics!

MOTTI: Dangerous to your starfleet, not to this battle station.

TAGGE: The Rebellion will continue to gain the tacit support of the Senate as long as—

Sound: The door swishes open, then closes as Vader and Tarkin enter. Vader's breathing.

TARKIN: *(APPROACHING)* The Imperial Senate will no longer be of any concern to us. I've just received word that the Emperor has dissolved the council permanently.

Sound: A buzz of quiet exclamations goes up.

TARKIN: The decree was carefully worded, of course, invoking the current emergency and the Rebel violence. But the last remains of the Old Republic have been swept away.

TAGGE: But how will the Emperor maintain control?

TARKIN: Fear will keep the worlds of the Empire in line, fear of this battle station.

TAGGE: And what of the Rebellion? If the Rebels have a complete technical readout of the Death Star, it's possible, however unlikely, that they might find a weakness and exploit it. If it's destroyed or even severely damaged, our main deterrent power will be gone.

VADER: The plans to which you refer will soon be back in our hands.

MOTTI: That is beside the point. Any attack made by the Rebels against this battle station would be a useless gesture, no matter what technical data they've obtained. The Death Star is now the ultimate power in the universe.

VADER: Don't be too proud of this technological terror you've constructed. The ability to destroy a planet is insignificant next to the power of the Force.

MOTTI: Don't try to frighten us with your sorcerer's ways, Lord Vader. Your sad devotion to that ancient religion hasn't helped you conjure up the stolen data tapes or given you clairvoyance enough to find the Rebels' hidden fortr—

Sound: Motti abruptly begins to choke.

VADER: Are you having difficulty breathing, Motti? Is your throat constricting . . . as though some *force* were at work?

Sound: The other officers murmur, amazed, among themselves. Motti's practically rattling his last.

VADER: I find your lack of faith disturbing, Motti.

TARKIN: Enough of this! Vader, release him!

VADER: As you wish, Governor.

Sound: Motti suddenly begins gasping for breath in huge gulps, then slumps to the table with a thud.

TARKIN: This bickering is pointless. Lord Vader will interrogate the Princess Leia and provide us with the location of the Rebel fortress by the time this station is operational. That should take no longer than two more work shifts. We will then show the power of this station and crush the Rebellion with one swift stroke.

Music: In.

Sound: The cell door suddenly raises with a brief, loud hiss. Vader's respirator is heard, and Leia's regular breathing.

VADER: I hope you find your quarters adequate, Princess Leia.

LEIA: Vader, I demand that I be released from this cell and given access to formal legal proceedings!

VADER: You can spare me your indignation, Your Highness.

Sound: A loud beeping and buzzing in background. It grows louder as the torture robot floats into the cell.

LEIA: What . . . ?

VADER: This machine? It is called an interrogation device, but there are those who call it other things.

LEIA: A torture robot! This violates every rule of law—

VADER: *(INTERRUPTING)* The law no longer applies to you! You're a Rebel, and you've refused your one chance at clemency. And now, Your Highness, we *will* discuss the location of your hidden Rebel base.

Sound: The torture robot's beeping increases in volume.

LEIA: Vader! Keep it away from me . . .

VADER: See the injection arm? Do you wish to avoid it? Then tell me . . . *(MOVING CLOSER)* . . . where is the Rebel fortress?

LEIA: *(BREATHING RAPIDLY IN FEAR, TRYING TO CONTROL HER-SELF)* I don't know what you mean.

VADER: So be it.

LEIA: No!

LEIA: *(HER VOICE QUAVERING AS VADER SHAKES HER)* Let go! S-stop!

VADER: Hold still, you little fool! There is *no* escape! One moment . . .

Sound: The beeping of the torture robot grows louder still, finally reaching a high squeal. There is a brief hiss of its injector arm. Leia cries out, then falls backward, moaning, to slump against the cell wall with a thud.

LEIA: You can't . . . you c—

Sound: Leia's breathing subsides to a regular rhythm like sleep.

VADER: Your Highness, do you hear my voice?

LEIA: *(AS IF IN TROUBLED DREAMS)* Hmm? Ah, no . . .

VADER: Princess Leia Organa, listen to my voice. Pay attention to my voice!

LEIA: V-voice . . .

VADER: That's right. You hear only my voice. Listen to it . . . trust it. I am your friend.

LEIA: Wha—friend? No . . .

VADER: Yes! You trust me, you can confide in me. All your secrets are safe with me.

LEIA: Mmmm? Safe?

VADER: That's right, safe. You are safe here; you're among friends. You can trust me. I am a member of the Rebel Alliance, like you.

LEIA: Rebel?

VADER: Yes. And we must know what you did with those tapes.

LEIA: Tapes . . .

VADER: The Death Star technical plans; what did you do with them? Where are they? The Rebels need to know! Help us, Leia!

LEIA: What? No . . . no.

VADER: We need them, Leia! What happened to those tapes? Where are they?

LEIA: Can't!

VADER: You must. It's your duty.

LEIA: My . . . my duty?

VADER: Yes! Your duty to our Rebel Alliance. Your obligation to Alderaan and to your father. It's your duty to tell us where those tapes are!

LEIA: My duty *not* to tell . . .

VADER: *Not* to tell the *Empire*. But it is your duty to tell us, the Rebel Alliance.

LEIA: What? Dunno. Leave me 'lone. Please . . .

VADER: When you've told me where the plans are.

LEIA: Can't!

VADER: You must! It's your responsibility.

LEIA: My . . .

VADER: Your responsibility. Tell us where the plans are or lives will be lost, and it will be your fault.

LEIA: No!

VADER: Yes! Your fault! Tell us where the tapes are or all those Rebel deaths will be your fault!

LEIA: Please . . . leave me alone . . .

VADER: Your father commands you to tell us!

LEIA: Father . . . father?

VADER: Yes. He orders you to tell us! Don't you want to obey him? Don't you wish to please your father?

LEIA: Yes. Yes!

VADER: Then tell me what you did with those plans. Say the words.

LEIA: But . . .

VADER: Your father orders you to tell us!

LEIA: Father . . . wouldn't. *(CHOKING)* Wouldn't!

VADER: You try my patience. Tell me what was done with those plans.

LEIA: N-no!

VADER: *(ICILY)* Listen to my voice. You are now in great pain . . . excruciating pain.

LEIA: Please . . .

VADER: Pain! A universe of it! Your world is nothing but pain.

LEIA: *(CRIES ALOUD)* Make it stop!

VADER: Tell me what I wish to know!

LEIA: *Help me!*

VADER: Tell me what I wish to know. Where are the plans?

LEIA: *(BREATHING IN GULPS)* I can't! Can't tell!

VADER: Your skin is afire.

LEIA: *(ALMOST A SCREAM)* No!

VADER: You're burning . . . your nerve endings are in flames. Your flesh is being torn apart.

LEIA: *(SCREAMS)* Make it stop! Please make it stop!

VADER: I will when you've told me where the Death Star plans are.

LEIA: Wo-*won't*!

VADER: Quickly; your death is near! Your body is in agony, and you can barely breathe!

LEIA: Please . . .

VADER: You're dying in torment. Where are the Death Star plans? Where is the Rebel fortress?

LEIA: *(SOBBING)* I can't tell.

VADER: There are only seconds left! Your heart is about to burst, and the breath of life is nearly gone!

LEIA: *(A WHISPER)* I . . . *won't tell!*

Sound: Vader's fist smashes against the cell wall with a resounding impact.

VADER: You must!

Sound: Leia can't answer, her breathing faint, mixed with strangling.

VADER: Stop! You are no longer dying, no longer in pain. Blank your mind!

LEIA: What . . . how . . .

VADER: Your mind is a blank. You float without a thought or concern.

Sound: Leia's breathing becomes normal.

GUARD: Lord Vader, is anything wrong?

VADER: Eh? No, get out . . . wait!

GUARD: Yes, Lord Vader!

VADER: Have a medical tech see to the prisoner. Make sure that she's suffered no serious damage. Have her fortified so that she can take another round of interrogation.

GUARD: Yes, Lord Vader!

Sound: Vader strides out.

VADER: I shall be back. Soon.

Sound: The cell door slams shut, ringing down a moment's silence.

Sound: The conference room up in background.

MOTTI: The engineering officers have reported that all final construction details were completed during the past work shift.

TARKIN: Is the final checkout finished?

MOTTI: Yes, sir. The Death Star is 100 percent functional.

TARKIN: Including our Prime Weapon?

MOTTI: Completely operational. This station can destroy any planet you care to select. The entire starfleet, in pitched battle, couldn't stop us. You now have in your hand the power of life and death over every living thing in the galaxy.

TARKIN: Life and death . . .

MOTTI: Ultimate power. It rests with you now.

TARKIN: *(NONCOMMITTALLY)* And with the Emperor, of course.

MOTTI: To be sure, Governor; that's what I meant.

Sound: The conference room door opens, then closes as Vader enters.

TARKIN: Lord Vader . . .

VADER: Ah, Lord Tarkin, I am informed that the station is now fully operational.

TARKIN: Yes, Vader, that's correct.

MOTTI: It only needs the governor's word to get under way and . . .

VADER: Serve the Emperor?

MOTTI: Er, quite so. To serve the Empire.

VADER: And the *Emperor*. He chose well when he selected you to oversee construction of the Death Star, Lord Tarkin. Other men might have harbored some mad thought of betrayal of the Emperor's trust. Ambition has been the downfall of many.

TARKIN: Indeed. But the Emperor knows my loyalty, is that not so, Motti?

MOTTI: Implicitly, Governor Tarkin.

TARKIN: Now, Vader, what of the Princess?

VADER: She resisted the first interrogation session. Her inborn willpower is formidable, and it has been augmented with certain physical and mental disciplines. No matter, I shall wear her down in time.

TARKIN: But how can that slip of a girl defy *you*? It's ludicrous!

VADER: I believe that she still holds hope that the stolen plans will eventually be delivered into Rebel hands. Though it is futile, it sustains her.

TARKIN: But you've broken hardened, resolute *men* with relative ease.

VADER: It is difficult to crush a prisoner's will until one has obliterated their *hope*.

TARKIN: I think you are too easy with her, Vader! Put aside your mind drugs and tele-suggestions . . . there are old methods, tried and true ways of making a captive speak. Phantom pain is something against which she can defend herself, but against the real thing, her resistance will collapse.

VADER: I think not. She is a member of the Royal House of Alderaan and of the Imperial Senate. She has had access to many family and governmental secrets; she has been specifically trained and prepared to withstand conventional questioning. I would have to apply levels of pain so high as to risk killing her.

TARKIN: And what of it? She must be disposed of in time, anyway.

VADER: But the Princess is my one lead to the Rebels. I cannot chance losing her just yet.

TARKIN: You haven't much time, Lord Vader. With the Death Star completed, I must take vigorous action against the Rebels as soon as possible. The Emperor expects great things of this battle station, and of me.

VADER: Without the information that Leia Organa is protecting, your best efforts will be a waste of time. But I will demolish her defenses, rest assured.

TARKIN: I've always found your methods rather needlessly elaborate, Vader.

VADER: They are effective. Nevertheless, I am open to suggestions.

TARKIN: That is wise. Stubbornness such as the Princess Leia's can often be circumvented by applying threats to some third party.

VADER: Meaning?

TARKIN: That I think it is time we demonstrated the full power of the Death Star. I have it in mind to do so in a fashion that will be doubly useful. Admiral Motti!

MOTTI: Yes, sir!

TARKIN: Tell your programmers to set a course for the Alderaan system.

MOTTI: With pleasure, Lord Tarkin!

TARKIN: You see, Vader? Our third parties, whom we'll threaten, are the entire population of her home planet.

VADER: Alderaan is one of the foremost of the inner systems. The Emperor should be consulted.

TARKIN: Do not think to challenge *me*! You're not confronting Tagge or Motti now! The Emperor has placed me in charge of this affair with a free hand, and the decision is mine! And you will have your information that much sooner.

VADER: Just so.

TARKIN: I'm glad you agree. The Empire is vast, and even a weapon as magnificent as the Death Star can only be in one place at a time. A major part of this station's value is as a deterrent. We must prove to the galaxy that we are prepared to use it at the slightest provocation.

VADER: If your plan serves our purpose, it will justify itself.

TARKIN: The stability of the Empire is at stake. A planet is a small price to pay.

Sound: Death Star's engines come up, then fade to silence.

Sound: Operational noise of the observation deck up and under:

MOTTI: *(SLIGHTLY OFF)* We've entered Alderaan's solar system, Governor Tarkin, and assumed orbit around the planet.

TARKIN: Make sure we're well out of range of the explosion. Is our Prime Weapon prepared?

MOTTI: Primary ignition can proceed immediately upon your command, sir. And Lord Vader will be here with the prisoner at any moment.

TARKIN: Splendid.

Sound: Power door opens, closes as Leia, Vader, and guards enter.

VADER: Here is the prisoner!

LEIA: *(APPROACHING)* Governor Tarkin! I should have expected to find you holding Vader's leash. I recognized your foul stench when I was brought onboard.

TARKIN: Charming to the last. You don't know how hard I found it signing the order to terminate your life.

LEIA: I'm surprised you had the courage to take the responsibility yourself.

TARKIN: Princess Leia, before your execution I would like you to be my guest at a ceremony that will make this battle station operational. No star system will dare oppose the Emperor now.

LEIA: The more you tighten your grip, Tarkin, the more star systems will slip through your fingers.

TARKIN: Not after we demonstrate the power of the Death Star. In a way you have determined the choice of the first planet to be destroyed, and it is for that reason that I've had you brought here to the observation deck. *(ASIDE)* Admiral Motti, have the viewscreens activated!

MOTTI: At once!

Sound: A soft humming begins.

TARKIN: Since you are reluctant to provide us with the location of the Rebel base, Your Highness, I have chosen to test the Death Star's destructive powers on that lovely blue world you see on our viewscreens . . . your home planet of Alderaan.

LEIA: But Alderaan is peaceful. We have no weapons . . . You can't possibly . . .

TARKIN: You would prefer another target? A *military* target? Then name the system!

LEIA: No! I . . .

TARKIN: Vader! Hold her!

Sound: A brief scuffle.

LEIA: Please . . .

TARKIN: I grow tired of asking this. So, for the last time . . . where is the Rebel base?

LEIA: *(A NEAR WHISPER)* Dantooine. They're on Dantooine.

TARKIN: There, you see, Vader? She *can* be reasonable. *(ASIDE)* Continue with the operation, Admiral Motti. You may fire when ready.

LEIA: *What?*

TARKIN: You're far too trusting. Dantooine is too remote to make an effective demonstration. But don't worry . . . we shall deal with your Rebel friends soon enough.

Sound: Prime Weapon building power in background.

MOTTI: Commencing primary ignition, Lord Tarkin.

LEIA: Tarkin, *please*! I beg you, in the name of mercy—

MOTTI: Prime Weapon firing . . . now!

Sound: Leia's scream is lost in the report of the Prime Weapon.

VADER: Our Prime Weapon is even more powerful than we'd calculated, Lord Tarkin.

TARKIN: Indeed.

MOTTI: Sensors indicate total destruction of the planet, Lord Tarkin.

LEIA: Father! Oh, my poor, poor Alderaan . . .

TARKIN: Return her to the detention level!

LEIA: Tarkin, if there ever was a shred of humanity in you or these twisted creatures of yours, it's dead now. You're at war with life itself. You're enemies of the universe . . . your Empire's doomed.

TARKIN: Take her away!

Music: In.

Sound: Vader's heavy footsteps and respirator.

VADER: *(APPROACHING)* You sent for me, Lord Tarkin?

TARKIN: Yes, Vader. We should be receiving word from our scouting expedition very soon.

VADER: Giving you your opportunity to—how did you put it?— "extinguish" the Rebellion?

TARKIN: Precisely. In the space of a single day I will effectively eliminate all organized resistance to the Empire.

VADER: Indeed.

TARKIN: What of the search for the plans?

VADER: I am convinced that the Princess sent them down to the planet Tatooine with a pair of droids. A short time ago a starship made a highly illegal blastoff from Mos Eisley Spaceport on Tatooine after her crew exchanged fire with a squad of stormtroopers. The ship got through our blockade somehow and entered hyperspace, evading pursuit. The droids in question were thought to be aboard her.

TARKIN: And our stormtroopers were outfought, our starfleet evaded? How is this possible? Whose ship was it?

VADER: That is difficult to say. She had false identification markings and a forged registration. Moreover, she was an extremely fast and elusive vessel, probably one of the smugglers who congregate in that region.

TARKIN: So the traitors have joined hands with criminals. And once again you've failed to regain those plans.

VADER: Our enemies are resourceful. But if you destroy the Rebel base, as you've resolved to do, the plans become a secondary concern, is that not so?

TARKIN: Yes, when we've wiped out the fortress on Dantooine, the matter will be virtually settled.

Sound: The power door opens, then closes, as Motti enters.

MOTTI: *(APPROACHING)* Lord Tarkin! Lord Vader!

TARKIN: Well, what is it, Motti?

MOTTI: Our scout ships have reached Dantooine. They found the remains of a Rebel base, but they estimate that it has been deserted for some time. They are now conducting an extensive search of the solar systems.

TARKIN: She lied! Leia Organa lied to us!

VADER: I told you she would never consciously betray the Rebellion.

TARKIN: Then her life is forfeit. Motti, have the Princess Leia Organa terminated . . . immediately!

NARRATOR: The Death Star is now a reality, capable of placing the entire galaxy within the Empire's grip. But on their way to the Alderaan system, unaware of the planet's destruction, are Luke Skywalker and his companions, aboard the starship *Millennium Falcon*, holding the galaxy's single hope for an end to Imperial tyranny.

Music: Closing theme up and under preview and closing credits.

ANNOUNCER: CLOSING CREDITS.

COCKPIT - FALCON / SCALE REVISION

EPISODE NINE:

"ROGUES, REBELS,
AND ROBOTS"

CAST:

Ben	Chewbacca
Luke	Threepio
Han	Artoo

ANNOUNCER: OPENING CREDITS.

Music: Opening theme.

NARRATOR: A long time ago in a galaxy far, far away there came a time of revolution, when Rebels united to challenge a tyrannical Empire. In the Rebellion's most desperate crisis, plans for the Empire's mightiest weapon, the Death Star, were stolen by Rebel agents and placed in the memory banks of the astrodroid Artoo-Detoo. Artoo and his fellow droid, See-Threepio, are now under the protection of the young farmer Luke Skywalker and the veteran Jedi Knight Ben Kenobi. Their plan is to deliver the droids to Rebels on the planet Alderaan.

Sound: The Millennium Falcon's *booming passage through hyperspace. Then engine hum and noise of various instruments of forward compartment up in background.*

NARRATOR: In order to accomplish their objective, Luke and Ben have hired two reckless smugglers, Han Solo and his copilot, Chewbacca, along with their starship, the *Millennium Falcon.* Having fought her way past an Imperial blockade, the *Falcon* is now en route, via hyperspace, her passengers and crew unaware that the Empire is already moving against the Rebel Alliance with all the power at its command.

BEN: *(SIGHING)* That brief shock was the jump to lightspeed. I think we can unfasten our safety belts now, Luke.

LUKE: Fine with me. That was the wildest ride *I've* ever been on! Between those Imperial cruisers blazing away at us and Han's crazy piloting, I never thought we'd make it.

Sound: They unfasten their seat belts.

BEN: Captain Solo's flying may be rather on the daredevil side, but I would say that we owe our lives to it. Not many pilots *or* starships can make their way through an Imperial Starfleet blockade. I can see where his renown as a smuggler had its source.

THREEPIO: Well, it reminded me why I hate space travel! May I unbuckle, too, sir?

ARTOO: SIGNALS.

THREEPIO: Oh, and Artoo would like to know if he can let go of the bulkhead.

LUKE: Sure, Threepio. This trip will take a while. How *is* Artoo?

ARTOO: WHISTLES.

THREEPIO: Oh, he says he's quite in order, Master Luke.

LUKE: Good, he's sure been through enough in the last couple of days.

THREEPIO: We all have, sir, if I may say so.

ARTOO: BURBLES AGREEMENT.

LUKE: What'd he say?

THREEPIO: Artoo points out that there is a recharging unit over here and, might I suggest, that he and I recharge.

BEN: A good idea. We can't foresee how long it will be before another opportunity presents itself.

LUKE: Sure, Threepio; you and Artoo go to it.

THREEPIO: Thank you, sir!

LUKE: Just look at this compartment, will you? Shipping containers, spare parts, empty crates, and plain old *junk* all over the place. Some starship!

BEN: This is a working freighter, Luke, even if her activities *are* rather on the shady side. Independent captains like Solo run their ships to suit themselves and live as they see fit. But I'll tell you this: For all the clutter, the *Millennium Falcon* is in excellent shape and far faster than she was when she was built. Solo wasn't exaggerating about those "modifications" he's made on her.

LUKE: You know what I was surprised to find back at the techstation? That holographic game board. I wouldn't've expected Han to be the kind to play.

BEN: Spacers fill the hours they spend in transit in a surprising variety of ways, Luke. But the fact that a rough-and-ready fellow like Solo chooses such a pastime *does* indicate another side to him.

LUKE: But who does he play against? The machine?

BEN: Against his first mate, Chewbacca, in all likelihood.

LUKE: You mean that big, shaggy Wookiee can play the board game?

BEN: Games of skill and thought aren't restricted to human beings and machines, Luke. Don't let Chewbacca's great size and fierce appearance fool you. Wookiees are a species with great adaptability, and they're quick to learn.

LUKE: I guess you're right. But there's no other crew—just Han and Chewbacca?

BEN: Their arrangement seems to work well enough for them . . . captain-pilot and first mate–copilot. They strike me as a very competent pair for all their brashness. As long as they can get us to Alderaan, they suit our needs.

LUKE: Yeah, for seventeen thousand!

BEN: Price is insignificant, Luke. What's important is getting Artoo-Detoo to Alderaan so that we can pass the information in his memory banks along to the Rebel leaders.

LUKE: I suppose. What d' you think this information is, anyway?

BEN: I cannot say, but if it weren't of the utmost urgency, we would never have been instructed to take it directly there. Things are coming to a crucial juncture in the war of Rebel against Empire.

LUKE: It's still hard to believe that a Princess of the Royal House of Alderaan *and* her father could both be members of the Rebel Alliance.

BEN: I think it's best to leave that subject for now, Luke, for a more guarded place and time.

LUKE: Huh? Do you think Han . . .

BEN: Captain Solo's loyalties obviously lie more with himself than with the Empire, but it's better not to test that by letting him know just what it is he's carrying in the form of Artoo . . .

HAN: *(CALLING)* The lightspeed jump came off without a hitch, gents and droids . . . Hey, what're those two doing at the tech-station?

BEN: The droids are merely recharging, Captain.

HAN: Well, make sure they don't mess with anything. Me and Chewie are gonna repair a little minor damage we did blasting out of Mos Eisley and dodging those Imperials, make sure we're not being followed. *(MOVING OFF)* So make yourselves comfortable, and we'll have you to Alderaan before you're through dusting the Tatooine sand off you.

BEN: Thank you!

LUKE: I guess I'll take a look around the *Millennium Falcon.* I've never been aboard a starship before, but I've sure thought about it enough.

BEN: Perhaps a little later, Luke. For now there are other, more important things for us to do. I don't know what our mission will bring or what we'll encounter on Alderaan, but it's best we begin your training.

LUKE: Right now? *Here?*

BEN: Didn't you tell me you wanted to be instructed in the ways of the Force in order to become a Jedi Knight like your father was?

LUKE: Well, yes, but . . .

BEN: Well, the way of the Jedi is a lifelong education, Luke. I began learning it when I was younger than you. I have achieved a certain mastery, and yet I am no less a pupil for all of that, even now.

LUKE: You've taught a lot of students, haven't you, Ben? Even this Darth Vader, the Jedi who turned traitor and killed my father.

BEN: Darth Vader . . . started out as my pupil, yes.

LUKE: I want to know about Vader, Ben. Who he is and why he went over to the dark side of the Force. I want to face him when I'm a Jedi Knight and tell him whose son I am.

BEN: If you wish to be a Jedi, you'll have to put aside your desire for revenge.

LUKE: But . . .

BEN: Anger and hatred . . . yes, and fear, too . . . these can help you draw power from the Force, but only from its dark side. And in the end the dark side of the Force exacts a terrible price from those whom it seduces.

LUKE: But . . . but tell me about Vader, Ben. I want to know who he is and why he gave in to the dark side . . .

BEN: Luke, Luke, you're reaching far ahead of yourself. The workings of the Force aren't always so direct. Above all else, mastery of the Force demands patience.

LUKE: I've felt short of that ever since you told me about Vader and how he betrayed my father and the other Jedi. But I didn't mean to sound like I'm impatient with you. I'm grateful that you cared enough about me to watch over me and to teach me.

BEN: I haven't had a student since before the dark times, before the Empire all but exterminated the Jedi. There were many times since when I thought I would never teach another, and I feared that the way of the Jedi would die out. This is a more significant occasion than you can appreciate yet.

LUKE: Do you mean . . . there are no other Jedi?

BEN: We are not altogether alone in the galaxy, you and I, but I doubt that we can count on help from others of our kind.

LUKE: *(WONDERINGLY)* Our kind . . . How do we start?

BEN: When the Jedi were guardians of peace and justice, back in the days of the Old Republic, an initiate would spend a great deal of time in contemplation, learning to open himself to the Force, before studying the more warlike aspects of our order. But this is a different day, with its own urgencies. Now, take your father's lightsaber in your hand.

LUKE: How do I hold the grip?

BEN: Watch . . . emulate me.

Sound: A rustle of Ben's robes as he draws out his saber.

BEN: Hold the grip *so,* so that the blade, when it comes into existence, will be high and ready.

LUKE: How did you do that quick draw in the cantina, when you cut those two killers down? I never saw anybody move so fast . . .

BEN: Basics first, Luke. You must—

LUKE: Crawl before I can run?

BEN: Just so . . . . good. Now, take up this stance.

LUKE: Like this?

BEN: That's it. Now, watch me. I push this button in the grip of the lightsaber to activate it. Energy is liberated.

Sound: The quick, sibilant hum of the saber.

BEN: And the blade comes into existence, you see? Now, from this basic position, you can launch into any movement of the blade . . .

Sound: The saber moans as Ben moves it through the air.

BEN: . . . in attack or defense, advance or withdrawal.

Sound: Ben switches the saber off.

BEN: Now, you try it.

LUKE: Okay. Let's see . . .

BEN: No, no . . . bring your feet together. Too wide a stance robs you of speed and agility. That's better. Can you feel your center of balance?

LUKE: Uh, it feels pretty good.

BEN: Watch, and I shall demonstrate the basic drill.

Sound: Ben's blade switches on again. Throughout the next speech, we hear his graceful steps, the flutter of his robes, and the swirl of his saber.

BEN: From the ready position, into the first defensive posture . . . and the second . . . third . . . and the fourth. Continuing the circular motion with a sweep of the blade, like so . . . and back again into the ready position.

Sound: The saber switches off.

BEN: You see?

LUKE: I think so. Can I try it?

BEN: *(LAUGHS)* Very well, *but carefully.* Never forget, a lightsaber blade will cut through anything it contacts. *Anything.* Now . . . your blade.

Sound: Luke's blade hisses on.

LUKE: This lightsaber . . . it feels kind of like it's alive.

BEN: It is, in a way, through you. Ready? First defensive posture . . .

Sound: Luke clumsily imitates Ben's performance.

BEN: And the second; it requires a deeper step forward, Luke. The third, no, keep your blade higher! That's right . . . and into the fourth. Bring it all the way around; a parry must be a *full* movement!

Sound: Luke's saber switches off.

LUKE: It's a lot harder than you make it look.

BEN: Learning to use a lightsaber properly is a long, meticulous process. Still, you haven't begun all that badly. I can see you inherited your father's dexterity and coordination.

LUKE: But I'm not sure I can get the hang of this, at least not soon enough to make it useful right now. I know how to use a blaster pretty well from survival school back home; maybe I'd better stick with that.

BEN: One can do things with a lightsaber that cannot be done with a mere firearm, Luke. But more than that, the lightsaber is a discipline for the mind and a schooling for the body and spirit. It's one of the ways in which a Jedi contacts the Force.

LUKE: I see. It's just that it's not like anything I ever tried before. Let me go through that drill again.

BEN: Just a moment, Luke. I've a feeling we may need our every resource when we reach Alderaan. I have it in mind to accelerate your training by opening you to the Force.

LUKE: Huh? How?

BEN: By building your trust in it and in yourself. A great part of a Jedi's power is derived from the Force by a firm conviction, a trust.

LUKE: I'll try whatever you want me to. What do I do?

BEN: Simply believe. I'm going to help you. I'll be your guide and your intermediary with the Force. Now, I'm going to stand here behind you. I want you to listen to my voice and empty your mind of everything else. Focus on my voice and concentrate on the open area of the deck, where you will try the drill once more.

LUKE: Yes . . .

BEN: Envision yourself going through the drill. Don't move, but feel the shape of the sequence, how your arms and legs will move, how nerves and muscles will cooperate. Try to make the sensations as real as you can . . . the wide, rotary motions of the lightsaber, the placement of your feet, and where your center of balance will be. Now, activate your blade.

Sound: Luke's saber switches on.

BEN: Good. Now, open yourself and create the flow of those movements in your mind. Let the drill's pattern carry your mind along. How does it feel?

LUKE: Like I can do it automatically, without thinking. No, not that exactly . . . more like . . . that I don't have to worry, something will move me through the drill . . .

BEN: That's fine, Luke. Hold that thought and focus on the drill. Don't worry about speed, don't worry about indecision, don't worry about anything. Feel the life of the lightsaber in your hands and anticipate the flow of it. *(AN EMPHATIC WHISPER)* And when you feel that you're ready . . . begin . . .

223

Sound: After a moment Luke moves confidently through the drill: rhythmic, coordinated, graceful.

BEN: *(CHANTING SOFTLY)* First defensive posture, that's right . . . second, good, Luke . . . and the third, *very* good . . . into the fourth, exactly! And back around to the ready position.

Sound: Luke's saber switches off.

BEN: Well done, Luke! How did it feel to you?

LUKE: So smooth . . . natural. But I wasn't thinking about it, really. The drill just . . . carried me along.

BEN: And so it should. You have a strong aptitude, Luke, a powerful affinity for the Force. What do you say to some more practice?

LUKE: Yes. I'd like that.

BEN: Excellent. Now, again, take up the ready position and feel the flow of the events to come . . .

Sound: Hum of the Falcon's *engine, machinery, etc., fades to silence.*

Music: In.

Sound: Falcon background up. Luke is moving through another drill.

BEN: Now, into the seventh attack position . . . pivot and parry! Fine! I think you should take another short rest, Luke. We've been at this for quite some time now.

LUKE: But I don't feel tired. I feel like I could do this forever.

BEN: Then take pity on your elders, son. I could use a respite myself . . .

BEN: Ah, here's Chewbacca. How are things in the cockpit?

CHEWIE: *(APPROACHING)* GROWLS A RESPONSE.

LUKE: What's he say?

BEN: He and Captain Solo have repaired all the damage.

CHEWIE: GROWLS AGAIN.

BEN: He says there's time before we reach Alderaan for a quick match at the holographic game board back in the tech-station. I'm sorry, Chewbacca, but Luke and I have other work to do.

ARTOO: WHISTLES ENERGETICALLY.

THREEPIO: Oh, be quiet, Artoo, and stop bragging!

LUKE: What's Artoo want, Threepio?

THREEPIO: Well, Master Luke, he claims to have been programmed to play a competent holo-game when he was assigned as a maintenance droid at a one-man refueling station in order to provide a diversion for the attendant.

LUKE: Then, why don't you play Artoo, Chewbacca?

CHEWIE: BARKS.

LUKE: Sounds like you're on, Artoo.

ARTOO: BEEPS CONFIDENTLY.

Sound: Artoo's treads across the deck, with Threepio following.

THREEPIO: *(MOVING OFF)* I hope you know what you're doing for a change.

CHEWIE: GROWLS.

LUKE: *(CALLING)* You'd better leave Chewbacca plenty of room back there on the acceleration couch, Threepio.

THREEPIO: *(FAR OFF)* I quite agree, sir.

LUKE: Now, how about a practice duel, Ben? If we took it real slowly, and I'll be careful, we could—

BEN: I don't think you're quite ready for that yet, Luke, though you *could* use more advanced practice at this point. Hmmmm. I noticed that Captain Solo wears his blaster in a fast-draw holster. He must keep a remote around for target practice. I wonder where he . . . ah!

(CROSSING) Here we are.

(CROSSING BACK) Have you ever used one of these little remote target globes before, Luke?

LUKE: Well, once or twice.

BEN: I'm resetting it. It will maneuver in the air, darting back and forth, and fire harmless sting bursts at you. They're a bit painful but not dangerous. I want you to try to block them with your lightsaber. When I release the remote into the air, it will commence an attack. Ready?

Sound: Luke's saber activates.

LUKE: Ready.

Sound: The remote moving on puffs of forced air and squirts of repulsor power, darting up and down, back and forth. Suddenly there's a hiss of a sting burst.

LUKE: Ouch! That hurt!

BEN: Not as much as a real enemy would, I assure you. I've set the remote to attack so long as your lightsaber blade is activated. Continue, Luke. You must reach out and make contact with the Force, to anticipate its attack, so that—

Sound: Ben suddenly gasps in shock.

LUKE: Ben!

Sound: Luke's saber switches off, and the remote become immobile.

LUKE: *(APPROACHING)* Ben, are you all right? Here, sit down. What's wrong?

BEN: I felt a great disturbance in the Force . . . as if millions of voices suddenly cried out in terror and were suddenly silenced . . . as if an entire world had died in an instant. I fear that something terrible has happened.

LUKE: Is there anything I can do?

BEN: No, I'll be all right.

HAN: *(APPROACHING)* Well, you can forget your troubles; we'll be at Alderaan pretty soon. I told you I could outrun those Imperial slugs! Hey, don't everybody thank me at once! Anyway, we should make Alderaan around oh-two-hundred-hours. I see Chewie found himself an opponent. Your little droid's not bad at that game. He'll have to watch out. He might win.

CHEWIE: *(COMING ON)* ROARS IN OUTRAGE.

HAN: Well, what'd I tell you, Chewie? It was a trap.

CHEWIE: SNARLS AGAIN.

THREEPIO: *(COMING ON)* But Artoo made a fair move, Chewbacca! If you fell for it, it's your fault. Screaming about it won't help you!

HAN: Better let Chewie have his way. It's not wise to upset a Wookiee.

THREEPIO: But sir, nobody worries about upsetting a droid!

ARTOO: WHISTLES.

HAN: That's 'cause droids don't pull people's arms out of their sockets when they lose. Wookiees are known to do that.

CHEWIE: RUMBLES IN AGREEMENT.

THREEPIO: I see your point, sir. *(MOVING OFF)* Might I suggest a new strategy, Artoo . . . let the Wookiee win!

CHEWIE: YEOWLS SMUGLY.

LUKE: Ben, are you feeling any better?

BEN: Yes. Let's continue with your drill, Luke. Saber ready?

Sound: Luke's saber switches on, and the remote becomes active.

LUKE: Ready.

BEN: Remember, a Jedi can feel the Force flowing through him.

Sound: The saber moans as the remote darts.

LUKE: You mean it controls your actions?

BEN: Partially, but it also obeys your commands. Careful now . . .

Sound: The remote moves in and sends out a sting burst.

LUKE: Ow, my leg!

HAN: *(LAUGHS)* Hokey religions and ancient weapons are no match for a good blaster at your side, kid!

Sound: Luke's saber switches off.

LUKE: You don't believe in the Force, do you, Han?

HAN: Kid, I've been from one side of this galaxy to the other. I've seen a lot of strange stuff, but I've never seen anything to make me believe there's one all-powerful Force controlling everything. There's no mystical energy field controlling *my* destiny!

BEN: Then what does?

HAN: Huh? Look, this stuff you're telling him, it's all a lot of simple tricks and nonsense.

BEN: I suggest you try again, Luke. Here . . . we'll try it with you wearing this crash helmet. I'll lower its blast shield into place.

Sound: Ben adjusting the helmet.

BEN: This time, let go of your conscious self and act on instinct.

LUKE: *(LAUGHS)* But with the blast shield down like this, I can't even see. How am I supposed to fight the remote?

BEN: Your eyes can deceive you . . . don't trust them.

HAN: Gonna try for *two* sore legs, huh, kid?

BEN: Now, let's try again, Luke.

Sound: Luke's saber activates. The remote comes at him and fires a sting burst.

LUKE: Ouch!

CHEWIE: GRUNTS IN LAUGHTER.

HAN: *(LAUGHS)* Seat of the pants! You're doing just great, kid!

BEN: Again, Luke. Listen to my voice and trust me. Reach out with your feelings.

Sound: The remote maneuvers again. Luke remains stationary. The remote fires three quick shots, which Luke parries with the lightsaber, making a new and different sound of the clash of energies.

THREEPIO: Master Luke, you did it!

Sound: The saber switches off.

HAN: Yeah, but going against remotes is one thing. Going against the living? That's something else.

BEN: You parried all three shots by trusting your feelings, Luke. You see? You *can* do it!

HAN: Oh, yeah? Well *I* call it luck!

BEN: In my experience, there is no such thing as mere "luck."

HAN: It's as good a faith as any, old man . . . luck and money.

BEN: Ah, yes, wealth. I'd forgotten how important that is to you.

HAN: Don't knock it. If me and Chewie weren't hard up for it, you two and the droids'd still be playing tag with the stormtroopers back on Tatooine. As it is, you get where you want to go and we clear our debts.

BEN: *(LAUGHS)* You're quite a paradox, Captain Solo. You prize above everything else the cardinal freedom of star travel, yet you're held back from it by something as trifling as money. Come to think of it, there are entire worlds in just that same predicament.

CHEWIE: ROARS ANGRILY.

HAN: You said it, Chewie! *(TO BEN)* So money's "trifling," huh? Well just *you* try getting along without any!

BEN: Oh, but I do!

HAN: Wha . . .

BEN: Have you ever seen a credit come into or leave my hand? I haven't had any . . . and haven't missed it . . . in, oh, quite some years now . . . and wanted for nothing.

HAN: Now . . . no, well . . . all right, so the kid there paid your way, but you wouldn't've gotten anyplace if he hadn't come up with the cash.

BEN: Perhaps I'm . . . lucky?

HAN: What'm I doing arguing with an old coot like you? You haven't even got the price of a meal. We'll talk it over when you get hungry.

Sound: Bleeping sound from the tech-station.

HAN: Anyway, we're coming up on Alderaan. You measure your freedom in this life in *cash*, old man. If you have enough, you can go as far and as fast as you want. Come on, Chewie!

BEN: *(CALLING)* Captain Solo!

HAN: *(OFF)* Yeah?

BEN: Even the universe itself is curved, my friend. If you run far enough and fast enough, you end up . . . right where you began.

HAN: Now just hold on there—

CHEWIE: *(OFF)* INTERRUPTS WITH A GROWL.

HAN: All right, all right, Chewie, I'm coming. *(MOVING OFF, MUTTERING TO HIMSELF)* Should've known better than to argue with a crazy old desert grubber, anyway . . .

LUKE: Don't pay any attention to him, Ben. All the money in the Empire wouldn't stop me from helping you deliver the droids and . . . doing what I can for Princess Leia.

BEN: I know that, Luke. I have great confidence in you.

LUKE: You know, I really *did* feel something during that lightsaber drill. I could almost see what the remote was going to do.

BEN: That's good. You have taken your first step into a larger world.

Music: Up.

Sound: Cockpit background up, with instrumentation beeping, engines louder, sensor readouts clicking, ocilloscopes, etc.

HAN: That old guy and the kid get on my nerves. If there's anything I hate, it's being saddled with a dewy-eyed idealist. They're nothing but trouble!

CHEWIE: GRUNTS IN A MILD TONE.

HAN: Oh yes they *are* "that bad"! They're hot, too. You saw how badly those Imperial cruisers wanted us!

CHEWIE: GRUNTS AGAIN.

HAN: What're you, getting soft in your old age? Maybe we should quit the smuggling business and open a soup kitchen?

CHEWIE: RUMBLES ANGRILY.

HAN: Okay, okay, calm down. The navi-computer says we're about ready to revert to normal space. Stand by, here we go. Cutting in sublight engines . . .

Sound: The ship's engines change pitch downward.

HAN: . . . Good. Now we can—

Sound: The ship abruptly shudders, setting off alarms and sending the instrumentation into hysteria.

CHEWIE: HOOTS IN DISMAY.

HAN: What the flamin', flyin' . . . aw, we've come out of hyperspace into some kind of meteor shower! Sky's full of them! Increase power to deflector shields!

CHEWIE: GRUNTS.

Sound: Switches being thrown.

HAN: Maybe there was an asteroid collision, only . . . it's not on any of the charts.

LUKE: *(APPROACHING)* What's going on?

HAN: We stopped off to pick up a load of gravel; what else?

BEN: *(APPROACHING)* There shouldn't be any navigational hazards this near Alderaan.

HAN: *(MUTTERING)* Our position is correct, only . . . no Alderaan.

LUKE: What d' you mean? Where is it?

HAN: That's what I'm trying to tell you, kid; it ain't there. It's been totally blown away.

LUKE: But how could that be?

BEN: Destroyed . . . by the Empire! I should have realized it when I felt it earlier . . .

HAN: An entire starfleet couldn't destroy the whole planet. It'd take a thousand ships, with more firepower than I've ever . . .

Sound: Insistent beeping begins.

LUKE: What's that light on the console?

HAN: Sensors say there's another ship closing on us.

LUKE: Maybe they know what happened to Alderaan.

BEN: It's an Imperial fighter.

HAN: What makes you so sure? Sensors don't have a clear ID on it . . .

Sound: The Falcon *shakes again.*

LUKE: It's firing on us! Look, there it goes!

HAN: And it's a TIE fighter, right enough. Good guess, old man.

LUKE: It must have followed us from Tatooine!

BEN: No, it's a short-range fighter.

HAN: But there aren't any bases around here. Where'd it come from?

LUKE: Maybe it wandered away from a convoy. Look! It sure is leaving in a big hurry! If that pilot identifies us, we're in big trouble.

HAN: Not if I can help it. Chewie, jam his transmissions.

CHEWIE: GROWLS.

Sound: Han and Chewie begin working at the console. The engines increase in volume.

BEN: It would be as well to let it go. It's too far out of range.

HAN: Not for long. You may think you know everything, but you've got a lot to learn about the *Millennium Falcon.* Hang on . . .

Sound: The ship's engines roar.

HAN: Chewie, switch weapons systems over to sensor gunlock. Let me know when we've got him ranged. A couple of salvos and our worries'll be over. His, too.

LUKE: Look, the TIE fighter's headed for that small moon!

HAN: Yeah, but we're gaining. I think I can bag him before he gets there. We're almost in range.

BEN: That's not a moon out there! That's a space station!

Music: Under to end of scene.

HAN: What? You're even crazier than I thought. Look at the size of it! It's way too big to be a . . . a space . . .

CHEWIE: MOANS IN DISTRESS.

HAN: . . . station. Uh-oh . . .

LUKE: Ben, you're right. I have a very bad feeling about this.

HAN: So you get those, too?

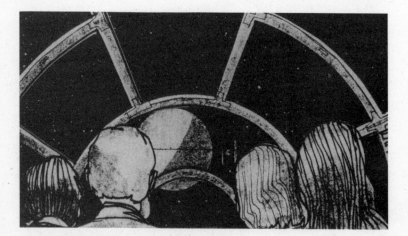

BEN: Turn the ship around!

HAN: Yeah . . . I think you're right. Full reverse!

CHEWIE: GROANS.

HAN: Chewie, lock in auxiliary power.

Sound: The ship begins shaking.

CHEWIE: HOWLS.

HAN: Chewie, I said *lock in auxiliary power*!

BEN: It's too late . . .

LUKE: Why are we still moving toward that station?

HAN: The *Falcon*'s not answering her helm! Whatever that thing is out there, it's got us caught in a tractor beam and it's hauling us in!

LUKE: Well, do something!

HAN: Kid, there's nothing I *can* do against a beam with that much juice! I'm on full power now, gonna have to shut down or I'll melt the engines. Chewie, full deflector shields, angle 'em forward!

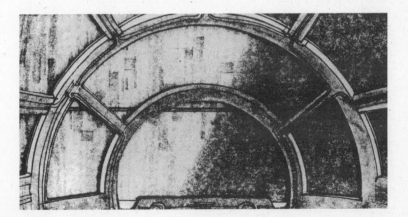

CHEWIE: RUMBLES.

Sound: He throws more switches.

HAN: They're not gonna get me without a fight!

BEN: But you can't win.

HAN: No, but I can shorten a few Imperial careers.

BEN: There are alternatives to fighting, though. Alternatives that might mean survival.

CHEWIE: GRUNTS HOPEFULLY.

HAN: All right, you got yourself an audience. What's the scheme?

BEN: You're a smuggler, are you not? Along with speed, your specialty is concealment. Let us take advantage of that.

HAN: How . . .

BEN: Quickly, jettison some escape pods before we come into close sensor range of that station. And prepare to make an entry into the ship's log. Luke!

LUKE: What, Ben?

BEN: Get the droids. Hurry. There's little time left.

LUKE: Right!

HAN: If you're planning what I think you are and we pull it off, I'll give you half fare on your next ride.

BEN: I only hope this works.

HAN: If it doesn't, they'll let us know at the firing squad!

Music: In and under:

NARRATOR: Caught in the grip of the Empire's awesome Death Star, the *Millennium Falcon* and her passengers and crew are drawn into the center of the web of galactic events. There, the

Princess Leia Organa is held captive pending her execution, and there, too, Darth Vader waits. Luke Skywalker is soon to meet the woman whose image has summoned him across light-years of space and the enemy whose destiny was tied to his own before his birth.

Music: Closing theme up and under preview and closing credits.

ANNOUNCER: CLOSING CREDITS.

EPISODE TEN:

"THE LUKE SKYWALKER
INITIATIVE"

C A S T :

Ben	Leia	Officer
Luke	1st Crewman	2nd Officer
Han	2nd Crewman	3rd Officer
Chewbacca	1st Trooper	Soldier
Threepio	2nd Trooper	Console Voice
Artoo		

ANNOUNCER: OPENING CREDITS.

Music: Opening theme.

NARRATOR: A long time ago in a galaxy far, far away there came a time of revolution, when Rebels united to challenge a tyrannical Empire. In the Rebellion's most desperate crisis, plans vital to the defeat of the Empire were hidden in the memory banks of the astrodroid Artoo-Detoo. Artoo and his companion droid, See-Threepio, have come into the hands of young farmer Luke Skywalker and the veteran Jedi Knight Ben Kenobi. Having resolved to deliver Artoo and Threepio to the planet Alderaan, Luke and Ben have hired a pair of daring smugglers, Han Solo and his copilot, Chewbacca, along with their starship, the *Millennium Falcon*.

Sound: The Falcon's *forward compartment in background, along with the rumble of the ship, without engines, as she's drawn along, with her warning sirens, alarms, etc.*

NARRATOR: But forces of the Empire have reached Alderaan's solar system first with their ultimate weapon, a huge spacegoing fortress called the Death Star with which they have destroyed the entire planet. The *Millennium Falcon*, arriving on the scene only to find Alderaan obliterated, is now being drawn into the Death Star by a tractor beam.

Sound: Distant noise of the escape pods being jettisoned.

THREEPIO: Listen, Artoo! It seems that Captain Solo is jettisoning the escape pods!

ARTOO: CONCURS.

THREEPIO: But what if they leave us behind?

ARTOO: OFFERS NO HELP.

THREEPIO: Oh, I simply hate space travel! Why is it that every time we're onboard a vessel, somebody seems determined to demolish us?

LUKE: *(OFF)* Threepio! Artoo!

THREEPIO: We're over here, Master Luke!

ARTOO: WHISTLES.

THREEPIO: Have we reached the planet Alderaan yet?

LUKE: *(FADING ON)* There *is* no Alderaan, Threepio!

THREEPIO: I beg your pardon, sir, but I feel it my duty to point out that you're in error. Why, I was there myself, just—

LUKE: Somebody's blown it to bits! Now will you shut up and c'mon?

THREEPIO: Yes, sir!

LUKE: Fast, or we're all dead!

THREEPIO: Oh, dear!

BEN: *(COMING ON)* Luke! Chewbacca and Captain Solo will be here in a moment. We're going to take refuge under the deck plates.

LUKE: *Deck plates?*

BEN: The *Millennium Falcon* is a smuggling ship, Luke. Since we cannot avoid being drawn into the battle station, our only chance is to hide in the ship's concealed compartments.

CHEWIE: *(OFF)* GROWLS.

BEN: Chewbacca! How much time do we have?

CHEWIE: *(OFF)* SNARLS.

BEN: Then we'd best move quickly.

LUKE: How do we get under the deck plates?

BEN: You will see. Chewbacca, open them, please.

CHEWIE: GRUNTS.

Sound: Chewie opens the latches.

LUKE: Huh! Hidden is right . . . I'd never've seen them.

BEN: Lend a hand here, Luke . . .

Sound: The heavy deck plates.

BEN: Threepio, help Chewbacca lower Artoo down there.

THREEPIO: Very well, sir. Hold still, Artoo!

CHEWIE: RUMBLES.

ARTOO: SIGNALS.

Sound: Artoo being lowered in the hold space.

THREEPIO: Carefully now.

CHEWIE: BARKS FIERCELY.

THREEPIO: There, Artoo, are you all right?

ARTOO: CHIRPS.

LUKE: The hold space looks pretty cramped, Ben. Are you sure there's enough room in there for all of us?

BEN: There will have to be.

LUKE: Where's Han?

BEN: Making final preparations . . . Ah! Here he is!

HAN: *(APPROACHING)* That's it ... we're ready. There are TIE fighters closing on us.

BEN: How close are we to the battle station?

HAN: At the rate they're hauling us toward that oversized ball bearing, they'll have us aboard it in no time.

BEN: You might as well leave the *Falcon*'s main hatch unlocked, or they'll simply blast their way in.

HAN: It's done.

BEN: Good. Did you make an entry in the ship's log?

HAN: Yeah, yeah, and I shot off a few escape pods, too. Think you're the only one who's ever conned Imperials? Now, if you don't mind, we're gonna have to continue this conversation in my private office. Hop in.

BEN: Indeed. I know how busy your schedule is, Captain.

Sound: Ben eases himself into the hold space.

HAN: In you go, Chewie, and hang on to your bowcaster. And the droid, what's your name ...

THREEPIO: See-Threepio, sir.

HAN: Just move it!

Sound: Chewie and Threepio get into hold space.

THREEPIO: Move over, Artoo!

ARTOO: BEEPS INDIGNANTLY.

HAN: You and me last, kid. Hope you remembered to stretch your legs a bit. We could be down there for a while.

LUKE: Uh, as a matter of fact ...

HAN: Forget it! Now hop in. Move over, Chewie.

Sound: Han and Luke hopping into hold space.

HAN: Just pull that deck plate into place over you. It'll seal and lock automatically.

Sound: The deck plates being dragged into place, locking with a hollow metallic clang. Ship's engines, etc., are muted, and the characters' voices reflect their confinement. Chewbacca's keening to himself softly. All are shifting and moving to try and find comfort.

HAN: Quit your griping, Chewie! And get yer toe outta my ear.

CHEWIE: BELCHES.

BEN: What's your estimate of our progress, Captain Solo?

HAN: They're probably clearing us through their outer defensive zones right about now. It looked like they had landing bays around the equator of that station. I'd guess they'll dock us there.

LUKE: What was all that about the escape pods and the ship's log?

HAN: I doctored the log to make it look like we abandoned ship in those pods right after liftoff and sent the *Falcon* along on automatics as a decoy.

LUKE: D' you think they'll believe it?

HAN: At first, maybe; these compartments are shielded and hidden pretty well.

Sound: Muffled clangs.

HAN: Okay! Here we go!

Sound: A loud clang reverberates through the ship.

BEN: That's it. We've been set down in a landing bay.

HAN: You guys keep your lightsabers handy. If they find us now, there'll be nothing to do but stand tall.

BEN: It will take a few moments for the pumps to replace the atmosphere in the docking bay, and then . . .

Sound: A clank and long whine of hydraulics as the ship's ramp is lowered with a thud.

HAN: Well, they got the ramp down. Quiet now!

Sound: A brief hiss.

HAN: *(WHISPERING)* That's the main hatch.

Sound: Boots overhead.

LUKE: *(WHISPERING)* Stormtroopers!

HAN: Shut up! One, two, three . . .

Sound: Steps continue.

CHEWIE: HOOTS SOFTLY.

HAN: Keep still! You're spoiling my count! Let's see . . .

Sound: Steps continue and fade.

HAN: I . . . I can't tell how many . . .

BEN: Six stormtroopers came onboard, and six have left.

HAN: *(SLIGHTLY LOUDER)* You've got good ears, old-timer.

LUKE: They bought it!

BEN: Yes, but we still . . .

LUKE: Ben! What's the matter? Are you all right?

BEN: Yes. Luke, I . . . recognized a presence just outside the ship. He's gone now, but his being here explains a good deal.

LUKE: Who was it?

HAN: Never mind that now! We've still got plenty of problems! Let's get outta here.

Sound: The deck plates being pushed aside and closed under as group starts to get up, their voices reflecting the difference.

LUKE: Boy, it's lucky you had these compartments!

HAN: What'd I tell you about luck, kid? Never thought I'd be smuggling *myself* in 'em, though. This is ridiculous! Even if I could take off again, I'd never get past that tractor beam.

BEN: Leave that to me.

HAN: Old fool . . . I knew you were going to say that.

BEN: Who's the more foolish, Captain Solo, the fool or the fool who follows him?

CHEWIE: YEOWLS A COMPLAINT.

HAN: It'll be okay, Chewie.

BEN: I assume they'll be sending a scanning crew onboard for a more thorough search and withdrew the stormtroopers so as not to confuse their instruments.

HAN: *(MOVING OFF)* I'll take a look.

Sound: He steps softly to the main hatch, then returns.

HAN: *(COMING ON, WHISPERING)* You called it. There's a two-man crew at the bottom of the ramp with an equipment case.

BEN: Hmmm. Then we'll have to . . .

HAN: Relax, this is *our* department. Get set, partner.

CHEWIE: SNARLS.

HAN: The rest of you get back out of sight!

Sound: The scanning crew comes up the ramp.

HAN: *(WHISPERING)* Chewie, here.

1ST CREWMAN: *(OFF)* Okay, set it down here.

2ND CREWMAN: *(OFF)* Watch your foot . . .

Sound: They set the cases down.

HAN: Evening, boys!

1ST CREWMAN: What? Who . . .

CHEWIE: SNARLS.

Sound: The two crewmen are slammed together, groaning and falling.

HAN: Sleep tight! Nice work, Chewie!

LUKE *(OFF)* You did it!

HAN: Stay where you are. There're two stormtroopers guarding the ramp. Hey, you guys down there!

1ST TROOPER: Huh?

HAN: Could you give us a hand for a minute? Our reciprocator's stuck in the optical refraction!

1ST TROOPER: *(COMING ON)* What's the problem . . . hey!

2ND TROOPER: Look out!

Sound: Concurrently, Han fires twice. Both troopers drop to deck.

HAN: Okay! Come on!

LUKE: You're really fast, Han.

HAN: Didn't I tell you it's better to count on a blaster than hokey religions and lightsabers?

LUKE: Now what?

BEN: In order to escape, we'll have to eliminate the tractor beam.

HAN: There's got to be a control office here in the docking bay. We're gonna have to get to it somehow.

BEN: The stormtroopers' armor . . . you won't be recognized in it.

HAN: What?

BEN: You'll be marching the rest of us ahead of you; we'll take them by surprise.

HAN: Now wait! This wasn't in the deal!

BEN: There's no telling when someone will come looking for these men. If we argue much—

HAN: Aw, for . . . all right. Help me get his armor off, Chewie!

Sound: Han and Chewie stripping off armor.

HAN: *(MUTTERING)* Whew! The things I do to stay in business!

BEN: Luke, you'll have to wear the other man's armor. It will be a bit large, but it will do.

LUKE: Right, Ben!

BEN: You stay behind, and if the command officer tries to contact his men by helmet comlink, step out from the end of the ramp and point to your transmitter to indicate that it's out of order.

Sound: Luke struggling into the armor.

LUKE: Where's the transmitter? Oh, right.

HAN: *(UNDER HELMET)* I hope yours took a bath once in a while, kid. This guy's armor smells like he lived in it!

Sound: Fade to silence.

Sound: Command office in background.

OFFICER: I don't see the sentries out there.

SOLDIER: Maybe the scanning crew found something aboard the captured ship, sir.

Sound: Snap of a comlink switch.

OFFICER: TX-four-two-one, why aren't you at your post? TX-four-two-one, do you copy? *(PAUSE)* Okay! There he is . . . he's pointing to his transmitter. Looks like we've got another bad comlink. *(MOVING OFF)* Take over here.

SOLDIER: Yes, sir.

OFFICER: I'll go and see what I can do.

Sound: A switch is thrown, and the door swoops up. A sudden ear-splitting yeowl from Chewie. The officer yells in pain.

HAN: Look out, Chewie!

Sound: Han fires, and the soldier screams, then drops to the floor.

HAN: Now let me get this stupid helmet off. See any more of 'em, old man?

BEN: *(COMING ON)* I think there were only these two. Luke, Threepio, Artoo, come in here quickly.

Sound: The doors slams down.

LUKE: You know, Han, between that Wookiee's howling and you blasting everything in sight . . . it's a wonder the whole station doesn't know we're here.

HAN: Bring 'em on! I'd prefer a straight fight to all this sneaking around!

ARTOO: *(OFF)* BEEPS A SIGNAL.

THREEPIO: *(OFF)* Artoo says he's found an outlet to the main computer, sir!

BEN: Excellent. Now, have Artoo plug into the outlet.

THREEPIO: Yes, sir!

BEN: His information-retrieval capacity should enable him to interpret the entire Imperial computer network.

Sound: Artoo bleeps as he activates readouts, data screens, etc.

THREEPIO: *(CALLING SLIGHTLY)* Artoo says he's found the main control to the tractor beam that's holding the *Millennium Falcon* here. He'll try to make the precise location appear on the monitor.

Sound: Monitor running through schemata and images at.high speed.

ARTOO: BLEEPS.

THREEPIO: *(CALLING SLIGHTLY)* That's it, there on the screen. Artoo says the tractor beam is coupled to the main reactor in seven locations. A power loss at any one of the terminals will deactivate the beam and allow us to leave.

BEN: Hmm. I don't think anyone else can help me with this particular job. I must go alone.

HAN: Whatever you say, old man. I've done more than I bargained for on this trip already.

LUKE: But Ben, I want to go with you!

BEN: Be patient, Luke. Stay here and watch over the droids.

LUKE: But Han and Chewbacca can—

BEN: Artoo and Threepio must be delivered safely or other star systems will suffer the same fate as Alderaan. Your destiny lies along a different path from mine . . . Captain Solo. Chewbacca. *(MOVING OFF)*

Sound: Power door swoops up.

BEN: The Force will be with you . . . always!

Sound: The doors hisses down.

CHEWIE: LOWS A DERISIVE COMMENT.

HAN: You said it, Chewie! Where did you dig up that old fossil, kid?

LUKE: Ben is a great man!

HAN: Yeah, great at getting us into trouble!

LUKE: I didn't hear you come up with any ideas . . .

HAN: Well, anything'd be better than just hanging around waiting for stormtroopers to pick us up!

LUKE: Who do you think got us this far—

ARTOO: BLEEPS URGENTLY, INTERRUPTING.

LUKE: Threepio, what is it? What's Artoo so excited about?

THREEPIO: I'm not quite sure, sir. He was searching the computer network, and now he keeps saying, "I've found her" and "She's here!"

LUKE: Well, who? Who's he found?

THREEPIO: Princess Leia, sir.

LUKE: The Princess? She's *here?*

HAN: Princess?

LUKE: Where? Where is she?

HAN: Princess? What's going on?

ARTOO: CHIRPS.

THREEPIO: Artoo says she's on level 5, detention block AA-23. He's mapped the location there on the screen. I'm afraid he says she's scheduled to be terminated, Master Luke.

LUKE: *Terminated?* Oh, no! We've got to do something!

HAN: What're you talking about?

LUKE: The Princess Leia of Alderaan . . . the droids belong to her. She's the one in the message . . . Oh, never mind . . . we've got to help her!

HAN: Now look, let's not get any funny ideas. The old man wants us to wait right here.

LUKE: But he didn't know *she* was here! We've got to figure out a way to get into the detention block!

HAN: I'm not going anywhere!

LUKE: They're going to execute her. Look, a few minutes ago you said you didn't want to just wait here to be captured, you wanted to do something.

HAN: Well, marching into the detention level is *not* what I had in mind!

LUKE: But they're going to kill her!

HAN: Better her than me!

LUKE: But . . . we can't let 'em do it! If you only knew her, Han. She's beautiful.

HAN: So's life!

LUKE: *(ENTICINGLY)* She's rich, Han.

CHEWIE: HOOTS, FORESEEING DISASTER.

HAN: Rich?

LUKE: Rich, powerful . . .

HAN: Wait a second. She was rich on Alderaan, but Alderaan ain't there anymore, remember? Who'd pay?

LUKE: The Rebel Alliance, that's who! And the Imperial Senate! And she's sole surviving heir to the off-world holdings of the Royal House of Alderaan! If you rescue her, the reward will be . . .

HAN: What?

LUKE: Well, more than *you* can imagine!

HAN: Don't bet on it. I can imagine quite a bit!

LUKE: You'll get it!

HAN: I'd better! What about the droids?

LUKE: They'll be all right here. We've got to save the Princess . . . she's more important right now!

HAN: What's your plan?

LUKE: Uh . . . Threepio, hand me that pair of wrist binders over there, will you?

THREEPIO: Yes, sir!

Sound: The clank of wrist binders.

LUKE: Thanks.

HAN: What're you gonna do with a pair of cuffs?

LUKE: Okay now, I'm going to put these wrist binders on Chewbacca, and—

CHEWIE: AN EMPHATIC SNARL THAT NO, HE WON'T, EITHER.

LUKE: Ah, right. Han, y-you put them on him.

HAN: *(LAUGHING)* Don't worry, Chewie, I think I know what he's got in mind. Get your helmet, kid.

CHEWIE: SNUFFLES A BIT.

Sound: The binders close on his wrists.

LUKE: Threepio, use that handheld comlink to keep in touch with us. Let's go.

THREEPIO: Master Luke, sir! Pardon me for asking, but what are Artoo and I supposed to do if we're discovered here?

LUKE: *(OFF)* Lock the door!

Sound: The door hisses up.

HAN: *(CALLING)* And hope they don't have blasters.

THREEPIO: *(CALLING)* That isn't very reassuring!

Music: In.

Sound: The door slams down. All sound out.

Sound: Various military personnel and automata.

HAN: How long are we gonna have to wait for these lift tubes?

LUKE: They should be here soon. *(PAUSE)* This helmet's too big for me. I can't see a thing in it!

Sound: Doors swishing open.

HAN: Here they are. In you go, Chewie!

Sound: They step into tube.

2ND OFFICER: *(APPROACHING)* Hold that car!

HAN: Uh, sorry, sir, we've got a prisoner here. You'll have to take the next car. Regulations, y' know.

2ND OFFICER: Oh. Very well . . .

Sound: The doors close. The lift hums as it drops them quickly.

LUKE: Nice work, Han.

HAN: I can't get these binders to stay closed on Chewie's wrists. This isn't gonna work.

LUKE: Why didn't you say so before?

HAN: I did say so before!

LUKE: Okay. We're here.

Sound: Doors slide open.

LUKE: Let's go.

3RD OFFICER: *(OFF)* Just stop right there, you two! Where do you think you're taking this . . . *thing*?

CHEWIE: GROWLS AT THE SLIGHT.

LUKE: Uh, prisoner transfer from detention block 1138.

3RD OFFICER: Well, nobody notified me, and *I'm* the duty officer here. *(MOVING BACK)* I'll have to clear it.

Sound: Switch is thrown.

3RD OFFICER: *(OFF)* This is detention block AA-23, duty officer speaking. Put me through to the detention level commander.

LUKE: *(WHISPERING)* They're not going for it.

3RD OFFICER: Sir, we have an irregularity here. There's apparently been a foul-up on a prisoner transfer . . . that's right, sir . . . yes, I'll hold.

HAN: *(WHISPERING)* There're only three guards and the duty officer. Chewie, you grab my rifle and make it look like you're making a break. Go!

CHEWIE: ABRUPTLY ROARS.

HAN: Look out! He's got my rifle!

LUKE: He's loose! He'll tear us all apart!

Sound: All three begin shooting. Alarmed cries from the guards: "That thing's loose," "look out," etc., and shouts of pain.

HAN: Shoot out the camera eye!

LUKE: Get the officer before he sounds an alarm!

3RD OFFICER: Fire back, you fools!

Sound: A firefight breaks out, blasts originating from both up close and distant. Chewie howls, and blaster bolts go back and forth, drawing more cries from the guards as they crash to the floor. Finally the guards are silenced and the firing dies away, leaving only the wail of an alarm.

HAN: Shoot out that last camera eye! Let's get these helmets off. *(VOICE NORMAL)* It really stinks in there!

Sound: Luke blasts the alarm. The commo console is spewing demands.

CONSOLE VOICE: Detention level AA–23, what's happening? What's going on there? *(CONTINUES UNDER:)*

LUKE: *(VOICE NORMAL)* I got the camera eye . . . do something about that alarm!

HAN: *(MOVING OFF)* Why'd he have to pick an alarm switch to die on? Stupid officers . . .

Sound: The alarm stops, but the console demands continue.

HAN: Now, we'd better find out which cell this Princess of yours is in. Here we go . . . cell number 21–8–7. You go get her, kid, and I'll try to keep a lid on things here.

LUKE: *(MOVING OFF)* I'll be right back!

HAN: I hope! Let's have a little peace and quiet here . . .

Sound: A switch being thrown.

HAN: Ahem. This is detention level . . . uh . . . AA–23. Ah, everything is under control down here. Situation, uh, normal.

CONSOLE VOICE: What's going on? What's happened?

HAN: We had a slight, um, weapons malfunction, but, uh, everything's perfectly all right now. We're fine, we're all fine here now, thank you. Um, how are you?

CONSOLE VOICE: We're sending a squad to your location!

HAN: Oh, negative, negative. We had a, a reactor leak here. Give us a few minutes to lock it down. Large leak . . . very dangerous.

CONSOLE VOICE: Who is this? What's your operating number?

HAN: Um . . . ah . . .

CHEWIE: GROWLS SOFTLY.

HAN: *(WHISPERING)* Good idea.

Sound: He blasts the console, which sputters and sizzles.

HAN: Boring conversation, anyway. *(PAUSE)* Let's hope the kid moves fast, Chewie. We're gonna have company!

Music: Up and under:

LUKE: *(BREATHING HARD)* . . . .eight-five, eight-six . . . twenty-one-eight-seven! This is it!

Sound: He pushes control button, the cell door slides up.

LEIA: *(OFF, AWAKENED)* Well? What do you want?

LUKE: Ah, um . . .

LEIA: Aren't you a little short for a stormtrooper?

LUKE: Huh? Oh, the uniform . . . I'm Luke Skywalker! I'm here to rescue you!

LEIA: You're . . . *you're what?*

LUKE: Here to rescue you! I've got your R2 unit . . . I'm here with Ben Kenobi!

LEIA: *(COMING ON)* Ben Kenobi? Where is he?

Sound: An explosion off.

LUKE: No time to explain! Come on!

Sound: Blaster fired off.

HAN: *(OFF)* Luke! Get back! *(COMING ON)* The stormtroopers blew the door, and we couldn't hold 'em! We can't get out this way! In here, quick!

Sound: Blaster bolts.

LEIA: Looks like we just lost our only escape route!

HAN: Maybe you'd prefer to stay here in your cell, Your Highness?

CHEWIE: GROWLS IRRITABLY.

LUKE: I'll try to raise Threepio on the comlink!

Sound: He flicks the comlink on.

LUKE: Hello, Threepio? See-Threepio?

THREEPIO: *(OVER COMLINK)* Yes, Master Luke?

LUKE: We've been cut off in the detention block! Is there any other way out of the cell bay?

THREEPIO: I'll check with Artoo.

ARTOO: WHISTLES OVER COMLINK IN BACKGROUND.

LUKE: What was that? I didn't copy!

THREEPIO: Artoo says all systems have been alerted to your presence, sir! The entrance to the detention block seems to be the only way in or out . . . all other information on your level is restricted . . . Oh! Sir, there are stormtroopers pounding on the door up here!

Sound: The comlink clicks as Threepio signs off.

LUKE: Threepio? Threepio?

Sound: He clicks off the comlink. Blaster bolts are still flying.

LUKE: There's no other way out of here!

LEIA: This is some rescue! When you came in here, didn't you have a plan for getting out?

CHEWIE: BARKS THAT HE'S OFFENDED.

HAN: The *kid* is the brains, sweetheart! We just drive the bus!

LUKE: I, that is . . .

LEIA: You, Luke, give me your blaster.

Sound: She grabs it and fires at the wall.

HAN: What are you blasting the wall for?

LEIA: Somebody has to save our skins! I've opened a hole to the garbage chute. Here's your gun, Luke . . . catch!

Sound: She tosses the gun to Luke and goes into the refuse duct, her voice echoing on:

LEIA: Follow me, flyboy!

HAN: She's crazy! But . . . okay, Chewie, you're next!

CHEWIE: OBJECTS IN A TORRENT OF GROWLS.

HAN: Get in that garbage chute, you big, furry oaf! Move, I said! I don't care what you smell!

CHEWIE: BALKS.

HAN: Oh you *won't*, huh?

Sound: A solid kick and Chewie's hoot echoing down the chute.

HAN: Wonderful girl you dragged us after, kid! Either I'm going to kill her or I'm beginning to like her! Get goin'!

LUKE: HOOTS. *(ECHOING DOWN THE CHUTE.)*

HAN: Look ooooooooout . . .

Sound: Intense fire.

Music: Up and under:

Sound: Wading in muck. Symphony of coughing and retching.

LUKE: Princess. *(CHOKES)*

HAN: BELCHES.

LEIA: Are you all right, Luke? I can't see a thing!

HAN: A garbage dump! Wonderful idea, Your Highness!

Sound: He struggles up under:

HAN: What an incredible smell! *(COUGHING)*

CHEWIE: GROWLS IN DISGUST.

Sound: Han wading through the swill.

HAN: Where's my blaster? I'm getting outta here! Chewie, get away from that door!

LEIA: No! Don't do that!

LUKE: Wait! Han!

Sound: Han fires, and the bolt begins ricocheting around the room.

HAN: Ricochet! Heads down!

Sound: Splish-splashing as they dive for cover. The ricocheting finally stops. Luke splashes up angrily.

LUKE: Will you forget it? The room's magnetically sealed!

LEIA: Put that thing away before you get us all killed!

HAN: Oh, absolutely, Your Worship! Look, I had everything under control until you led us down here! Y' know, it's not gonna take them long to figure out what happened to us!

LEIA: It could be worse.

Sound: A loud ferocious bellow echoes through the room.

HAN: It's worse!

LUKE: There's something alive in here!

LEIA: Can you see anything? There's not much light . . .

HAN: It's your imagination.

Sound: Small, rippling sounds in the swill.

LUKE: Hey! Something just brushed past my leg!

Sound: Another swirl.

LUKE: Look! Did you see that . . . tentacle or something?

HAN: Where?

CHEWIE: WHIMPER.

LUKE: Something's grabbed my—

Sound: Luke is yanked under the water.

HAN: Luke! Luke!

Sound: Han thrashes the water, searching. Luke suddenly breaks the surface, choking and barely able to speak.

LEIA: Luke! Grab hold of something!

LUKE: *(STRANGLING)* It's choking me! Shoot it, will you! My gun's jammed!

HAN: Where?

LUKE: *Anywhere!*

Sound: Han fires two or three times.

LUKE: *(SCREAMING)* Ah . . .

Sound: He's cut off as he's drawn under again.

CHEWIE: HOWLS.

HAN: Luke! Kid!

Sound: Han wades around for a moment as silence descends. Then the room resounds with a metallic booming of giant push rods locking into place.

LEIA: What . . .

Sound: Luke breaks the surface again, coughing and spitting.

LEIA: Grab him! Don't let go!

Sound: Splashing and flailing as Luke is pulled to his feet.

LEIA: What happened?

LUKE: I don't know. One minute that . . . whatever it was, had me, and the next, it just let go of me and disappeared.

LEIA: That booming sound must have scared it, but I don't understand . . .

Sound: Machinery being activated.

HAN: I've got a very bad feeling about this . . .

Sound: Machinery begins to whir and grind, and the walls rumble.

CHEWIE: HOWLS IN FRIGHT.

LUKE: The walls . . . they're moving!

HAN: They're closing! I don't believe this. We're inside a *compactor*!

LEIA: We'll be crushed! Try and brace the walls with something!

Sound: As the machinery grinds, Chewie and the others scavenge frantically in the muck for braces, etc.

Music: Up and under:

NARRATOR: Luke, Leia, Han, and Chewbacca can find no escape; elsewhere on the Death Star, Threepio and Artoo are in the hands of Imperial stormtroopers and Ben Kenobi continues his lone mission. And if they fail, if they die, the galaxy will come permanently under the yoke of the Empire.

Music: Closing theme up and under preview and closing credits.

ANNOUNCER: CLOSING CREDITS.

EPISODE ELEVEN:

"THE JEDI NEXUS"

C A S T :

Ben	Vader
Luke	Tarkin
Leia	Comm Voice
Han	1st Trooper
Chewbacca	2nd Trooper
Threepio	3rd Trooper
Artoo	

ANNOUNCER: OPENING CREDITS.

Music: Opening theme.

NARRATOR: A long time ago in a galaxy far, far away, there came a time of revolution, when Rebels united to challenge a tyrannical Empire.

Sound: Death Star up in background.

NARRATOR: Now many strands in the web of galactic events have come together onboard the Empire's ultimate weapon, an enormous spacegoing fortress called the Death Star. At large in its vast interior, pursued by Imperial stormtroopers, is a strange assortment of Rebels: Luke Skywalker, and his droids, Artoo-Detoo and See-Threepio; the Princess Leia Organa; and the veteran Jedi Knight Ben Kenobi. Allied with them by necessity are Captain Han Solo of the *Millennium Falcon* and his copilot, Chewbacca, a pair of reckless smugglers. And arrayed against these seven are the powers of a determined and merciless Empire and its most feared agent, Darth Vader.

Sound: Conference room up in background. Vader's respirator.

VADER: I tell you, Governor Tarkin, he *is* here!

TARKIN: Obi-Wan Kenobi? What makes you think so, Vader?

VADER: I sensed his aura clinging to that starship we captured, a tremor in the Force. The last time I felt it was in the presence of my old master.

TARKIN: If there is anyone on that starship, the scanning crew will detect them. But surely Kenobi must be dead by now!

VADER: Do not underestimate the power of the Force. Kenobi is a

Jedi Knight and can use it superlatively well. He can, therefore, do things that would seem impossible to ordinary men, men who understand only their machines and the things they can see and touch.

TARKIN: Men like me; is this what you're implying? I tell you, the Jedi are extinct. Their fire has gone out of the universe, as you should well know, having brought that about. You, my friend, are all that's left of their religion.

VADER: I think not.

TARKIN: Enough! When we captured that starship, I thought the Princess Leia might still be of use to us in locating the Rebel base, but since the ship appears to be empty, her reprieve is canceled. I'm going to have her executed at—

Sound: He's interrupted by the comlink. A switch is heard.

TARKIN: Well? What is it?

COMM VOICE: Governor Tarkin, we have an alert in detention block AA-23. It seems the Princess has escaped somehow. We're not quite sure yet . . .

TARKIN: The Princess! Put all sections on alert! Locate her and any other Rebels at once!

Sound: He snaps off the comlink.

VADER: Obi-Wan Kenobi *is* here. The Force is with him!

TARKIN: If you're right, he will not be allowed to escape.

VADER: Escape may not be his plan. Still, the other Rebels can be of use to us in the manner we discussed. I suggest you make the necessary arrangements at once.

TARKIN: And General Kenobi?

VADER: Patterns are emerging that have great meaning for the Jedi. This is a nexus of events brought about by the Force itself. I must face Obi-Wan Kenobi alone.

Music: Up and under:

3RD TROOPER: One of the duty crew's been shot! The other's been knocked cold!

2ND TROOPER: A couple of you get them down to sick bay!

Sound: Bodies being carried out as trooper snaps on console.

1ST TROOPER: Patch me through to the security commander.

Sound: A clicking.

COMM VOICE: What's your situation there?

2ND TROOPER: Sir, we're in the command office overlooking the captured starship. The scanning crewmen on the ship were knocked unconscious, and the guards have been shot.

COMM VOICE: Any sign of the Rebels?

2ND TROOPER: None, sir.

COMM VOICE: Check the place out thoroughly, then search the area!

2ND TROOPER: Yes, sir!

Sound: Com-patch clicks off.

2ND TROOPER: All right, let's check this place over top to bottom!

3RD TROOPER: There's a storage locker over here!

2ND TROOPER: Stand back, men! Okay . . . open it!

Sound: The locker door slides open.

2ND TROOPER: What the . . .

THREEPIO: *(FROM LOCKER)* Oh! They're madmen! They broke in and attacked the duty crew and locked us in here!

ARTOO: WHISTLES EARNESTLY.

THREEPIO: They're headed for the prison level! If you hurry, you might still catch them!

2ND TROOPER: You, stay on the console and report that!

1ST TROOPER: *(OFF)* Will do!

2ND TROOPER: The rest of you, follow me!

THREEPIO: Come along, Artoo.

1ST TROOPER: *(OFF)* Where're you two going?

THREEPIO: Oh, er . . .

ARTOO: WHISTLES.

THREEPIO: Yes, that's it . . . All this excitement has overrun the circuits in my counterpart here.

ARTOO: COMPLAINS ELABORATELY.

THREEPIO: If you don't mind, sir, I'd like to take him down to maintenance.

1ST TROOPER: *(OFF)* Oh. All right.

ARTOO: SIGNALS QUICKLY.

THREEPIO: What? Oh, the handheld comlink!

Sound: Threepio snatches it off a control bank.

THREEPIO: Got it!

1ST TROOPER: *(OFF)* What's that, droid?

THREEPIO: Nothing, sir. Nothing! Come on, Artoo!

Music: Up and under:

THREEPIO: Well, Master Luke and the others don't seem to have made it back here to the docking bay yet. Something must have happened to them.

ARTOO: WHISTLES.

THREEPIO: How should I know? Is there another computer outlet around here anywhere?

ARTOO: SIGNALS.

THREEPIO: Good! Plug into the network and see if they've been captured.

Sound: Artoo extends his adapter arm and works at the outlet.

THREEPIO: Hurry!

ARTOO: BEEPS.

THREEPIO: Well, thank goodness they haven't been found, anyway. But where could they be?

ARTOO: BEEPS A SUGGESTION.

THREEPIO: Use the comlink? Oh! I'd forgotten I'd turned it off before.

Sound: Click of the comlink being turned on.

THREEPIO: Are you there, Master Luke?

LUKE: *(OVER COMLINK)* Threepio?

THREEPIO: Yes, sir. We've had some problems . . .

LUKE: *(INTERRUPTING)* Will you shut up and listen to me? We're stuck in a garbage compactor, and it's closing in on us! Shut down all the trash-masters on the detention level, do you copy? Shut down all the garbage mashers on the detention level! We're going to be crushed!

ARTOO: BEEPS.

Sound: Artoo working at the computer outlet.

THREEPIO: No, no, Artoo. Shut them all down! Hurry!

ARTOO: SIGNALS.

THREEPIO: They're dying down there! Oh, curse this metal body. I wasn't fast enough! It's all my fault! My poor master . . . eh?

Sound: Crackle of the comlink.

LUKE: Threepio, we're all right. It's stopped! We're all right! You did great!

THREEPIO: Oh! They're alive, Artoo!

ARTOO: WHISTLES HAPPILY.

LUKE: Now, you have to let us out of here. Open pressure maintenance hatch on unit number . . . *(ASIDE)* . . . where are we? Three-two-six-eight-two-seven.

THREEPIO: Three-two-six-eight-two-seven. Have you got that, Artoo?

ARTOO: BLEEPS.

Sound: More of Artoo's maneuvering at the computer.

LUKE: That's it! Now wait near the ship; we'll meet you there!

THREEPIO: Yes, sir!

Sound: Comlink snaps off.

THREEPIO: Come along, Artoo!

Music: Up and under:

Sound: Luke and company stripping off armor.

HAN: I figured for a while there that we were all gonna be a whole lot thinner. I never thought those droids'd pull it off!

LUKE: And you said you hate machinery that talks back!

HAN: No more. Okay, dump the armor over there but hang on to your belt . . . it's got survival gear on it.

Sound: Armor tossed aside.

HAN: Now we can get out of here . . . *if* we can just avoid any more female advice. C'mon, Chewie . . .

LEIA: *(INTERRUPTING) Listen!* I don't know who you are or where you came from, but from now on you do as *I* tell you, understand?

HAN: Now look, Your Worshipfulness, let's get one thing straight! I take orders from one person . . . me!

LEIA: Well, then, it's a wonder you're still alive. Now, will somebody get this big walking carpet out of my way.

HAN: No reward is worth this! After you, Your Highness!

Music: Up and under:

HAN: There's the *Falcon*, down there!

CHEWIE: GROWLS WITH DELIGHT.

HAN: Me, too, Chewie!

Sound: Snap of the comlink.

LUKE: Threepio, hello. Do you copy?

THREEPIO: *(OVER COMLINK)* For the moment, Master Luke. Artoo and I are directly across the hangar from the ship.

LUKE: We're on the level right above you. Stand by.

LEIA: You mean to tell me that you flew here in *that* old relic? You're braver than I thought!

HAN: Nice, isn't she! C'mon.

1ST TROOPER: *(OFF)* There they are!

HAN: Uh oh! Stormtroopers! Let 'em have it, Chewie!

1ST TROOPER: Fall back, fall back!

HAN: Keep 'em running, Chewie!

CHEWIE: GROWLS FEROCIOUSLY.

HAN: *(CALLING)* You two run for the ship!

LUKE: *(OFF)* Han!

LEIA: *(OFF)* Come back!

LUKE: Come on, Princess.

Sound: Han and Chewie continue firing on the troopers, yelling, running, and whooping. Suddenly the return fire becomes more intense and focused.

HAN: *(PANTING)* They're coming back!

CHEWIE: HOOTS IN APPREHENSION.

HAN: Let's get out of here! Up ahead! They're closing those blast doors!

CHEWIE: HOWLS.

HAN: Move it! Gotta make those doors . . . 'fore they close! C'mon, Chewie!

Music: Up and under:

Sound: Door clangs shut.

HAN: Hold . . . hold it . . . . *(BREATHING HARD)* We gotta shoot . . . the lock!

Sound: The firing of their blasters and sputtering of circuitry.

HAN: *(STILL PANTING)* Hah! Whichever . . . of those geniuses back there . . . thought of having the blast doors . . . shut ain't gettin' a . . . promotion for it!

CHEWIE: HOWLS GLEEFULLY.

HAN: *(MORE NORMALLY)* Listen, I think we can work our way around to the ship. That squeak was too close for me. If we get back to 'er, I say we make a break right away, whether the rest of them are there or not!

CHEWIE: GROWLS FIERCELY.

HAN: C'mon, we don't owe nobody nothin'! Nobody but us, that is! Did *they* care about *us* when they dragged us into this crazy deal?

CHEWIE: SNARLS DUBIOUSLY.

HAN: So why should we stick around and maybe get burned down for them? One chance to get out of here with our skins may be all we *get*, Chewie!

CHEWIE: GROWLS.

HAN: Ah, you big softy! You're gonna ruin our reputations. All right, let's get back first and see what happens from there. *(MOV-ING OFF)* But whatever those Rebels offer us for getting that Princess back, I want at least twice as much . . .

CHEWIE: LOWS CONSOLATION.

Music: Up.

Sound: Death Star background up.

LEIA: Are those stormtroopers still out in the corridor?

LUKE: I'll take another look. *(HIS VOICE STRAINS AS HE LOOKS)* Yep. *(PULLS BACK)* But they're not heading this way. I think they're guarding that junction down there.

LEIA: They're between us and the ship. We'll have to find a way around them.

LUKE: We're safe enough in this utility compartment for now. If we wait a minute or two, they may be ordered away to chase Han and Chewie. If not, we can always duck out and try another route.

LEIA: I suppose you're right. *(BEAT)* Luke, how did you get involved in all this?

LUKE: *(LAUGHS)* It's sort of complicated; Artoo wound up at our farm back on Tatooine. I found your message when I was cleaning him up. Artoo ran off to find Ben, and I followed him, but Ben found us instead. We hired Han to bring us to Alderaan . . . I mean . . . that is . . .

LEIA: And when you got here, Alderaan was gone, destroyed.

LUKE: You know about that?

LEIA: I was forced to watch it happen to my family . . .

LUKE: I'm so sorry . . .

LEIA: The important thing now is to see that it never happens again . . . Listen!

LEIA: *(WHISPERING)* They're coming this way!

LUKE: *(WHISPERING)* Quick, get over beside the door!

LEIA: *(WHISPERING)* Are they gone?

LUKE: *(WHISPERING)* I'll check. *(CROSSING)* Yeah, probably after Han and Chewbacca. And the corridor junction looks clear.

LEIA: Then we'd better go! Do you remember the way?

LUKE: I think so . . .

2ND TROOPER: *(OFF)* You there!

LUKE: What . . . ?

2ND TROOPER: Stand where you are!

LUKE: *(MOVING OFF)* Run! C'mon, quick!

Sound: They take off as blaster bolts come at them and cries of "Halt!" etc., come from distance.

LUKE: *(COMING ON)* Around that turn to the right! I'll try and slow 'em down!

Sound: Luke fires back as they run.

LEIA: *(SHOUTING)* Which way, Luke?

LUKE: *(SHOUTING)* Next right! Up that ramp!

Sound: Shooting up.

LEIA: *(PANTING)* Luke . . . *stop*!

LUKE: Whoooooooooooa . . . *(PANTING)*

LUKE: *(DEEP ECHO)* Where d' you think we are?

LEIA: This must be the central core shaft! There's no way across!

LUKE: I think we took a wrong turn . . .

Sound: Troopers start firing in far background.

LEIA: We can't go back. They're blocking our way!

LUKE: Shut the hatchway! Quick!

Sound: A click, and the hatchway hisses shut and mutes the blaster fire.

LEIA: There's no lock!

LUKE: I'll shoot the hatch controls! Stand back!

Sound: Luke fires, the controls explode.

LUKE: That oughta hold it for a while.

LEIA: But not for long. We've got to find the control that extends the bridgeway across the shaft!

LUKE: Uh, I think I may've just blasted it . . .

Sound: An ominous sizzling.

LEIA: They're trying to burn their way through the hatch!

LUKE: Sounds like they might succeed. You'd better stand off to one side, Princess, out of the line of fire. I'll try and hold them off.

LEIA: Luke, *no!* There must be some other way!

LUKE: None that I can see . . .

Sound: A blaster bolt, then another.

LEIA: Look out!

LUKE: What . . .

LEIA: Up there, across the shaft! More troopers!

LUKE: Just what we needed . . . wait! That's it! My belt!

Music: In and under:

LEIA: Belt?

LUKE: I took it off a stormtrooper . . . Look, it's got a grappling hook on it! We'll *swing* across the shaft!

Sound: More bolts explode around them.

LUKE: Here, take the blaster and keep them busy!

Sound: The weapon being passed and Leia beginning to fire.

LUKE: *(SHOUTING)* Now, let's just hope the hook's strong enough . . .

Sound: Luke's working at it.

LUKE: . . . and there's enough line on the spool.

LEIA: *(SHOUTING)* But where—

Sound: She's interrupted by incoming bolts and fires a few shots:

LEIA: —where will you secure it?

LUKE: *(SHOUTING)* Those outlet clusters up in the shaft . . . there.

Sound: The line whistles as Luke whirls it in a circle.

LUKE: Here goes!

LUKE: HOOTS.

LEIA: Luke, they're getting the hatch open!

LUKE: The hook caught! We're in business. Grab hold of me, tightly.

LEIA: Wait . . .

Sound: She kisses him.

LUKE: W-what'd you kiss me for?

LEIA: For luck!

LUKE: Hang on!

Music: Up.

LUKE/LEIA: LAUGHTER AND CHEERING.

LUKE: We made it!

LEIA: Now what?

LUKE: Lemme get rid of this line . . .

LEIA: How do we get to the ship from here?

LUKE: There's a service hatch down there, if I remember, to the left . . . come on . . .

Sound: Cross-fade to:

LUKE: *(PANTING)* Come on . . . here it is. *(PANTING)*

Sound: The hatch slides up.

LEIA: Oh! There's the ship! I take back everything I said about her!

LUKE: And there're Han and Chewbacca.

HAN: *(COMING ON)* What kept you? Me and Chewie were thinking of starting the party without you!

CHEWIE: SNARLS.

LEIA: We ran into some old friends.

LUKE: Is the ship all right? Where's Ben?

HAN: The *Falcon* seems okay, and the droids are right over there. Haven't seen the old man, though. Let's just hope he put that tractor beam out of commission and he's on his way back.

LEIA: But that still leaves all those stormtroopers in the hangar to worry about.

HAN: Yeah, we've been trying to figure out an angle on that.

LUKE: What about the hangar-bay doors?

HAN: I'm counting on 'em still being on auto. They should open when the *Falcon* gets to 'em.

LEIA: But the stormtroopers . . .

HAN: We won't get another chance like this. If nothing changes in the next few minutes, we're gonna have to take them on!

LUKE: What about Ben?

CHEWIE: HOOTS.

HAN: We can't do a job on everybody in the garrison, Luke! If he's not back by the time we go, tough luck.

LUKE: But . . .

HAN: Look, you do what you want! Me and Chewie are giving it a couple more minutes, and then we're gonna make a break for the ship.

Sound: Fade to silence.

Music: Vader's theme.

Sound: Death Star corridors. Vader's respirator up.

BEN: Darth Vader!

VADER: I've been waiting for you, Obi-Wan Kenobi!

Sound: Vader's lightsaber flares on.

VADER: We meet again at last. The circle is now complete. . . . When I left you, I was but the learner . . . now *I* am the Master.

Sound: Ben's saber activates. Vader's steps halt.

BEN: Only a master of evil, Darth.

VADER: Have you finished whatever petty errand it is that brings you here? The tractor beam, perhaps?

BEN: I have deactivated it, yes.

VADER: Little good that will do you, Obi-Wan! Ready?

BEN: Ready.

Sound: Vader's saber flashes and Ben's answers. Ben's breathing, Vader's respiration. The match goes on with starts and stops, rapid fencing alternating with feinting and circling. The sabers hiss and crackle as they clash, spit and ripple as they slide along one another, and hum and moan eerily. Then they separate for a moment.

VADER: Your powers are weak, old man!

BEN: You can't win, Darth. If you strike me down, I shall become more powerful than you can possibly imagine.

Sound: They engage again, then withdraw.

VADER: Why don't you stand your ground? Patterns of the Force have reached a nexus! Do you think you can retreat all the way into the hangar? You've learned fear in your old age.

BEN: A Jedi never forgets how to die, Darth.

LUKE: *(OFF)* Ben!

Sound: They duel again. Then disengage.

LUKE: Ben!

VADER: Why do you glance aside, Obi-Wan? Your young friends? You will have to forget them . . . your life is over!

LUKE: Ben!

BEN: *That* rests with the Force.

Sound: Ben's saber moans as he brings it up in a final salute.

VADER: Why do you salute? . . . Obi-Wan?

LUKE: *(OFF)* Ben! Defend yourself!

LEIA: *(OFF)* Come on, Luke! Run for the ship! It's too late!

Sound: Vader's saber cuts the air. Ben's robes rustle to the deck, and his saber clatters.

LUKE: *(OFF)* Noooooo! Nooooo! No! No!

BEN: *(DISEMBODIED)* Run, Luke! Run!

VADER: What's this? His robes . . . empty!

Sound: Luke begins blasting at the troopers.

HAN: *(OFF)* Luke! Come on, kid! Quick!

Sound: The Falcon's engines begin to roar under:

VADER: So, that was Obi-Wan's intent . . . a diversionary tactic! A fool's sacrifice! They made their escape . . . and now they think they've won!

Sound: The Millennium Falcon's engine rises, reverberating, overriding all background noise.

BEN: *(DISEMBODIED)* By striking me down, you've made me more powerful than you can possibly imagine!

Sound: Fade to silence.

Sound: The Falcon's forward compartment, the engines rumbling.

LEIA: Luke?

LUKE: He just stood there, Leia. Just stood there and let himself be cut down . . .

LEIA: Oh, Luke! I can't begin . . .

LUKE: Why wouldn't he defend himself?

LEIA: I can't explain it to you, Luke. The Jedi lead their lives according to what they believe the Force demands of them, and it's not always something the rest of us can understand.

LUKE: But . . . that still doesn't . . .

LEIA: I know that Ben must have had some reason, some overriding purpose in allowing Darth Vader to take his life.

LUKE: *Vader?* That was *Vader* who killed him?

LEIA: Yes, he's the Emperor's personal agent. He's the one who's been trying to recover the plans of the Death Star—

Sound: Luke's fists smash down on the table.

LUKE: Vader killed my father! Vader helped wipe out the Jedi, and Vader's troops killed my uncle and aunt!

LEIA: Luke, Luke, calm d—

LUKE: Vader's taken away everything I ever had! And I ran from him. Don't you understand that? *Vader took away everything I ever had!*

LEIA: Everthing I had, too, Luke.

LUKE: . . . Alderaan, your whole world, destroyed . . . How can you live with that? How do you go on?

LEIA: You find a purpose, to justify the sacrifice.

LUKE: Like Ben did.

LEIA: Yes. Mine's to stop Vader and Tarkin and the Empire. I think that's . . . worthwhile. What about you?

LUKE: Yes . . . yes, I do, too. It's just that Ben seemed like he'd always be there, you know? Like he was one thing that wouldn't change. I . . .

LEIA: What, Luke?

LUKE: I even thought I heard him. After he was cut down, I thought I heard him. I was shooting at the stormtroopers, and . . . and all of a sudden it was as if Ben was at my shoulder. Like when he was teaching me to use the lightsaber . . . he wasn't in my line of vision, but he was *there!* Talking to me!

LEIA: We were all calling to you; you probably mistook—

LUKE: I heard you! And Han! But this was *Ben!* He said, "Run,

Luke, run!" And . . . I did. *(PAUSE)* I can't believe he's gone; I just can't believe it.

LEIA: There was nothing you could've done, Luke!

HAN: *(APPROACHING)* C'mon, buddy, we've got work to do! We're not out of this yet.

LUKE: Huh?

HAN: We'll be coming up on their sentry ships in a minute . . . We'll have to take 'em head-on. I'd rather have live gunners in the turrets than trust computers.

LUKE: What do you want me to do?

HAN: Chewie's flying, and I'm taking the top gun turret. I want you to man the belly guns.

LUKE: Ummm . . .

HAN: Look, I'd love to chat all day, but we've got a date with those Imperial TIE fighters.

LUKE: Oh, sure.

HAN: As for you, Your Wonderfulness, Chewie could use a hand in the cockpit right about now.

LEIA: I'll do what I can, *Captain.*

HAN: I'm sure you will, sweetheart! Well, Chewie doesn't like to be kept waiting . . .

Sound: She goes.

HAN: Save us from princesses! Okay, you ever fire a quad-gun mount before?

LUKE: Oh, well, I . . .

HAN: Luke!

LUKE: No!

HAN: Well, it's simple. The servos and targeting instrumentation are all standard. Don't rely on your computer alone; eyeball it once in a while.

LUKE: If you say so.

HAN: Just climb down the ladder into the belly turret and shoot anything that's not *us*. Clear enough for you?

LUKE: Right!

HAN: Off you go. When you're in, put on your headset and we'll run you through a couple of test traverses!

LUKE: I'm on my way.

Sound: Cross-fade to:

HAN: *(OVER COMM)* You in, kid?

LUKE: Yeah.

Sound: Luke throws switches, gun servos begin to whine.

HAN: Okay, take the firing grips and get the feel.

Sound: The quad-mount whines back and forth.

HAN: Run 'em top to bottom and left to right. Make sure the tracking servos answer properly.

Sound: The guns traverse.

LUKE: Um, feels okay.

HAN: Got your targeting computer engaged?

LUKE: Uh . . .

Sound: Another switch thrown, followed by active beeping of computer.

LUKE: . . . of course!

HAN: Good. Your sensors'll give you an audio simulation for a rough idea of where those fighters are when they're not on your screen. It'll sound like they're right there in the turret with you.

LUKE: Got it.

HAN: And I don't care what the tracking compensators say . . . *lead* your targets! Invest in the future.

Music: Softly under and building.

LEIA: *(OVER COMM)* We've got four TIE fighters on the screens, closing fast.

HAN: Check; you never did anything like this before, Luke?

LUKE: I . . . no.

HAN: I oughta be charging you for vocational training.

LUKE: Look, I can do it!

HAN: Sure, sure. It's nursery school stuff.

LEIA: *(OVER COMM)* The fighters are breaking! They're almost on us!

HAN: Stay sharp, Luke!

LEIA: Here they come!

Sound: The wail of a TIE fighter comes in and past. The Falcon *shudders.*

HAN: *Hit 'em!*

Sound: Luke's quad-mount fires, cannon barrels slamming away in alternating pairs, servos whining.

LUKE: Missed!

Sound: More firing. A fighter swoops by, and another comes in. The starship rattles.

HAN: One coming your way!

Sound: Luke's servos whir.

LUKE: Where . . .

Sound: A TIE fighter screams in.

LUKE: I see him!

Sound: The cannons pound away.

HAN: Lead 'im! Lead 'im!

LEIA: They're all around us!

LUKE: They're coming too fast!

HAN: Well, they're not about to slow down for you!

Sound: The cannon fires again. The Falcon *trembles and bucks. The servos complain.*

HAN: Pay attention to your audio and pick 'em up on their approach runs, Luke!

Sound: Luke blasts at another fighter as it comes in. He misses, and it streaks off.

LUKE: Han, one coming your way!

Sound: The distant report of the top turret. More fighters circle, and the ship quakes.

LEIA: Chewbacca says we've lost lateral controls!

HAN: Don't worry . . . she'll hold together!

Sound: The Falcon *takes another blast.*

HAN: *(MURMURS)* Come on, baby, you heard me! Hold together!

Sound: Luke's cannon salvo again. Han's guns blast, and there's a loud explosion outside that rocks the ship.

HAN: *(HOOTS)* That's one! Three to go!

Sound: Cannons fire again, servos whine, and the ship's engines roar.

HAN: One coming at you, Luke!

Sound: Luke's targeting computer beeps, he fires, and the explosion.

LUKE: Got him! Han, I got him!

HAN: Great, kid! Don't get cocky!

LEIA: There are still two more out there!

HAN: One's under your guns, Luke!

Sound: Luke tracking and firing. Another explosion rocks the ship.

HAN: *Nail* 'im! I have to pay for all these repairs!

LUKE: I'm trying!

Sound: A TIE fighter coming around for another run. Luke fires again, with the computer beeping, and the fighter explodes.

LUKE: Han! I nailed him!

Sound: A TIE screeches by.

LUKE: Han! One coming your way!

Sound: Han fires, and the last fighter explodes.

HAN: That makes four! Clean sweep!

CHEWIE: HOWLS HAPPILY IN COMLINK.

LEIA: You did it!

HAN: Nice work, Luke! Chewie, punch in the jump to lightspeed! We made it!

Sound: Cheers.

Music: In and under:

NARRATOR: The *Millennium Falcon* speeds off with her disparate passengers and crew after victories and losses. But the Death Star dogs her track as a final confrontation takes form and patterns emerge from the Force. And freedom and peace are to live or die with the final contest of Death Star against Rebels.

Music: Closing theme up and under preview and closing credits.

ANNOUNCER: CLOSING CREDITS.

X-WING FIGHTER, ATTACK POSITION

EPISODE TWELVE:

"THE CASE FOR

REBELLION"

CAST:

Luke	Vader	Red Leader
Leia	Tarkin	Dodonna
Han	Willard	Gold Leader
Chewbacca	Motti	Wedge
Threepio	Rebel	Biggs
Artoo	2nd Rebel	PA

Music: Opening theme.

NARRATOR: A long time ago in a galaxy far, far away, there came a time of revolution, when Rebels united to challenge a tyrannical Empire. In the Rebellion's greatest crisis, the Empire unleashed its ultimate weapon, the Death Star, a spacegoing fortress capable of destroying entire planets. An oddly met group of Rebels have managed to penetrate to the heart of the Imperial stronghold and escape with information that may hold the key to victory.

Sound: Death Star up in background.

NARRATOR: But disaster looms, too, as the Death Star dogs their tracks, intent on pursuing them to the hidden Rebel base and obliterating the Rebel Alliance forever.

Sound: The Death Star conference room up, with Vader's respirator. Tarkin enters.

TARKIN: *(APPROACHING)* Are the Rebels well on their way, Vader?

VADER: Their starship just engaged our sentry fighters and fought her way clear. They're about to make the jump to lightspeed.

TARKIN: Indeed? What were our losses?

VADER: I withdrew all except four TIE fighters from that defensive zone to make the Rebels' escape more plausible. All four of our pilots were killed . . . These traitors to the Empire are formidable opponents.

TARKIN: We're fortunate that they themselves weren't slain. It's a pity about the casualties, but they're no great sacrifice to make in return for a lead to the Rebel base.

VADER: An insignificant price.

TARKIN: You're sure the homing beacon is secure aboard their ship? I'm taking a considerable risk in allowing them to escape, Vader. Your plan had better work.

VADER: We will follow them to their base, rest assured, and eliminate these Rebels.

TARKIN: I'm uneasy about having left the Death Star plans in that droid of theirs.

VADER: There was no alternative, Governor Tarkin. The Rebels might not try to return to their base if they didn't have the plans. Besides, they might already have been duplicated . . . Flushing the R2 unit's memory banks would be no guarantee of security.

TARKIN: As you say.

MOTTI: *(APPROACHING)* Lord Tarkin!

TARKIN: Well, Motti?

MOTTI: The homing beacon is transmitting a perfect signal, sir. What are your orders?

TARKIN: Follow it, Motti, and have all personnel placed on standby alert. We are about to wipe another planet out of existence . . . the Rebels' base world. Then the galaxy is ours.

Sound: Conference room and Death Star background fades to silence.

Sound: Millennium Falcon *engine rumbles up in background. Sputtering circuitry, sparking wire, etc.*

THREEPIO: Help! I think I'm melting!

ARTOO: BEEPING POINTLESS SUGGESTIONS.

THREEPIO: Oh, this is all your fault, Artoo!

HAN: *(APPROACHING)* Hey! What're you two doing playin' around there?

THREEPIO: I assure you, sir, this is no game! Please, before I'm severely impaired . . .

HAN: All right, all right. Artoo, hit that cutoff switch over there.

ARTOO: BEEPS.

Sound: A switch being thrown. The sputtering and sparking stop.

THREEPIO: I am forever in your debt, sir!

HAN: Yeah, yeah. Gimme a hand getting him untangled from all these wires, Artoo.

ARTOO: WHISTLES.

Sound: The two extricating Threepio and helping him up.

HAN: How'd you get into this, anyway?

THREEPIO: During our engagement with the Imperial fighters, when the ship was being jolted by cannon fire, I was propelled into all those exposed control elements.

HAN: You shoulda sat tight.

THREEPIO: I was attempting to assist Artoo in extinguishing a minor fire, sir.

HAN: That so? Well, you two are pretty handy to have around, after all.

THREEPIO: I must say, that battle didn't do our circuitry any good!

HAN: Don't knock your luck. We canceled all four of those TIE fighters.

THREEPIO: I suppose you're right, sir. Where is Master Luke?

HAN: Looking over some minor damage for me. He'll be along in a second.

THREEPIO: Shall Artoo and I . . .

HAN: *(MOVING OFF)* Do whatever you feel like. I've gotta get up to the cockpit.

THREEPIO: Well, Artoo, perhaps we'd better investigate my circuitry damage.

Sound: Cross-fade above to bridge sounds and:

LEIA: Can you get lateral controls back, Chewbacca?

HAN: *(FADING ON)* Me and him can do anything with this ship except lose!

CHEWIE: GROWLS AGREEMENT.

HAN: Okay, partner, I'll take over here. You run aft and see what you can do about the laterals. We can get by on auxiliaries for now.

CHEWIE: BARKS.

Sound: He rises from his seat.

HAN: I'll punch up the jump to lightspeed.

CHEWIE: *(OFF)* GRUNTS.

HAN: *(CALLING)* And get those droids to help! Well, not a bad bit of rescuing, huh? Y' know, sometimes I even amaze myself!

LEIA: That doesn't sound too hard. Look, use your head . . . The Imperials *let* us go! It's the only possible explanation for the ease of our escape.

HAN: *Easy?* You call that easy?

LEIA: They're tracking us now.

HAN: Not this ship, sister!

LEIA: Oh, you're impossible! Well, at least Artoo-Detoo is still intact.

HAN: What's so important about the droid? What's he carrying?

LEIA: The technical readouts of that battle station. I only hope that when the data are analyzed, a weakness can be found.

HAN: Listen, if you're so afraid we're being tracked, we'll lay over someplace and search the ship.

LEIA: There's no time! If the Empire isn't stopped, other planets will be destroyed as Alderaan was. That's why I've got to risk going directly to the Rebel base. The fight isn't over yet!

HAN: It is for *me*, sister! Look, I ain't in this for your revolution and I'm not in it for you, Princess. I expect to be well paid . . . I'm in it for the money!

LEIA: You needn't worry about your reward. When you get us to our destination, you'll receive it.

HAN: Don't you think it'd help if you told me where we're going?

LEIA: The fourth moon of the planet Yavin . . . that's where the base is. Then you can go do whatever you like. *(MOVING OFF)* If money is all you love, then that's all you'll receive!

LUKE: *(MOVING ON)* Princess . . .

LEIA: Your friend here is quite a mercenary, Luke! *(STILL MOVING OFF)* I wonder if he really cares about anything . . . or anybody!

LUKE: *(CALLING)* I care . . . *(SITTING)* So . . . what d' you think of her, Han?

HAN: I'm trying not to, kid.

LUKE: Good.

HAN: Hmm? *Oh.* Still, she's got a lot of spirit. I dunno, do you think a Princess and a guy like me could . . .

LUKE: *No!*

HAN: CHUCKLES.

Sound: Han begins throwing switches. The Falcon's *engines build.*

LUKE: Where are we headed?

HAN: Fourth moon of someplace called Yavin. It's where *all* the idealists hang out, I hear.

Music: In and out.

Sound: Falcon's *engines roaring in descent.*

HAN: Those Rebels sure picked themselves a planet in the middle of nowhere, didn't they?

CHEWIE: GRUNTS.

LUKE: *(COMING ON)* How're we doing, Han?

HAN: I dunno about you, but I'm doin' fine. *(LEANING ACROSS)* 'Scuse me, sister. That was Yavin we just ducked around. We're in the fourth moon's atmosphere now. Set-down's in a coupla seconds.

LEIA: Did you transmit the recognition code I gave you?

HAN: Naw, we decided to get blasted out of the sky. What d' you think? *(PAUSE)* Coming up on landing coordinates now, Chewie.

CHEWIE: GROWLS.

Sound: The pitch of the engines changes.

HAN: Well, the place has a decent atmosphere. Mostly jungle, though. The landing zone's right there by those temples.

Sound: The engines roar as the Falcon *sets down with a slight thud. Han and Chewie work the console, and the engines die.*

HAN: At least nobody's shot at us. Yet. Looks like there's a reception committee coming out to meet us.

LEIA: If you'll open the hatch, we won't trouble you any further. I'll have the money brought out to you.

HAN: *(LAUGHS DRYLY)* If you don't mind, my partner and I will come along . . . just to protect our investment, you understand. After you.

LEIA: Anything, as long as you stop wasting my time!

HAN: Cash on delivery was the deal, if I recall right.

LUKE: What's the matter, don't you trust us?

HAN: Nothing personal; we don't trust anybody.

CHEWIE: YAWPS.

THREEPIO: *(FADING ON)* Have we arrived, Master Luke?

LUKE: This is it, Threepio.

THREEPIO: At last, a place of refuge!

HAN: *(LAUGHS)* With that Death Star on our trail? I'd set you straight, Threepio, but I'd hate to ruin your day.

LEIA: Just open the hatch.

HAN: Oh, instantly, Your Highness!

Sound: The controls click, the hatch rolls up. As the ramp hisses down, jungle-fauna noises come from distance.

HAN: *(INHALES DEEPLY)* Whew! It's a jungle planet, all right!

LEIA: Let's go, Luke.

LUKE: Threepio, Artoo, come on.

Sound: Luke, Leia, and the droids start down the ramp.

HAN: After you, partner.

CHEWIE: SNARLS.

Sound: Han and Chewie go down the ramp. As the group reaches the bottom of the ramp and steps out onto the paving, the jungle noises grow louder.

HAN: Some fortress! Those temples look like they're a million years old.

REBEL: *(APPROACHING)* Princess Leia! Your Highness! We'd hoped it was you! Commander Willard is waiting to greet you all.

LEIA: Thank you. These droids must come, too . . . The R2 unit is carrying vital information.

ARTOO: WHISTLES SMUGLY.

REBEL: Of course. *(ASIDE)* Take these droids to the speeder and help them aboard.

2ND REBEL: Sir!

REBEL: Carefully!

2ND REBEL: Sir!

REBEL: Your Highness, if you would follow me to the speeder, we can take you directly to Commander Willard . . .

Sound: Cross-fade to:

Sound: Inside the underground area of the temple-fortress. Room is busy with mech-techs at work, flight crews, engines being tested, etc.

HAN: *(OVER NOISE)* Your Rebellion's got some great equipment, Princess! No heavy combat ships at all, and every one of those snub fighters is older than you are!

LEIA: Some day you'll learn that it's people and not *things* that decide history.

HAN: You'd better teach that to the Empire first!

WILLARD: *(APPROACHING)* Leia! Princess Leia!

LEIA: Commander Willard! Oh . . .

Sound: They embrace.

WILLARD: Leia, you're safe! We'd feared the worst! *(MORE COMPOSED)* Welcome, all of you. Is General Kenobi with you? We'd had word that you were to contact him.

LEIA: Obi-Wan Kenobi has been killed, Commander. He gave his life in a diversionary action so that the rest of us could escape the Death Star.

CHEWIE: HOOTS SOFTLY.

HAN: *(SOMBERLY)* Hush, Chewie.

WILLARD: That is sad news, indeed. When we heard about Alderaan, Your Highness, we were afraid that you were . . . *lost*, along with the others. It was a terrible calamity . . .

LEIA: We haven't time for our sorrows, Commander. I have no doubt we are being tracked here by the Death Star . . . We were allowed to escape so that we could lead them here. The technical data on the battle station are stored in the memory system of the R2 unit. You must use them to plan an attack . . . they're our only hope.

WILLARD: We're badly unprepared for pitched battle, Your Highness. Perhaps we should evacuate instead.

HAN: *(SLIGHTLY OFF)* Smart boy!

CHEWIE: WOOFS.

LEIA: There isn't time! Commander, if we fail to stop the Death Star now, other planets will be annihilated.

WILLARD: Then you're right. We have no choice but to fight. *(ASIDE)* Take the R2 unit to the techs for special information retrieval!

REBEL: Yes, Commander!

Sound: The men hop to it, leading off Artoo.

ARTOO: *(OFF)* WHISTLES URGENTLY.

THREEPIO: I beg your pardon, Princess Leia. May I go along with Artoo?

LEIA: Of course.

THREEPIO: Thank you.

WILLARD: *(CALLING)* Have that information brought to the briefing room as soon as it's retrieved!

REBEL: *(CALLING)* Yes, sir!

WILLARD: We can wait for it there. This way, Your Highness, gentlemen.

Sound: As they walk.

WILLARD: Our main problem here is personnel. We're desperately lacking pilots, trained or otherwise.

LEIA: Yes, so I'd heard.

WILLARD: But now, what of you, Your Highness? Our last word of you was that you'd intercepted the Death Star data transmissions.

LEIA: My ship was attacked by an Imperial cruiser over Tatooine . . .

Sound: Cross-fade to:

Sound: The briefing room up.

LEIA: *(COMING ON)* . . . then, after Alderaan was . . . was destroyed, the Grand Moff Tarkin ordered me executed.

WILLARD: Executed!

LEIA: Yes. I was in my cell, awaiting the executioner, when the door opened and in stepped this man right here. Commander Willard, Luke Skywalker.

WILLARD: Young man, this is more of a pleasure than you can imagine! Even if we'd known the Princess's whereabouts, I doubt we could've mounted an operation to get her out!

LUKE: It was actually sort of improvised.

WILLARD: All the more to be admired! The ability to think on one's feet isn't common.

LUKE: Well, Han and Chewbacca here had as much of a hand in it as I did, and so did Ben Kenobi.

CHEWIE: GROWLS.

WILLARD: Han . . . ah, yes, your captain and his friend, here. Sir, allow me to congratulate—

HAN: Why don't we skip the formalities? I'm gonna push ahead to the important part of the Princess's story . . . That planet killer is on its way here, and personally, I don't plan to stick around and get reacquainted.

WILLARD: I don't quite follow you.

HAN: You'll live a whole lot longer if you do . . . believe me! Look, I got dragged into this mess. I'm just a guy with a starship for hire. I was promised payment, and I want it.

LUKE: Han!

HAN: The rest of you can do whatever you want, but I kept my end of the bargain. Now you keep yours, Princess.

WILLARD: Princess Leia, I—

LEIA: Captain Solo may have no morals whatsoever, Commander, but he's right. Both Luke and I promised him payment for his and Chewbacca's help in this matter.

WILLARD: Very well. I see I misjudged you, Solo.

HAN: I'll cry later. Right now, I'll settle for cash. In small, used notes if you've got 'em.

WILLARD: But this is a Rebel camp! We're hunted people, with very little Imperial currency among us!

HAN: Oh. Well, your tech facilities must have stocks of precious metals.

WILLARD: Yes . . .

HAN: They'll do.

WILLARD: But those are critical matériel! We need those metals for repairs, to keep our weapons and equipment functioning!

HAN: Look, I lived up to my end of a *deal*! You live up to yours! Even a Rebel Alliance has to do business with us independents from time to time. If I put the word out that you're a bunch of swindlers . . .

LEIA: Commander, see that he's paid, please. Not all your stocks, but whatever you can possibly spare.

WILLARD: Very well, Your Highness.

LEIA: It won't be wealth unlimited, Solo, but it ought to satisfy even you.

HAN: What d' you say, Chewie?

CHEWIE: BARKS SUCCINCTLY.

HAN: Okay, box it up for us and we'll be on our way.

WILLARD: It will take some time to have it measured out and put in containers.

HAN: I know, but make it fast . . . that Death Star's not gonna stop to chat once it gets here. Anyplace I can clean up a little while I'm waiting?

REBEL: There's a basin in the pilots' ready room, down that corridor. You'll have it all to yourself.

HAN: *(MOVING OFF)* C'mon, Chewie.

CHEWIE: YEOWLS.

HAN: *(OFF, CALLING)* Sing out when you're ready!

LUKE: I can't believe it! I know he always talks tough, but I thought that when it came right down to a decision . . .

WILLARD: The man's amoral . . . no conscience at all.

LUKE: No! Commander, you don't know him like I do! He's wrongheaded about a lot of things, but inside . . .

LEIA: Luke, you heard Han. He's made up his mind.

LUKE: Let me talk to him. *(MOVING OFF)* I know I can bring him around.

REBEL: Commander Willard, sir?

WILLARD: What is it?

REBEL: Sir, that matériel may be critical to the Rebellion. If it's only Solo and the Wookiee, sir, they could be compelled to leave without their payment.

LEIA: No. I gave my word . . . It *would* hurt outsiders' faith in the Alliance.

WILLARD: Besides, the man already knows a good deal about our activities. He might take revenge by revealing it to the Empire.

LEIA: No, he'd never . . .

REBEL: Then, there's a more permanent solution, sir. I could arm a squad of men and—

LEIA: No! That's just what this Rebellion is about!

WILLARD: See that he's paid.

REBEL: Yes, Commander.

Music: Up.

Sound: Water, washing, etc.

HAN: It's open skies from now on, partner!

CHEWIE: SNARLS.

HAN: Aw, keep your pelt on! Once we get out of this place, we'll be able to afford a nice, long rest . . .

LUKE: *(APPROACHING)* Han!

HAN: *(SIGHS)* What now? *(MORE ALERT)* Hey, they're not trying to back out of the bargain, are they?

LUKE: Will you stop being suspicious of the whole galaxy? I told them I'd come and talk to you. I said I could change your mind.

HAN: Then you fibbed. This ain't my fight.

LUKE: Don't you think it will be when the Empire takes over everything? You think the men who built the Death Star are going to leave people like you and Chewbacca alone?

CHEWIE: GRUNTS.

HAN: If we mind our own business . . .

LUKE: Stop lying to yourself!

HAN: Careful, Luke. And what're *you* gonna do? Sit here and hold the Princess's hand while the Death Star turns this whole planet into a gas cloud?

LUKE: I . . . Commander Willard said they need pilots. I'm going to volunteer.

CHEWIE: WOOFS IN SURPRISE.

HAN: What? Luke, d' you know what I saw when I was getting us out of that battle station?

LUKE: I don't care . . .

HAN: Besides all the cannon and missile tubes and that big planet killer, it's got fighter boys. Lots of them. And those Imperial pilots are *pros*!

LUKE: I know it'll be dangerous . . .

HAN: And d' you happen to know what a green pilot's life expectancy is in combat? A minute or so!

LUKE: At least I'll try! What about you? You and Chewbacca and the *Millennium Falcon* could make all the difference. Han, you're a crack pilot, a veteran! Why can't you—

HAN: *(INTERRUPTING)* Because I used up my time! And more, long ago.

Sound: Silence, broken only by a single mournful keen from Chewie.

LUKE: I see.

HAN: You only think you do.

LUKE: You won't help us?

HAN: Look, I did what I could, but that's the limit. I'm not dying over somebody's *cause*!

LUKE: Others will. Others *have*!

HAN: Others . . . You're talking about the old man, aren't you? Ben?

LUKE: Ben said there was more to you than you wanted to admit.

HAN: Then he was as crazy as you are! I'm still raising ship.

LUKE: The least you could do is leave the metals behind. These people need everything they can lay their hands on.

HAN: Those metals'd only be blown away with the rest of the place. With me, they'll do somebody some good.

LUKE: But you could keep that from happening! You could stay and fight!

HAN: Look, me and Chewie've *finally* made our pile! Our luck's turned good, and I'm not gonna question it.

LUKE: That's why you're afraid—

HAN: Afraid? Listen, that little stroll through the Death Star was light exercise. *We've* been through scrapes that—Oh, never mind; just don't talk to me about "afraid."

LUKE: *(MOVING OFF)* Then I guess there's nothing more to talk about. I'll see—

HAN: *(INTERRUPTING)* And this ain't even a risk . . . it's a sure thing. This place won't even be here an hour or two from now. So why should we stick our necks out?

LUKE: *(OFF)* To give your life some meaning, Han.

CHEWIE: RUMBLES A COMMENT.

HAN: *(CALLING)* Yeah, well, who asked *you*? *(TO CHEWIE)* Hey, you see a towel around here anywhere?

CHEWIE: ROWFS.

HAN: Ah, my shirt'll do.

LEIA: *(APPROACHING)* Han, are you sure you won't reconsider—

HAN: *(INTERRUPTING)* Great. Now you. Look, forget about me. I've made my decision. You want to do somebody a favor? Luke's going to volunteer to fly a fighter.

LEIA: *Luke?*

HAN: Go talk him out of it . . . save his life.

LEIA: I . . . don't need to. Luke's made the right decision. What about you?

HAN: I've had my fill of playing hero, thanks. It's a sucker's game.

LEIA: That's your final word?

HAN: You'd better go say good-bye to Luke, Princess. That "right" decision's gonna be the last one he ever makes.

Music: Up.

Sound: The Rebel training room. Simulator-computers, AV aids, etc.

LUKE: *(COMING ON)* Sir, I was told to report here for flight testing . . .

BIGGS: Sir! *(LAUGHS)* "Sir," he calls me . . .

LUKE: Biggs? *Biggs!* Biggs Darklighter!

BIGGS: Hi, hotshot!

LUKE: What're you doing here?

BIGGS: That's my line. *I* was the one who went off to join the Rebellion, remember? You're supposed to be back on Tatooine.

LUKE: Oh, Biggs! Have I got some stories to tell!

BIGGS: Yeah, I'll bet. The whole base is talking about the new arrivals: smugglers, droids, and a renegade Princess. You got here in strange company, but you got here!

LUKE: I told you I'd throw in with the Rebels one day, didn't I?

BIGGS: Luke, I never doubted you for a second. I know you too well. Now, what's this about testing?

LUKE: Commander Willard sent me; I volunteered when he said you're short of pilots.

BIGGS: Desperate's more like it.

LUKE: You know how good I was with a T-16 back home. . . .

BIGGS: We're sending up pilots with less experience than you. And T-16s are a lot like the snub fighters we're using.

LUKE: I know; I looked one over. I'm sure I could handle it.

BIGGS: But there hasn't been much time or fuel for training, and there's none to spare for testing you. Besides, we couldn't risk losing a ship . . .

LUKE: Sure, I understand . . .

BIGGS: No, no; what I meant was that I'll have to test you here, hotshot, in this flight simulator.

LUKE: *(BRIGHTENS)* All right.

BIGGS: Hop in.

Sound: Luke climbs into simulator.

BIGGS: I'm going to run a full combat simulation, Luke. Buckle in tight; you're going to be pulling realistic gee forces.

LUKE: *(ECHOING)* Check! All set, Biggs.

BIGGS: Close 'er up . . . and good luck.

Sound: Hatch being closed.

BIGGS: *(TO HIMSELF)* Okay, Luke, here . . .

Sound: Throws switches to activate simulator.

BIGGS: . . . you . . . go!

Sound: The simulator begins the test sequences.

BIGGS: Attack sequence . . . now!

Sound: Another switch is thrown. From inside the simulator are heard the roars of TIE fighters under:

BIGGS: *(MURMURS TO HIMSELF)* First attacker . . . destroyed; good. Second . . . direct hit! Very good. Third . . . hmm . . . yeah, excellent! All right, let's see how you do against increased gee forces, buddy.

Sound: More switches thrown, and the simulator's racket increases, with the whining rising in pitch.

BIGGS: . . . and multiple attackers . . .

Sound: More switches. The firing grows more intense.

BIGGS: Not bad . . . go get 'em, Luke! Not bad at all . . .

Sound: The attack sequence ends, and the simulator gradually halts, the hatch opens, and Luke pulls himself out under:

LUKE: Uh! What a ride! How'd I do, Biggs?

BIGGS: A lot better than most of the guys who're going on this next mission, I'll tell you that. But I have to show your test results to Commander Willard, Luke.

LUKE: Sure.

BIGGS: You wait here . . . Oh! Oh, excuse me . . .

LEIA: *(COMING ON)* No; my fault entirely . . .

LUKE: Biggs Darklighter of Tatooine, meet Princess Leia Organa. Your Highness, this is my best friend.

BIGGS: Uh, pleased to meet you, Your, um, Highness. . . .

LEIA: And you, Biggs; Luke's spoken of you.

BIGGS: *(MOVING OFF)* Well, ah, I have to go . . . that is . . . pardon me.

LEIA: How did the flight test go, Luke?

LUKE: He has to check with Commander Willard, but it looks like I made it!

LEIA: Oh?

LUKE: Well? Aren't you going to—

LEIA: I . . . spoke with Han. He wouldn't change his mind . . .

LUKE: I know!

LEIA: And he said that . . . that I should talk you out of flying a fighter. I said that you'd made the right decision.

LUKE: But you don't sound so sure.

LEIA: Luke, you've never flown in combat before!

LUKE: Neither have some of the others. Biggs is fresh out of the Academy!

LEIA: But he and the others have been training.

LUKE: Well, you're looking at the hottest gully-jumper on Tatooine.

LEIA: Bush piloting isn't the same as combat flying! *(PAUSE)* Luke, you've done so much for the Rebellion already . . . nobody could blame you if you didn't go on this mission. I wanted you to know that.

LUKE: Leia . . . thank you. But it's what I want; so much depends on this . . .

RED LEADER: *(APPROACHING)* Skywalker, Biggs here just showed Commander Willard and me your test results.

LUKE: And?

RED LEADER: You only got killed twice.

LUKE: Oh . . .

RED LEADER: Cheer up; that's surprisingly good, since Biggs was tossing the whole starfleet at you. You know the techniques, and your body can stand the strain. Looks like you've got yourself a bird.

LUKE: I *have*?

BIGGS: Yeah, I'm your flight leader. Welcome to Red Flight.

LUKE: Thanks!

RED LEADER: You'll be Red Five, Luke. Biggs is Red Three, your wingman.

BIGGS: *(LAUGHS)* Together again, hotshot!

RED LEADER: Let's go, Luke; the mission briefing starts in a few minutes. Your Highness, if you'll excuse us . . .

LEIA: Of course. Luke . . . I'll see you before you leave . . .

Sound: The briefing room up: R2 units beeping, pilots murmuring, etc. Luke and Biggs enter.

BIGGS: Have a seat, Luke. The show's about to start.

Sound: Chairs scraping. Dodonna goes to speakers' podium.

DODONNA: May I have your attention?

Sound: Conversations stop.

DODONNA: We have analyzed our new information and formulated our attack strategy. Please direct your attention to the screen.

Sound: The screen hums down.

DODONNA: This is the Death Star.

Sound: The pilots exclaim among themselves.

DODONNA: *(OVERRIDING THEM)* This battle station is heavily shielded and carries a firepower greater than that of half a starfleet. Its defenses are designed, as you can see, around the concept of a direct, large-scale assault. But small, one-man fighters should be able to penetrate its outer defenses.

Sound: The pilots mutter their doubts.

GOLD LEADER: Pardon me for asking, General Dodonna, but what good are snub fighters going to be against that thing?

DODONNA: Well, the Empire doesn't consider a small fighter to be any threat, or they'd have a tighter defense. But an analysis of the design plans provided by Princess Leia has demonstrated a weakness in the battle station. Now, watch this enlarged view carefully.

Sound: The projector clicks.

DODONNA: The approach for your attack run will not be easy. You're required to maneuver down this trench in the station's structure and skim the surface to the point you're seeing now. This target area is only two meters wide.

Sound: The pilots shift nervously. Chairs squeaking and muttering.

DODONNA: The target is a small thermal exhaust port right below the main port. Its shaft leads directly to the Death Star's reactor system. A precise hit down this shaft will strike the reactor and start a chain reaction which should destroy the entire station.

Sound: Pilots now mutter openly.

DODONNA: I cannot stress too strongly the point that *only* a precise hit will reach the bottom of the shaft and strike the reactor.

The thermal port is ray-shielded, so you'll have to do this job with photon torpedoes.

Sound: The pilots exclaim to one another about that.

WEDGE: *(TO LUKE)* That shot is impossible, even for a targeting computer!

LUKE: It's not impossible, Wedge. I used to bull's-eye womp rats in my T-16 back home, and they're not much bigger than two meters!

WEDGE: And were the womp rats shooting at you with turbo-laser cannon?

DODONNA: Gentlemen! Gentlemen!

Sound: The chatter dies away.

DODONNA: We've just gotten word that the Death Star has entered this solar system! It is orbiting the planet Yavin now and will be within firing range of this moon in just over thirty minutes.

Sound: Chatter once again breaks out.

DODONNA: *(OVERRIDING THEM)* Man your ships, and may the Force be with you!

Sound: Chairs scrape, equipment rattles, and talking as they hurry off.

RED LEADER: *(MOVING OFF)* Luke, Biggs, go suit up, then meet me in the hangar area.

BIGGS: Right away, sir! C'mon, hotshot. *(PAUSE)* Hey, aren't those two the ones who came in with you?

LUKE: Where? Oh, yeah . . . *(CALLING)* . . . Han! Chewbacca!

CHEWIE: *(OFF)* GROWLS.

HAN: *(COMING ON)* 'Lo, kid. Me and Chewie just dropped by to watch the fun. Our pay's almost ready. So, you really went and signed on, huh?

LUKE: That's right. Biggs Darklighter, this is Han Solo and that's Chewbacca.

CHEWIE: BARKS.

HAN: Biggs the hometown hero, eh? Luke talked about you. You're on the team, too?

BIGGS: Yes. And you?

HAN: Not a chance. Me and my friend have places to go and things to do.

BIGGS: So do we.

HAN: I know all about it. Let's go, Chewie. *(MOVING OFF)* Best of luck, hometown heroes! You're gonna need it all!

BIGGS: What was all that about, Luke?

LUKE: I'll explain it later.

PA: All flight crews, man your stations! All flight crews, man your stations!

LUKE: Let's go!

Music: Up and under:

NARRATOR: The Rebels are now committed to a desperate stand against the Death Star; the battle station rushes toward them, its commander determined to wipe the Rebel Alliance out of existence. In the next thirty minutes, Luke Skywalker and everything and everyone he cares about will know triumph or disaster.

Music: Closing theme up and under preview and closing credits.

ANNOUNCER: CLOSING CREDITS.

DEATH STAR / POLAR TRENCH

EPISODE THIRTEEN:

"FORCE AND

COUNTERFORCE"

CAST:

Luke	Motti	Red Four
Leia	Biggs	Red Six
Han	Dodonna	Gold Five
Chewbacca	Wedge	Gold Two
Vader	Crew Chief	Officer
Threepio	PA	Red Ten
Artoo	Red Leader	Red Twelve
Ben	Controller	Rebel
Tarkin	Gold Leader	

ANNOUNCER: OPENING CREDITS.

Music: Opening theme.

NARRATOR: A long time ago in a galaxy far, far away, there came a time of revolution, when Rebels united to challenge a tyrannical Empire.

Sound: Death Star up in background.

NARRATOR: Now that struggle has come to a decisive moment, as the Empire's huge spacegoing fortress, the Death Star, approaches the Rebel base on the fourth moon of the planet Yavin. The Rebels have elected to stand fast and engage the Death Star in a desperate battle in which they'll either triumph and save the galaxy from cruel Imperial domination or be utterly destroyed by the terrible power of the battle station's Prime Weapon. As the Rebels rush to scramble their tiny fleet of fighter craft for the assault, the Imperial lords prepare to wipe them out of existence.

Sound: Death Star observation deck up, with instrumentation, etc., and Vader's respirator.

PA: *(OFF)* The Death Star is now orbiting the planet Yavin at maximum velocity. The Rebel base will be within firing range in thirty minutes.

VADER: This will be a day long remembered, Lord Tarkin. It has seen the end of Obi-Wan Kenobi and will soon see the end of the Rebellion.

TARKIN: Yes, the Emperor will be pleased, Vader.

Sound: Portal opens and closes under:

MOTTI: *(APPROACHING)* The Prime Weapon is fully prepared,

Governor Tarkin. We'll be able to obliterate the Rebel moon the moment we're within range.

TARKIN: Very good, Motti. Are all our people at their battle stations?

MOTTI: We're on full alert status, sir.

VADER: With your permission, Governor Tarkin, I'll make a personal tour of inspection. Nothing must be left to chance.

TARKIN: As you wish, Lord Vader.

VADER: *(MOVING OFF)* I shall be back well before we fire the Prime Weapon.

Sound: Vader's respiration and heavy footsteps move off.

MOTTI: Lord Tarkin, may I compliment you on this achievement?

TARKIN: Thank you, Motti, although others contributed to it. Vader's efforts to locate this base, for example.

MOTTI: But you supervised construction of the Death Star, sir. And you command it. In destroying the Rebellion as you destroyed Alderaan, you'll prove that *you* hold the ultimate power in the galaxy.

TARKIN: In the name of the Empire, of course.

MOTTI: Of course, Lord Tarkin. But the Emperor is far from here, and you are in actual control.

TARKIN: This isn't the first time you've spoken in this fashion, Motti. Say what it is that's in your mind.

MOTTI: If you command it, Governor Tarkin.

TARKIN: I do.

MOTTI: Very well. This battle station has become the very source of the Empire's power. Not even the Imperial starfleet could stand against us. And all of that power lies at your command.

TARKIN: You are close to treason, Motti.

MOTTI: Is it treason to point out that you could demand a position of authority second only to that of the Emperor?

TARKIN: I would not care to have the Emperor as my enemy.

MOTTI: But command of the Death Star makes you his equal. You could share dominion of the galaxy.

TARKIN: With you at my right hand?

MOTTI: I'm your willing servant, Lord Tarkin.

TARKIN: And then, of course, there's Lord Vader to consider.

MOTTI: Formidable as he is, the Dark Lord of the Sith is hardly an insurmountable problem.

TARKIN: You think not?

MOTTI: The personnel of this battle station owe their allegiance to you. Lord Vader, for all his superstitious trickery, can be dealt with. Do not forget that you wield the ultimate power.

TARKIN: I shall consider what you've said, Motti. First, however, we must attend to the Rebels: When they have been eradicated, there will be time to think further about your suggestion.

Sound: Death Star background out.

Music: Up.

Sound: Rebel hangar background up, with techs working on the fighters. Chewie and Han are loading their boxes onto the speeder.

PA: *(OFF)* Flight crews, to your stations! All flight crews, man your stations!

HAN: *(WITH EXERTION)* Hurry up, Chewie!

CHEWIE: GROWLS.

Sound: Han sets another box on the speeder.

HAN: The faster we get this stuff loaded and get out of here, the better I'll like it. I want to be long gone when that Death Star starts firing.

CHEWIE: RUMBLES AN ANSWER.

HAN: I still can't believe these Rebels're gonna try and take that thing on with snub fighters!

LUKE: *(APPROACHING)* Han! Chewbacca!

CHEWIE: BARKS.

LUKE: So, you've got your reward.

HAN: You guessed it.

Sound: He sets another box down.

HAN: I see they found you a flight suit. You look just like an old hand, kid.

LUKE: You're just going to leave, Han?

HAN: Yeah, that's right. We found that homing beacon the Imperials hid onboard the *Falcon*. So, we've got some old debts we've got to go and pay with this stuff, right, Chewie?

CHEWIE: GRUNTS.

Sound: Han sets another box down.

HAN: Even if we didn't, you don't think we'd be fools enough to stick around here, do you?

LUKE: I was hoping you would.

HAN: Why don't you come with us, Luke? You're pretty good in a fight . . . I could use you.

LUKE: Come on, Han! Why don't you look around you? You know what the Rebels are up against. They could use a good pilot like you. You're turning your back on them.

HAN: What good's a reward if you ain't around to spend it? Besides, attacking that battle station ain't my idea of courage. It's more like suicide.

Sound: Han sets down another box.

LUKE: Well, take care of yourself, Han. I guess that's what you're best at, isn't it? *(MOVING OFF)* So long . . .

HAN: Hey, Luke!

Sound: Luke pauses.

LUKE: *(OFF)* What?

HAN: May the Force be with you.

LUKE: *(MOVING OFF)* Sure, Han.

CHEWIE: GROWLS.

HAN: What're you lookin' at, Chewie? I know what I'm doin'! C'mon, let's finish up and raise ship.

Music: Transition.

LEIA: *(APPROACHING)* Luke!

LUKE: Yes, Princess?

LEIA: What's wrong?

LUKE: Oh, it's Han! I don't know; I really thought I could change his mind.

LEIA: He's got his own path to follow . . . No one can choose it for him.

LUKE: *(MOVING)* I only wish Ben were here.

LEIA: Wait, Luke . . . before you go . . .

Sound: She kisses him.

LEIA: . . . a kiss for luck.

LUKE: Thanks!

BIGGS: *(OFF)* Luke! Come on!

LUKE: I'll . . . I'll see you later, Leia.

LEIA: Yes, Luke. *(MOVING OFF)* Good-bye.

BIGGS: *(COMING ON)* Luke, come on! We're lifting off in a minute or two.

LUKE: All set, Biggs.

BIGGS: So I saw. So you finally found your dream girl, huh?

LUKE: Hey, Biggs . . . THEY LAUGH.

LUKE: It'll be good to know we're up there together, though.

BIGGS: Just like back home on Tatooine, Luke, racing through the Stone Needle. Well, there's your ship, Luke.

LUKE: An X-wing! I always dreamed—

THREEPIO: *(APPROACHING)* Master Luke, sir!

LUKE: Oh, hi, Threepio.

THREEPIO: Sir, the Rebels are short of R2 units, and so they're putting Artoo-Detoo in the technical socket of your fighter.

ARTOO: *(OFF)* BLEEPS A GREETING.

LUKE: At least I'll have plenty of friends up there with me.

BIGGS: *(MOVING OFF)* See you upstairs, Luke!

LUKE: Right, Biggs!

THREEPIO: The very best of luck to you, Master Luke.

LUKE: Thanks, Threepio.

Sound: Luke climbs the ladder to his cockpit.

CREW CHIEF: *(OFF)* Say, Red Five, your R2 unit seems a bit beat up. Do you want me to see if I can't find another?

ARTOO: BEEPS INDIGNANTLY.

LUKE: Not on your life!

CREW CHIEF: *(MOVING OFF)* Whatever you say.

Sound: Luke climbs into the cockpit under:

LUKE: That little droid and I have been through a lot together.

Sound: Luke fastens his harness and puts his helmet on.

LUKE: You okay back there, Artoo?

ARTOO: BEEPS BACK THAT HE'S OKAY.

THREEPIO: *(OFF)* Hang on tight, Artoo! You simply have to come back, you know!

ARTOO: SECONDS THAT.

THREEPIO: You wouldn't want my life to become boring, would you?

ARTOO: BEEPS *NO*.

CREW CHIEF: *(OFF)* You're ready for liftoff, Red Five. Time to seal your canopy.

LUKE: Check!

Sound: Luke hits a switch; and the canopy is lowered by servos, filtering out much of the hangar noise. A few more switches are thrown, and the engine revs.

BEN: *(DISEMBODIED VOICE)* Luke, the Force will be with you.

LUKE: *Ben?* . . .

RED LEADER: *(COMMO)* Red Flight, this is Red Leader. Prepare for liftoff.

Sound: Engine noises up, then fade.

Sound: Rebel operations room up, with control personnel monitoring the mission, telemetry sounding, etc.

DODONNA: We'll be following the mission from right here, Your Highness. This screen is the main tactical display.

LEIA: I see, General Dodonna. See-Threepio, there's room for you right here.

THREEPIO: Thank you, Your Highness.

DODONNA: Those blips there are our fighters. They're closing on the Death Star now.

LEIA: What is their plan of attack?

DODONNA: The Y-wing fighters are our primary attack ships . . . that's Gold Flight. They'll be first to make photon torpedo runs on the target shaft.

LEIA: And the X-wing fighters?

DODONNA: That's Red Flight. They'll distract the Imperials, draw their fire, and fly flak suppression runs.

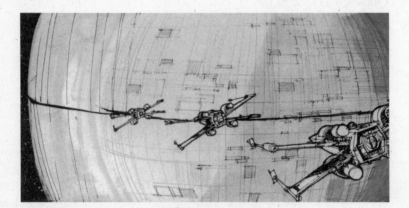

LEIA: And if the Y-wings don't manage to get a torpedo down that vent shaft?

DODONNA: Then the X-wing fighters are our contingency force. They'll take up the torpedo attack.

PA: *(OFF)* Death Star still approaching. Estimated time to firing range, fifteen minutes.

LEIA: Are you certain that even a direct hit down the shaft will stop the battle station?

DODONNA: Not the photon torpedo itself, but the chain reaction it will set off in the station's main reactor, yes.

CONTROLLER: *(OFF)* General Dodonna, Red Flight and Gold Flight are now in range of the Death Star.

DODONNA: Patch in their communications net over the main system.

CONTROLLER: Yes, sir.

Sound: The fighter's commo crackles over the operations room speakers. All pilots sound tinny.

RED LEADER: Red Flight, this is Red Leader. Lock all S-foils into attack position.

THREEPIO: I haven't had an opportunity yet to thank you properly, Your Highness, for allowing me to follow the attack here in the operations center.

LEIA: Hmm? Oh, you're welcome, Threepio. After all, you and Artoo have been through a great deal for the Rebel Alliance, even if it wasn't by choice.

THREEPIO: When the plans for the Death Star were being retrieved from Artoo's memory banks, we both learned the full story.

LEIA: Circumstances compelled me to use Artoo as a courier. I know it brought hardship and danger to you both, but it was the only thing I could do at the time.

THREEPIO: Oh, Artoo and I understand that, Princess Leia. I only hope that Artoo survives his current assignment.

LEIA: You care very much about Artoo-Detoo, don't you?

THREEPIO: I've . . . I've grown used to him, even though we've only been together for a relatively short time.

LEIA: It's possible to care for . . . someone . . . very much after only a short time.

RED LEADER: All right, we're passing through their magnetic field. Hang on tight; we'll be doing a little rattling.

DODONNA: Their countermeasures equipment should get them through.

CONTROLLER: They've made it through the magnetic field!

RED LEADER: All ships, switch on your deflector shields, double forward.

WEDGE: Look at the size of that battle station!

RED LEADER: Cut the chatter, Red Two. All ships, accelerate to attack speed. This is it, boys!

CONTROLLER: They're moving into range of the Death Star.

GOLD LEADER: Red Leader, this is Gold Leader.

DODONNA: That's the Y-wing flight leader, Your Highness.

RED LEADER: I copy, Gold Leader.

GOLD LEADER: We're starting for the target shaft now.

RED LEADER: Good hunting, Gold Leader. Red Leader to Red Flight, we're in position. I'm going to fly across the battle station's axis and try to draw fire.

DODONNA: That area is particularly well fortified. It will be up to Red Flight to keep the Imperials busy.

WEDGE: Heavy fire, boss! Twenty-three degrees!

RED LEADER: I see it! Stay low!

LUKE: Red Leader, this is Red Five . . . I'm going in!

LEIA: *(TO HERSELF)* Luke!

THREEPIO: And Artoo . . .

BIGGS: Luke, pull out! Pull out! *(PAUSE)* Are you all right?

LUKE: I got a little cooked in that fireball, but I'm okay.

Sound: Leia lets out a held breath.

DODONNA: Red Flight has a better than even chance against those heavy guns, Your Highness. Those X-wings are very agile ships.

LEIA: But if the Imperials send out TIE fighters for ship-to-ship combat . . . what then?

DODONNA: Well, then . . . our hopes would rest almost entirely with Gold Flight.

LUKE: Red Leader, this is Red Five. I'm going in again.

RED LEADER: Watch yourself, Luke! There's a lot of heavy fire coming from the right side of that deflector tower.

LUKE: I'm on it!

CONTROLLER: Flight leaders, we've picked up a new group of signals . . . enemy fighters, coming your way.

LEIA: Fighters!

RED LEADER: I copy, base.

LUKE: My scope's negative.

WEDGE: Same here.

RED LEADER: Maintain visual scanning, Red Flight. With all this jamming they'll be on top of you before your scopes can pick them up.

LEIA: General, can't we track the Imperial fighters for them?

DODONNA: Not at this range, Princess. There's too much jamming and counterjamming going on.

RED FOUR: Here they come! They're right behind us!

RED LEADER: Biggs, you've picked one up! Watch it!

BIGGS: I can't see him! Where is he?

RED SIX: John D., one coming up on your tail!

RED FOUR: I see him, Porkins!

BIGGS: This one's latched tight! I can't shake him!

LUKE: Hang on, Biggs, I'm coming!

RED LEADER: Stick tight to your wingmen, all of you!

LUKE: I got him, Biggs! You're clear!

BIGGS: Thanks, Luke!

RED SIX: Scissor right, Red Four! I'll get him off your back!

RED FOUR: Will do!

CONTROLLER: Gold Leader, three more fighters have left the Death Star. They may be after you.

GOLD LEADER: This is Gold Leader. I copy.

BIGGS: Pull in, Luke! Pull in!

WEDGE: Watch your back, Luke! Fighters above you, coming in!

THREEPIO: Master Luke! Artoo!

BIGGS: Got 'im! You all right, Luke?

LUKE: I'm hit, but not bad. Artoo's working on it.

LEIA: General Dodonna, isn't there anything we can do to help them?

DODONNA: Every fighting craft we have is out there already, your Highness. This is what the X-wings were sent to do . . . keep the Imperials occupied. At least they're not outnumbered.

LEIA: Not yet.

RED LEADER: Red Six, can you see Red Five?

RED SIX: There's a heavy fire zone over on this side. Luke, where are you?

LUKE: I can't shake this TIE fighter!

WEDGE: Hold on, Luke!

CONTROLLER: The Death Star is ten minutes from firing range.

LUKE: Thanks, Wedge!

WEDGE: Any time!

GOLD LEADER: Red Leader, this is Gold Leader. We are beginning our attack run.

RED LEADER: I copy, Gold Leader. Go to it.

GOLD LEADER: The exhaust port is marked and . . . *locked* in. All Y-wings, switch power to front deflector shields.

DODONNA: Good! The targeting computers have picked out the exhaust port!

GOLD LEADER: How many gun batteries do you count, Gold Five?

GOLD FIVE: I say about twenty guns, some on the surface and some in the towers.

GOLD LEADER: Switch over to targeting computers.

GOLD FIVE: Computer's locked on. I'm getting a signal.

DODONNA: We have a good chance now. Only a targeting computer has any real hope of scoring a precise hit.

LEIA: Because of their speed?

DODONNA: That's right. They'll be flying down that trench in the Death Star at such a rate that the shot's virtually impossible to an unaided pilot.

GOLD TWO: The guns! They've stopped!

GOLD FIVE: Stabilize your rear deflectors. Watch for enemy fighters.

GOLD LEADER: They're coming in! Three marks at two-ten!

LEIA: Can't the X-wings help them!

DODONNA: They're still engaging the other Imperials. Gold Flight is on its own now.

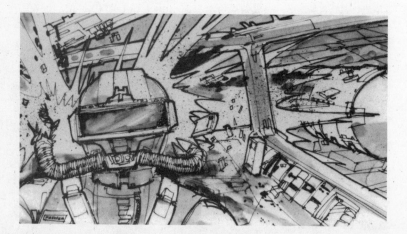

GOLD LEADER: They got Gold Two! This trench is too narrow! I can't maneuver!

GOLD FIVE: Stay on target.

GOLD LEADER: We're too close to each other . . .

GOLD FIVE: Stay on target!

DODONNA: *(TO HIMSELF)* Just a little longer . . . a few more seconds.

GOLD FIVE: Gold Five to Red Leader . . . lost Dutch, lost Tiree.

RED LEADER: I copy, Gold Five.

GOLD FIVE: I'm hit . . . The fighters came from behind—

Sound: He's cut off abruptly as his ship explodes.

CONTROLLER: He's gone. The Death Star is at five minutes and closing.

LEIA: What do we do now, General Dodonna?

DODONNA: Red Flight will have to try to make the attack run. They're all we have left.

Music: Transition.

Sound: Death Star observation deck up.

MOTTI: Governor Tarkin, the Rebel Y-wing fighters have been destroyed, but their X-wings have broken contact with our interceptors. We believe they're about to resume the attack the others were attempting.

TARKIN: Do you suppose they have any hope of succeeding?

MOTTI: No, sir. Lord Vader is still out there in his personal fighter, with his own wingmen. The other Rebels will meet the same fate as the first ones.

TARKIN: As you say. Still, perhaps caution *is* warranted. Prepare my ship in case it seems more advisable for me to depart the Death Star.

MOTTI: Lord Tarkin, pardon me, sir, but you mustn't consider relinquishing your command, even temporarily!

TARKIN: Why not?

MOTTI: This battle station is the source of your influence and power! If you show that you can be made to abandon it, you undermine your hope of gaining supreme rank in the Empire.

TARKIN: You seem certain about that.

MOTTI: I am, Governor Tarkin!

TARKIN: And you are equally certain that there's no danger?

MOTTI: No matter what the Rebel strategy is, they'll fail. Lord Vader has personally annihilated their first attack group, and he'll do the same for the other.

TARKIN: Yes. For one who professes to rely upon some unseen Force, Vader *is* extremely adept with our most advanced prototype fighter. Very well, Motti.

Sound: Portal opens under:

MOTTI: You won't regret this, Lord Tarkin.

OFFICER: *(COMING IN)* Lord Tarkin, we've analyzed the Rebel attack, sir, and it seems there *is* danger. Should I have your ship standing by?

TARKIN: Evacuate? In our moment of triumph? I think you overestimate these Rebels' chances!

PA: *(OFF)* The Death Star will be within firing range in three minutes.

Music: Transition.

Sound: Luke's X-wing cockpit, with his engines, maneuvering, instrumentation, etc. All voices, except Luke's and later Ben's, are over commo.

RED LEADER: Red Flight, this is Red Leader. Sound off.

WEDGE: Red Two here, Red Leader, off to your right.

BIGGS: Red Three, standing by.

LUKE: Red Five, at rendezvous mark six point one.

RED TEN: Red ten here, boss.

RED TWELVE: Red Twelve, right behind you, Red Leader.

RED LEADER: Looks like we're all that's left.

DODONNA: Red Leader, this is base one. Keep half of your group out of range for the next attack run.

RED LEADER: Copy, base one. Luke, I want you to take Wedge and Biggs. Stay up here and wait for my signal to start your run.

LUKE: I copy, Red Leader. *(TO HIMSELF)* Me?

BIGGS: Good luck, boss.

RED LEADER: Thanks. Okay, Red Flight, this is it!

LUKE: Artoo, how're things going back there?

ARTOO: WHISTLES A HARASSED REPLY.

LUKE: Just do your best to keep the damage under control!

BIGGS: Can you hang on, Luke?

LUKE: I think so, Biggs.

WEDGE: Good. It'll take all three of us to make a successful run.

RED TEN: We should be able to see the target location by now.

RED LEADER: Keep your eyes open for those fighters.

RED TEN: There's too much interference!

337

RED LEADER: Red Five, can you get a visual on them from where you are?

LUKE: There's no sign of any . . . wait! Coming in on you, point five three.

RED TEN: I see em!

RED LEADER: Targeting computer locked on! Target's coming up!

LUKE: *(TO HIMSELF)* Hurry, boss, hurry!

RED LEADER: Just keep those fighters off me for a few more seconds . . .

RED TEN: They're all over us back here!

RED LEADER: Almost there . . .

RED TEN: They got Red Twelve!

RED LEADER: Almost there . . .

RED TEN: I can't hold them!

RED LEADER: It's away!

RED TEN: It's a hit!

RED LEADER: Negative. The torpedo didn't make it down the shaft.

LUKE: Red Leader, we're right above you. Turn to point-oh-five. We'll cover for you.

RED LEADER: Stay there. They just got Red Ten, and I've lost my starboard engine. Their leader's flying a prototype fighter. He's a real killer.

BIGGS: But boss . . .

RED LEADER: Red Five, get set up for your attack run. It's over for me—

Sound: An explosion in Red Leader's commo. He roars as he goes up in flames. His voice is suddenly cut off.

DODONNA: Red Five, the Death Star will be within range in approximately one minute.

LUKE: Okay, Biggs, Wedge, let's close it up. We're going down that trench full throttle.

WEDGE: Right with you, boss.

LUKE: *(TO HIMSELF)* "Boss . . ."

BIGGS: Luke, at this speed, will you be able to pull out in time after you've fired?

LUKE: It'll be just like Beggar's Canyon back home, Biggs.

BIGGS: We'll stay back and cover for you.

LUKE: It's up to you guys to screen me from those fighters.

WEDGE: My scope shows the tower, but I can't see the exhaust port. Are you sure the computer can hit it?

LUKE: It'll hit it. *(TO HIMSELF)* Please . . . it's got to! *(TO THE OTHERS)* Watch yourselves! Increase speed full throttle!

WEDGE: We're right behind you.

LUKE: Artoo, that stablizer's broken loose again! See if you can't lock it down!

ARTOO: CHIRPS.

WEDGE: Look out!

BIGGS: TIE fighters! Right behind us . . .

WEDGE: I'm hit! Losing control . . . I can't hold course!

LUKE: Get clear, Wedge! You can't do any more good back there!

WEDGE: Sorry, Luke! The TIEs aren't following. They're staying on you. The leader's flying some kind of prototype ship.

BIGGS: Hurry, Luke! They're coming in much faster this time! I can't hold them!

LUKE: Artoo, try and increase the power!

ARTOO: SIGNALS.

BIGGS: Their leader's latched on to me! Luke—

Sound: He's cut off abruptly as he's shot down.

LUKE: Biggs! *Biggs!* Oh, Biggs . . .

Sound: Luke's ship is jarred by a near miss.

LUKE: Hang on, Artoo!

DODONNA: Luke, thirty seconds left!

LUKE: Targeting computer . . . locked on.

Sound: The computer begins beeping.

BEN: *(DISEMBODIED VOICE)* Use the Force, Luke.

LUKE: Ben? Ben!

BEN: Let go, Luke! Trust me! Reach out with your feelings!

LUKE: I . . . I trust you, Ben.

Sound: He flicks a switch, and the targeting computer stops.

DODONNA: Luke, this is base one! You've switched off your targeting computer! What's wrong?

LUKE: Nothing's wrong. I'm all right.

Sound: The ship is jolted again.

ARTOO: AN ELECTRONIC SHRIEK OF PAIN.

LUKE: I'm hit! I've lost Artoo!

DODONNA: The Death Star is nearly in range!

LUKE: Their leader's right on my back . . . I can't . . . what?

Sound: An explosion rocks the ship.

LUKE: Somebody's firing on them! Who . . .

HAN: *(OVER COMM)* Yahoo!

LUKE: Han! Han, you came back!

HAN: You're all clear, kid. Now let's blow this thing and go home!

LUKE: *(TO HIMSELF)* Reach out . . . with my feelings and . . . fire!

Sound: His fighter jolts as the torpedoes leave it.

LUKE: It's away!

HAN: Now get clear, kid! Pour it on!

Sound: Luke's engines roar. Suddenly, a series of loud explosions.

HAN: You did it! Great shot, kid! That was one in a million! You blew it right out of the sky!

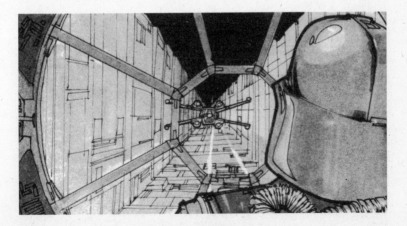

DODONNA: Sensors report total destruction of your objective.

HAN: Luke, let's go park these crates and celebrate!

LUKE: I'm right behind you!

BEN: *(DISEMBODIED VOICE)* Remember, Luke, the Force will be with you . . . always.

Music: Transition.

Sound: The Rebel hangar. Rebels are cheering, laughing, and back-slapping.

LEIA: *(COMING ON)* Luke! Oh, Luke, we won! We won!

LUKE: We never would have if Han hadn't changed his mind.

LEIA: You should've seen the looks on our faces in the operations center when we heard his voice. I don't think I've ever been so surprised in my life.

Sound: She's interrupted by more cheering as Han and Chewie come through the crowd.

CHEWIE: ROARS.

HAN: *(APPROACHING)* Luke—hey, Luke!

LUKE: *(LAUGHS)* Han! Chewbacca! I knew you'd come back! I just knew it!

HAN: Well, I wasn't gonna let you get all the credit and take all the reward.

LEIA: Han, I knew there was more to you than money!

CHEWIE: HOOTS.

HAN: Careful, you'll damage our reputation.

LUKE: Isn't it time you stopped—

CREW CHIEF: *(OFF)* Okay, lower that R2 unit carefully!

LUKE: Artoo, I forgot! He was hit! *(TO CHIEF)* Lower him right here!

Sound: Artoo being set down.

HAN: He sure took a bad one back there.

THREEPIO: *(APPROACHING)* Oh, my! Artoo, can you hear me? Say something. Sir, you can repair him, can't you?

CREW CHIEF: We'll get to work on him right away.

THREEPIO: You simply must repair him! Sir, if any of my circuits or gears will help, I'll gladly donate them.

LUKE: He'll be all right, Threepio.

LEIA: We'll see that our best people are working on him. He certainly deserves it.

Music: Transition.

LUKE: Will you quit pacing, Han? There's nothing to be worried about.

HAN: Me and Chewie ain't too comfortable around all these ceremonies and formal stuff.

CHEWIE: HOOTS AGREEMENT.

LUKE: Look, they're going to hang a medal around your neck, not stand you up against a wall and shoot you!

HAN: It's still not my line of work.

LUKE: You'll survive.

HAN: You're taking it pretty well. That's a real sharp outfit they scrounged up for you.

LUKE: *(CLEARING HIS THROAT)* Uh, well, the Princess went to all the trouble of arranging the ceremony, so I thought . . .

HAN: Thought you'd make a good impression on her? Smart boy!

LUKE: It still seems so strange to have met her. I remember the first time I saw her, just an image from Artoo's memory banks . . .

HAN: It led you a long, long way, Luke.

LUKE: It did. Everything's so different all of a sudden . . . So many things have changed.

HAN: I'm sorry about Biggs. And Ben, and all the others. They're the ones who deserve the medals.

LUKE: They died for something they believed in. What made you come back, Han?

HAN: Oh, the Wookiee here got stubborn about it.

CHEWIE: GROWLS.

LUKE: Come on, Han!

HAN: Well, he *did* give me an argument. Besides, I did some thinking about what you and Ben and Her Highness said and . . . a few things that've happened to me along the way. So I turned the *Falcon* around. Maybe it's time I tried a steady job.

LUKE: Oh, Han . . . anyway, I'm glad you did. That TIE fighter had me cold.

HAN: I couldn't quite nail their leader, the one in that prototype fighter . . . he was *good*. But I got one of his wingmen, and the other collided with him.

LUKE: And that knocked him out of the fight?

HAN: Yeah, but I don't think it disabled him. I guess he got clear.

LUKE: Whatever happened, it was good enough for me . . .

Sound: The throne room doors open.

REBEL: Sirs, the troops are assembled, and we're ready for the presentation.

CHEWIE: GRUNTS.

HAN: Now, what d' we have to do, again?

REBEL: Simply walk the length of the throne room to the dais, where the Princess Leia will award you your medals.

LUKE: You can do it, Han, you'll see.

HAN: Hope so. C'mon, Chewie.

CHEWIE: HOOTS.

REBEL: This way, gentlemen.

Sound: Martial music.

HAN: *(OUT OF THE SIDE OF HIS MOUTH)* Will you look at all these Rebels? We'd better not be last on the dinner line.

LUKE: You're supposed to be serious!

HAN: I bet they're tired of staring at each other. Chewie, give 'em "eyes front"!

CHEWIE: HOOTS A COMMAND IN WOOKIEE.

Sound: Either by coincidence or by cosmic predestination, the massed Rebels obey, facing the dais.

HAN: Good discipline, there.

LUKE: Han, behave!

Sound: Martial music ends.

LEIA: *(FADING ON)* Welcome, on behalf of the Rebel Alliance.

HAN: Glad we could make it, believe me.

LEIA: *(IGNORING HIM)* General Dodonna, the medals, please. Accept these, the highest decoration the Alliance can bestow, for your gallantry. Han Solo . . .

HAN: *(SOFTLY)* You still can't come up with any more cash, huh?

LEIA: *(STIFFLY, THROUGH HER SMILE)* Han, if you don't act like a grown-up, I'll strangle you with it. *(LOUDER)* And . . . Luke Skywalker.

LUKE: Thank you, Princess Leia.

LEIA: No, Luke, thank *you*. From the Rebel Alliance and from Leia Organa.

LUKE: What I did, I did for both, Leia.

ARTOO: *(SLIGHTLY OFF)* WHISTLES FOR ATTENTION.

LUKE: *(LAUGHS)* Artoo-Detoo!

THREEPIO: *(SLIGHTLY OFF)* Yes, Master Luke, he's completely repaired!

LEIA: And now you may turn to your comrades in arms and receive their ovation.

Sound: The assembled troops break into applause and cheering.

CHEWIE: GROWLS.

ARTOO: BEEPS.

LEIA: How d' you like being a hero, Han?

HAN: Some parts weren't too bad. I dunno; want to do it again sometime?

LEIA: What do you say, Luke? Shall we?

LUKE: It wouldn't surprise me at all!

Music: Closing theme up and under closing credits.

ANNOUNCER: CLOSING CREDITS.

ABOUT THE AUTHOR

BRIAN DALEY is the author of numerous works of science fiction and fantasy, including the Coramonde and Alacrity Fitzhugh books. He also scripted the National Public Radio serial adaptations of *Star Wars* and *The Empire Strikes Back*, dramatic recordings for Disneyland/Buena Vista, and a number of animated TV episodes.

In collaboration with his friend and fellow Ballantine novelist James Luceno—using the pen name Jack McKinney—Brian co-wrote the *Robotech*, *Sentinels*, and *Black Hole Travel Agency* series.

Brian has in recent years been laboring over an SF saga that's grown in the telling. He and his longtime companion, historical novelist Lucia St. Clair Robson, live in a quiet riverside community near Annapolis, Maryland.

JOIN THE **STAR WARS** FAN CLUB

For only $9.95 you can join THE OFFICIAL STAR WARS FAN CLUB! Membership includes:

- THE STAR WARS INSIDER, the quarterly magazine, packed with STAR WARS photos, interviews and articles! (one year subscription)

- THE JAWA TRADER, the official catalog of STAR WARS and INDIANA JONES collectibles, inserted in every STAR WARS INSIDER.

- Exclusive membership kit loaded with collectibles for members only!